A Redemption for the Baron

Barrington's Brigade
Book 3

Ruth A. Casie

ARE YOU SIGNED UP FOR DRAGONBLADE'S BLOG?

You'll get the latest news and information on exclusive giveaways, exclusive excerpts, coming releases, sales, free books, cover reveals and more.

Check out our complete list of authors, too!

No spam, no junk. That's a promise!

Sign Up Here

www.dragonbladepublishing.com

Dearest Reader;

Thank you for your support of a small press. At Dragonblade Publishing, we strive to bring you the highest quality Historical Romance from some of the best authors in the business. Without your support, there is no 'us', so we sincerely hope you adore these stories and find some new favorite authors along the way.

Happy Reading!

CEO, Dragonblade Publishing

Additional Dragonblade books by Author Ruth A. Casie

Barrington's Brigade Series
A Marriage for the Marquess (Book 1)
A Dilemma for the Duke (Book 2)
A Redemption for the Baron (Book 3)

The Ladies of Sommer-by-the-Sea Series
The Lady and Her Quill (Book 1)
The Lady and the Spy (Book 2)
The Lady and Her Duke (Book 3)
The Duke's Lost Love (Novella)

Pirates of Britannia Series
Donald
Hugh
Graham
The Pirate's Jewel
The Pirate's Redemption

The Lyon's Den Series
The Lyon's Gambit
The Lyon's Alliance

Chapter One

June 25, 1821
The Edge of Baycliff Woods
Sommer-by-the-Sea, England

T HE LUSH, EARLY summer countryside of Sommer-by-the-Sea was a welcoming sight, especially after the last grueling eighty miles. Captain Thomas Grenville rode along the familiar paths of Baycliff Woods. Now, away from the chaos of war, the Scottish Clearances, and their aftermath, he confronted the uneasy stillness of coming home. The boy who rode off to war had faded away a long time ago.

The terrain sloped upward, giving way to rolling hills thick with trees that stretched toward the horizon. As he rode beneath the green canopy, he glanced overhead, but the setting sun was obscured by the storm clouds gathering in the darkening sky.

He paused at the crossroads where the main road skirted Baycliff Mound. The roadway would be an easier ride, but it would add precious time to his journey. Thomas glanced up again. He'd never make it home without getting totally soaked if he followed the road. His decision made, he spurred his horse, Valor, forward. They veered off the path and began the steep but manageable climb up Baycliff Mound.

The wind picked up and howled through the trees the closer he got to the top of the hill. Halfway up the climb, the first raindrops fell. He pulled his coat around him in an effort to stay dry and cursed under his breath. "Welcome home, Captain. So much for getting home before the storm," he added with a mocking chuckle.

It was fitting, in a way. Sommer-by-the-Sea had never been known for its predictable weather. If anything, the countryside seemed determined to give him a baptismal return, though he might have preferred a quiet brandy.

Within minutes, the rain was lashing down, drumming against his coat as the trail churned and turned into sludge beneath Valor's hooves. For a disorienting moment, he wasn't in England at all, but in the rain-soaked fields of France, where mud was as thick as gun smoke.

Valor shook, sending a spray of water from his mane in every direction. His ears flicked back before he gave a deep, rumbling snort.

Grenville exhaled and wiped his face. His hand drifted to his coat pocket and closed around the familiar shape, the cool, etched gold coin. Barrington's calling card. A summons to action, but this time, the battlefield wasn't across the sea. It was here.

He had left the service to take up the title, now Baron Grey-stone, whether he liked it or not, and manage the estate his father could no longer oversee alone. His days were consumed with settling disputes, managing tenants, and navigating the layered intricacies of the family's holdings. The work kept him busy. Kept him focused. The responsibilities were better than pacing the halls at night. But they didn't settle the restlessness, the unease that remained bone-deep and familiar.

A crack of thunder rolled over the ridge, startling a flock of birds from the trees. Grenville's body tensed at the sound. Old instincts. He drew a breath and held it.

You're not there. You're here.

He let his breath out slowly, then drew in another. The scent was of rain on the rich soil and wet leaves, not the battlefield. He was in Baycliff Woods.

He'd be home soon, dry, with a glass of brandy. Not the cup of hot cocoa, Mrs. Cove, the family's housekeeper, gave him with a cluck of disapproval over his muddy boots on her clean floors. A smile tugged at his lips. He hadn't thought of Mrs. Cove in years.

"Come on, boy," he murmured softly to Valor. "Let's get home before this storm drowns us."

He was eager to leave the ghosts of the past behind, at least for the night. With a gentle nudge, he urged his horse forward, hooves squelching through the mud.

As they emerged from the woods, the horse's ears flicked sharply forward, muscles tensed under the saddle. Beneath him, his mount's muscles tightened. Grenville's gaze narrowed. *There's something ahead.* He tightened his grip on the reins. "Steady," he whispered. Through the downpour, a shape began to emerge.

"A carriage," he muttered, tilting his head to the right. "And it's listing awkwardly."

The rain eased just enough for him to see the problem. One wheel had sunk deep in the mire. A figure, undeniably feminine despite the soaked cloak, struggled beside an elderly coachman.

Grenville urged Valor forward, stopping a respectable distance away. "It's a nasty storm. Allow me to help you get out of this mess," he called out.

The woman turned toward him, rain dripping from the brim of her hat. "That won't be necessary." She turned away from him. When he didn't move, she glanced over her shoulder "We can manage on our own."

Grenville huffed a laugh, shaking his head. "Ah, but denying a gentleman the chance to be gallant? That, my lady, is a true scandal." He gave a mock bow, the rain spilling off his hat's brim as if nature itself disapproved of his jesting.

A crack of thunder split the air. Lightning followed, quick and sharp. The carriage horses startled, stamping and pulling against the wet reins. The elderly coachman struggled to calm the agitated team.

Grenville swung down from his mount, boots squelching into the mud. He moved quickly to the lead horse, murmuring steady nonsense in a low, firm voice. The reins jerked in the coachman's hands, tugged taut by the horses as another crack of thunder spooked them.

But the lead horse beneath Grenville's hand began to settle, ears twitching, head dipping slightly. A moment later, the others followed.

"I have them under control now, sir. Thank you," the coachman said, his grip easing as control returned.

Grenville released the bridle and stepped back. The coachman turned to the young woman. "This rain isn't letting up. One more pair of hands will make a difference."

He saw the way her jaw tightened, the flicker of irritation in her eyes. Clearly, the notion of accepting help, especially from him, clearly chafed.

"Tell me, Captain, do you make a habit of collecting wayward travelers?" Her tone was cool, and clipped, matching her words.

He arched a brow. "Captain?"

She tilted her head. "You sit a horse like a man trained for battle, but you don't wear your rank like a badge."

Grenville hesitated for the briefest moment, studying her. Most people made assumptions about rank and station based on uniform or reputation. But she had read his proof of command in his posture and his control, not as an ornament. It was an astute observation, sharper than he expected, and far more intriguing.

Amusement tugged at the edge of his mouth, tempered by curiosity.

"As for wayward travelers," he said at last, with a half-smile, "I only stop for the interesting ones. And you, my lady, are certainly more intriguing than the average highway mishap."

"Not so bold." She shrugged, murmuring almost to herself.

He raised a brow. "And you, I wager, don't much care for men who are."

A muscle twitched in her cheek, but she didn't flinch. "Care? No, Captain." She let the title linger, deliberate now. "I merely know the sort."

He observed as she gathered her sodden skirts and caught the smallest hesitation, the flicker of something else in her eyes. A challenge? A memory, perhaps? But more than likely, a warning.

The woman turned away, her skirts in hand, and he exhaled, shaking his head. Stubborn. Proud. He should have expected nothing less.

Still, he couldn't help but watch.

Her wide-brimmed hat did little to keep the rain at bay. Grenville noticed how her soaked clothes clung to her, revealing the graceful lines of her figure. Long tendrils of her fiery red hair had escaped, plastered to the curve of her long, slender neck. Her green eyes, sharp and bright, flashed with irritation and determination.

Stubborn and proud, admirable traits until they stranded one in the mire of their own pride.

Grenville stepped closer, shaking his head. Mud pulled at his boots with every step. "Battling the elements alone? Is a noble effort," he said, his voice low, "but even the fiercest warriors know when to accept an ally."

He watched the battle play out in her stance, the rigid set of her shoulders clashing with the flicker of resignation in her gaze. The fight was still there, but so was the sense. Her clenched fists loosened, and the rigid line of her posture began to ease.

At last, she spoke, her tone quiet but firm. "Very well."

Grenville nodded once, stepping toward the horses. He ran a steady hand down the nearest gelding's rain-slicked neck, murmuring quiet reassurances. The animal flicked an ear, muscles twitching beneath his palm.

Checking the harness, he made a minor adjustment to the traces to keep them from tangling.

As they worked side by side, the rain became little more than a distant drumbeat against the earth. Grenville stole a glance at her. Fiercely intent, her brows were drawn in quiet concentration. She did not fumble, did not hesitate. She met each challenge with steady hands and a sharp mind, adjusting tack, soothing the horses with quiet murmurs that even the downpour couldn't drown out."

The storm may have been relentless, but so was she. A woman like this would not bend easily, nor did she shrink from a challenge. He had fought alongside men who lacked her steadiness. That was an intriguing thought. If he were to choose allies in a fight, he would want her on his side.

Grenville held the reins firmly. "Easy now… easy." His voice was calm and steady, coaxing the horses as they struggled, but their hooves were unable to find solid footing. "Steady… that's it." The carriage rocked, but refused to move. "Good lads," he murmured, though the praise was hollow. The mud had it firmly in its grip.

Beside him, the woman moved with purpose. She scanned the roadside and gathered some good size stones with sharp, clean-edges and heavy enough to wedge beneath the wheels for traction.

He watched her wedge the first stone under the wheel. Her fingers were caked with mud, soaked to the wrist, but every movement was precise.

She bent again. Her boot slipped in the muck, and her footing gave way. With a soft gasp, she pitched forward, her arms flailing for balance.

Grenville moved without thinking. His hands found her waist, firm and sure, just before she fell.

For a single, breathless moment, the world stilled.

She froze in his arms. Rain drummed a steady rhythm around them, but between them, nothing moved. Not her breath. Not his.

Her body was rigid beneath his touch, tension coiled like a spring. He felt it as surely as he'd once felt the weight of his musket in his hands.

Then, in one sharp, breathless motion, she pulled away.

His hands fell back to his sides, fingers curling against the cold. The space between them felt abruptly colder. Emptier. She hadn't clung to him. Hadn't cried out. She just went still, quiet. Soft. It didn't fit the sharpness of her tone or the pride in her posture. That contradiction lingered, unsettling him.

She turned without a word and knelt beside the wheel as though nothing had happened.

But something had. He had seen it in her eyes, a flicker of something, before she looked away. Not fear. Not exactly. But not indifference either.

The coachman came around, reins still in hand. "This is worse than the downpour at Waterloo. We thought the sky would never clear."

Grenville blinked, the words yanking him backward.

Mud. Smoke. The coppery stench of blood. The cries of his men cut short. The signalman, motionless. A red hole in his chest.

He exhaled sharply. *Not here. Not now.*

Beside him, the woman straightened, smoothing her skirts, but her fingers trembled slightly as she brushed the mud away. Her gaze had gone distant, her breath caught just a second too long. A different battlefield, perhaps. But the echo rang the same.

He hesitated. Just long enough to ask, quietly, "Are you hurt?"

She stilled for half a heartbeat, then gave a short shake. "No, I'm fine. Thank you."

Her voice was steady, but something in the way she avoided his gaze told him that the moment had unsettled her, too.

A renewed gust of wind and rain whipped around them like a wild beast, refusing to be ignored, much like the unresolved tension between them.

She stepped forward again, brushing her skirts aside as she inspected the wheel. "If my coachman settles the horses, we might manage with a bit of leverage on the wheel?"

Grenville gave a short nod. "Then let's not waste time." Without a word, he passed her a thick branch he'd stripped earlier, its base solid and angled just right for a lever. She took it without hesitation.

"You're stronger than I am," she said. "I'll brace the stones."

He didn't argue. Together, they worked quickly. She knelt beside the wheel, hands steady despite the mud, slipping the stones into place with practiced precision. The coachman moved to calm the team. Grenville crouched, angling the branch beneath the axle.

He reached out, his hands firm on the lever. "You've got quite the fighting spirit, haven't you?" he remarked, gritting his teeth against the strain. "Stubborn as the mud itself."

She shot him a glance, her green eyes flashing. "I don't need your flattery, sir. If I wanted empty compliments, I'd chat with my mirror."

He chuckled, shifted his weight, and pushed down on the makeshift lever. "You've got to admit, this mud is being particularly stubborn."

She huffed, wiping a muddy strand of hair from her face. "I suppose it's fitting, considering the company." Her eyes flicked back to the task at hand. "We haven't got all day to play in the mud."

He grinned. "Let's outfox this mud and get you on your way."

With a coordinated effort, a lift from him, a pull from the coachman, and a strong push from the horses, the carriage jolted forward, the wheels catching traction. Inch by inch, it rolled free of the rut and onto firmer ground.

She stood tall beside it, her shoulders squared, her satisfaction unmistakable. Mud streaked her skirts, and damp hair clung to her cheek, but her poise never faltered.

Grenville pulled his handkerchief from his pocket and cleaned his hands as best he could. "The storm's been relentless, hasn't it? Almost feels like the battles I've seen. Mud and rain everywhere, making everything more difficult."

He paused, then extended the least-soiled corner toward her.

She hesitated for a moment, then accepted it with a nod that was almost regal. "I'll see it returned," she said, her voice composed.

"At your leisure," he replied, surprised by how much he meant it.

"It has been a challenge, but I suppose we Scots are used to weathering storms."

He paused, his gaze lingering on her.

"Aye, weathering storms and fighting battles, just like in the military. Sometimes, it's not about the strength you have, but the alliances you form and the people beside you."

She turned her face toward him. For a breath, her eyes weren't sharp. They were searching.

"It sounds like you've had your share of tough decisions."

"Indeed," he murmured, his voice quieter now as if speaking more to himself than to her. "It's often the responsibilities that shape our choices. Doing what's necessary to protect those we care about, even if it means making sacrifices."

There it was again, that flicker of tension in her jaw, like a question she hadn't decided to ask.

Then, he added, "I could accompany you to your destination."

"That won't be necessary," she said, waving away his offer with a flick of her wrist.

He gave her a smile. "Ah, you don't want anyone to know you needed help. Don't worry, your secret is safe with me."

As she adjusted her skirts, her hand brushed against something solid near his feet. A glint of gold. She picked it up and turned it over between her fingers. "You dropped this." Her tone had changed. It was softer now. "BB? Does that stand for 'Baron of Bother'?"

Their fingers brushed as she handed the coin back to him, a fleeting spark. Warm. Disarming.

"You might want to be more careful with your treasures," she remarked with a playful glint in her eyes.

He chuckled, a deep baritone sound, and pocketed the coin. "Thank you," he replied. "It was my pleasure, Bonnie Battler."

She arched a brow, a mix of irritation and curiosity flashing in her green eyes. "Bonnie Battler? If you intend to flatter me, Captain, you'll have to try harder than that."

He shrugged, a playful smile tugging at his lips. "You've got the fight in you, that's for sure. And 'Bonnie' fits you well, very well." He bowed to her as if she were a princess.

She couldn't help but laugh, a soft, genuine sound that surprised even her. "Fair enough, Captain. I'll take it as a compliment." There was a pause, reluctant but sincere. "I suppose I owe you thanks."

He tipped his hat. "Perhaps our paths will cross again."

She gave him a gracious nod, one warrior to another.

The carriage rolled on at last, the wheels moving smoothly now. Overhead, the clouds began to part, and a few stars pricked through the dark.

Grenville remained where he stood, watching until the carriage vanished into the distance.

Helping her had stirred something he hadn't felt in a long time. Not duty. Not war. Something quieter. Harder to name.

Her fire. Her pride. The way she'd stood her ground without flinching. He exhaled, just once. He didn't know her name. But he wanted to.

Chapter Two

B RIDGET MCCONNELL SAT alone in the dimly lit carriage, the lantern's flickering glow barely warming the velvet-lined interior. The road was damp and uneven, the steady rhythm of the carriage doing little to soothe the restlessness coiled inside her.

The rain had stopped, the clouds parted to reveal a star-scattered sky, but she was already soaked to the skin. Mud clung to her hem, her hands… and her thoughts.

She pulled her cloak tighter around her shoulders, but it offered no relief. The air inside the carriage felt thick, a mixture of stale upholstery and the faint lavender sachet tucked into the folds of her belongings. Her fingers toyed with the ribbon of her reticule, twisting it tighter with every passing thought.

As the carriage trundled forward, the surrounding landscape shifted from open countryside to dense woodland. Towering oaks lined the narrow road, their twisted branches stretching toward the sky like skeletal fingers. The mist had settled low, clinging to the earth, creeping between trunks and stones, blurring the path ahead.

She peered out the rain-streaked window, catching glimpses of movement beyond the trees. Likely nothing more than the wind disturbing the underbrush, but the unease that had plagued her since leaving home twisted tighter in her chest. She was a stranger here, venturing into a world that was not hers. The thought made her sit straighter, as if posture alone could shield her.

Her thoughts strayed, uninvited, to the man on the road. The one with steady hands and piercing blue eyes. He had touched her only briefly, steadying her when she slipped, but the memory of it lingered like warmth in her skin. Foolish. He was English. One of *them*. And yet, he had neither postured nor presumed. He had worked beside her in silence, not dismissive, not commanding, just… present.

She sighed and leaned back against the worn seat. Her father's parting words echoed in her mind, his voice steady, filled with the quiet authority he wielded so well.

It wasn't just memory. It was longing, for the Highland dawn, the bracing bite of the wind off the loch, the scent of peat smoke curling through the heather.

Those were her mornings, not this world of curtained coaches and careful expectations. Her world had been fierce and cold and bright. It had never made her feel… small.

And yet, this morning, she did.

The decision to leave had not only been a journey of miles, but of allegiance. Leaving Glencross hadn't just been saying goodbye to hills and kin. It had meant agreeing to a plan crafted in strategy and hope.

Her father had said it plainly. A Highland daughter, yes, but one bound by duty. If she did this well, the English might soften. The violence might ease. Her people might yet endure.

But it hadn't felt like power. It had felt like being bartered.

The memory of the captain rose again, uninvited. Not because of what he'd done, but because of what he hadn't. He hadn't insisted. He hadn't dismissed her. He had worked beside her, said little, and looked at her as if he saw her, not her name, not her title, just… her.

It had rattled her more than any challenge might have. She didn't know what to make of a man who met her strength with steadiness. That was not English. That was dangerous.

The carriage jolted, rousing her from her thoughts. She shifted in her seat and glanced out again. The mist was lifting. The landscape had changed to sculpted shapes. To the kind of land ruled by ledgers and topiary shears.

This was his world. And soon, it would be hers.

"Bridget, lass, you carry more than just your own fate on your shoulders. Remember that."

She did remember. Every mile of this journey weighed heavier than the last, not because of the roads, but because of what they meant. She wasn't here for comfort or companionship. She was here to serve a purpose. An alliance. A promise forged in ink and blood.

How could she forget? The burden of duty had never been a light one. She had left Scotland with the knowledge that her presence at Alastair Court was more than a mere visit. Her friend Lady Marjory Alastair needed her, of that much she was certain. And yet, there was something else, something unspoken, that had drawn her here.

Not him. Certainly not him.

But the image returned. The height of him. The line of his shoulders. The blue of his eyes, too clear, too sharp, too steady.

She pressed her fingers to her temple and forced the thought away. A uniform and a strong jaw didn't make a man less dangerous.

Bridget saw the estate as the carriage came up the Alastair Court drive. It was a far cry from the rugged Highlands she called home. In the dark, she could just make out the estate's manicured lawns and architecture. Stone walls stood in clean lines, shaped by order and wealth. Nothing like the wild crags of her childhood, but no less commanding. It was unfamiliar, imposing, yet impressive.

The carriage came to a halt with a jarring lurch at the grand entrance. Bridget, drenched and weary, cast a brief glance at the imposing façade as she stepped down. She squared her shoulders and pushed aside her discomfort. There was no place for hesitation now. Not here. Not in England. Whatever lay ahead, she would meet it standing tall.

The butler opened the door with practiced ease. "Welcome to Alastair Court, Lady Bridget." The butler bowed slightly. "Lady Alastair is expecting you. This way to the drawing room."

Her gaze drifted to the drawing room to her right before she decided she dared not move from the foyer's marble floor, where a muddy puddle was forming. "I'll wait here, thank you."

"Very well, my lady." The butler hurried down the hall.

As she waited for Lady Alastair, the gravity of her mission clung to her like an ill-fitting cloak, tugging her thoughts back to her father and the argument before she left Glencross.

The image of her father pacing the room, his jaw tight with frustration, played vividly in her mind. Every line of his face had been worn deeper that night. The memory of their heated exchange played in her mind, each word still fresh and vivid.

"Bridget, do you understand what's at stake here? The Clearances have ravaged our lands. We need an alliance to protect our people, our heritage!"

Anger surged through her, hot and unrelenting. Her hands curled into fists, nails biting into her palms as she stepped forward.

"And you think marrying me off to some English lord will solve all our problems? I suppose I should be grateful Viscount Huntington's wife still suffers him, or you would send me packing off to be his bride!"

A shadow passed over her father's face, his mouth setting into a hard line. "This isn't a game, Bridget. And you're not some piece of land to be traded."

"Then stop treating me like one!" Bridget turned sharply, staring out the window as if that would make the situation better. "I've seen English suitors in London, Father. They smile and charm, but they only want to smooth the edges, erase the fire, and make me something docile and English. I won't stand for it. I won't lose myself to their civility."

Her father's voice softened, but the gravity of his words remained. "You want our family torn apart?" He stepped in front of her, blocking her restless path. "You have no idea what that would do to you."

Her resolve wavered, if only for a heartbeat.

Her father's expression softened for a moment, his voice dropping to a more somber tone.

"Bridget, lass, you are the fiercest person I know. But there are times when strength isn't enough. We need alliances. You can make a difference, not just for yourself but for all of us."

She crossed her arms. "And what would some English nobleman want with the likes of me?" Bridget challenged, her eyes flashing with defiance. "They've already taken their tribute in coin, land, and people. They have left us little else."

Her father held her gaze. "Because, Bridget, you are a woman of extraordinary worth." He didn't raise his voice. He didn't need to. The certainty in it held her still.

"If I wanted empty flattery, Father, I'd speak to my reflection."

"It's not flattery. It's the truth." He exhaled. "You are fierce, unyielding, a trait that commands respect. You bring with you the resilience of the Highlands and the knowledge of how to manage land and people. That is no small thing. Our name still has influence, even across the border."

"And yet, I would still be the one expected to bend."

"Bridget, I don't wish to see you unhappy. But this doesn't have to be a sacrifice. Use your wit, your courage. Seek out someone who sees beyond titles and wealth, someone who values the woman you are."

Between them, the fire snapped and crackled, the only sound in the tense quiet. For the first time, she let herself consider his words.

"It's a heavy burden you place upon me," she said, still gazing at the flames.

He gave a small, rueful smile. "Aye, lass, I know. But you're strong enough to bear it. After all, you're the daughter of the Laird of Glencross."

Bridget tore her gaze from the flames, inhaling deeply as if steadying herself for battle. The air felt too thick and the room too small.

"I will consider it," she conceded quietly. "But I make no promises."

Her father gave her a small, knowing smile. "I wouldn't expect anything less from you."

Even now, his words echoed in her mind, lingering like an unfinished conversation. She had seen the men her father spoke of. They were filled with empty promises and empty smiles. No one had proven to be worthy. No one had met her fire without trying to extinguish it.

She had made the journey south not just as a daughter, but as an emissary, one who must tread carefully between expectation and her own resolve. Alastair Court was not merely a waypoint. It was a threshold, and whatever came next, she would face it on her terms.

And yet... the needs of her clan clung to her, heavier and more inescapable than she wished to admit.

Duty had always come at a cost. Lord Alastair had long standing business dealings with her father. Lady Alastair had become a good friend. Though their circumstances were vastly different, there was a quiet understanding between them that had always made Bridget feel comfortable.

And that comfort was rare. Precious. Invaluable in a place that expected her to shape herself to fit its mold.

Marjory's husband, Mark Alastair, was another matter. Though polite and amicable, he had always struck Bridget as a man whose mind was often elsewhere. He was the sort to immerse himself in his own pursuits, leaving the daily concerns of the household to his wife. Bridget had never thought much of it. There were plenty of men of his station who did the same. If anything, she had admired the quiet competence with which Marjory managed everything.

It gave Bridget hope. Hope that women might still carve out influence in a world ruled by men.

This visit, this carefully arranged stay, was not merely for her own benefit. Lord and Lady Alastair, actually Marjory, were to introduce her to suitors with no obligations. She would have the final word on who she accepted as well as the terms for the marriage agreement. She was determined to prove her worth beyond mere beauty and heritage, to find a way to honor her family without losing herself in the process. *Doing what's necessary to protect those we care about, even if it means making sacrifices.*

Footsteps echoed down the hall, pulling her from her thoughts. She squared her shoulders and prepared for whatever came next. Bridget smiled warmly the moment she saw Marjory coming down the hall.

"Bridget! Good heavens, you're soaked through. What a wretched night for travel!"

She was grateful for the warmth of Marjory's welcome. To her father's point, perhaps not all English people were uncaring or adversaries.

"Aye." She glanced down at her mud-stained skirt. "The weather wasn't kind. I apologize for my state."

Marjory gracefully waved off her apology.

"Besides," Marjory teased, "if you hadn't arrived like a ship-wrecked sailor, I'd hardly believe you'd come from Scotland at all. How many times have Mark and I come to you in no better condition? I'll have a hot bath prepared for you." Marjory turned toward the hallway she had exited. "Mrs. Simmons."

The housekeeper hurried to Marjory.

Where had the housekeeper been lurking that she appeared so quickly? In London, it took an entire five minutes for someone to reply.

"Bring Lady Bridget some warm towels and have a bath drawn for her." Marjory turned back to Bridget.

A downstairs maid appeared from the same place as Mrs. Simmons.

"My lady." She dipped a quick curtsey as she handed Bridget a towel, then proceeded to clean the floor with the other one she had in her hand.

Marjory took Bridget's arm with an easy familiarity, though a fleeting hesitation passed over her features. If Bridget had not known her so well, she might not have noticed it at all.

"You must be exhausted. I'll have a tray of hot tea with sup-per brought up to your room. You rest. We can talk in the morning." They climbed the staircase. "I'm so glad you're finally here."

"Thank you, Marjory. It's good to see you." Bridget's smile came without effort. Despite her reservations, she was genuinely happy to see her friend. "It seems the weather followed me all the way."

"It will be relatively dry by the morning. I think you'll enjoy being in Sommer-by-the-Sea more than London." Marjory leaned in with a conspiratorial glint in her eye. "I certainly do. You'll find country house parties far less... rigid than London soirees and galas."

Marjory chatted animatedly about the preparations for the weekend's events.

"The ballroom has never looked lovelier," Marjory said, adjusting the drape of her sleeve as she spoke. "The chandeliers have been polished until they sparkle, and I had the house staff bring in extra candelabras."

Bridget smiled faintly as she listened to Marjory continue, her voice bubbling with enthusiasm.

"I had the staff arrange the drawing room differently this time," Marjory went on. "Last year's gathering was far too cramped, and I cannot bear to see another guest practically wedged into the corner with no hope of escape. And the flowers, oh, Bridget, you must see them! Fresh from the hothouse, in the most stunning arrangements. Roses, lilies, even a few exotic blooms for the ballroom. I thought we would use flowers from our garden as centerpieces for the dining table."

Bridget chuckled as they reached the landing, where the scent of baking pastries drifted from the kitchens below.

"The menu is set," Marjory continued. "Pheasant, trout, roasted lamb with that spiced glaze everyone raved about last year. And the desserts! I told the cook to prepare an array, but I suspect the lemon tarts will vanish first. They always do."

"You've certainly thought of everything," Bridget said, taking in the energy in Marjory's voice.

"I had to," Marjory replied, smoothing her skirt as they walked toward the parlor. "The guest list is not as simple as it was last year. There are more, shall we say, strong personalities attending this time."

Bridget nodded, but her mind had begun to drift. The evening's events still clung to her thoughts, refusing to be dismissed.

She could still see him, those steady blue eyes, the quiet authority in his stance. The way he'd looked at her... as if he saw more than a stranger on the roadside. As if she wasn't merely passing through his day.

"Bridget? You've gone quiet."

Bridget's heart did a somersault at the sound of her name. For a fleeting moment, she felt as if she'd been caught practicing with her small blade, something her mother forbade her to do.

Marjory placed her hand on Bridget's arm. "You seem a bit distracted."

"I'm fine, just a bit more tired than I thought." Bridget forced a smile, though her mind was elsewhere. The man's determination and quiet strength had left an impression on her, one she couldn't easily dismiss. The memory hovered, uninvited and unshakable.

"There's still much to be done," Marjory continued. "I'd welcome your company as I make the final arrangements."

"Of course," Bridget replied, grateful for something else to focus on.

Marjory led her up the sweeping staircase, the mahogany banister smooth beneath her hand. At the top, they arrived at the landing, a circular space adorned with a plush rug and a vase of fresh roses atop a marble pedestal. "Your room is just down this hall." Marjory gestured to the left.

"Thank you for understanding my late arrival."

Marjory gave her a knowing look, a hint of mischief in her eyes.

"Well, it's not every day a Scottish lass turns up at my door looking like a drowned rat. Now, let's get you settled."

She exhaled, and the tightness in her chest eased. Relief, unexpected, but welcome, settled over her. Marjory's teasing grounded her, pulling her back from where her thoughts had strayed.

"Here we are." Marjory opened the door. "Now, get yourself warm and settled. We shall speak in the morning."

Bridget hesitated at the threshold. "I would ask you to have tea—"

Marjory's expression shifted, a flicker of sorrow crossing her face. "Perhaps tomorrow," she said softly. "There are a few things I need to take care of tonight with Mark."

She reached for Bridget's hand and gave it a gentle squeeze. "I'll see you in the morning." Then she gently kissed her cheek and was gone.

Bridget stood in the quiet, the offer still lingering on her tongue. She hadn't needed tea. She'd just wanted not to feel quite so alone.

Bridget stepped into her room and let the silence settle around her. She had to admit that despite the disappointment, she was grateful for time to herself.

Warmth wrapped around her the moment she stepped inside, a stark contrast to the wind that chilled her skin. Soft candlelight revealed delicate floral wallpaper in muted tones of cream and blue on the walls. It was the sort of room meant to soothe, not impress, and it was a welcome change.

A four-poster bed draped with lacy curtains that slightly billowed in the draft dominated one side of the room. The linens were crisp and white, accented with embroidered pillows that added a touch of elegance without being fussy. The intricate quilt pattern reminded her of the ones back home that lay at the foot of her bed. Her throat tightened, unexpectedly and unwelcome. A homesick sigh pushed through her lips.

The fireplace opposite the bed crackled softly, the flames casting shadows that flickered across the polished wooden floor. Above the mantel hung a simple mirror framed in dark wood, its surface slightly warped with age. To one side of the fireplace stood a comfortable armchair upholstered in deep burgundy fabric. A small table stood beside it with a vase of fresh wildflowers whose subtle scent mingled with the faint aroma of burning wood.

Heavy velvet drapes framed a large window that overlooked the estate's gardens. Though the night obscured most of the view, she could make out the silhouettes of neatly trimmed hedges and the gentle sway of trees still dripping from the rain. A writing desk sat beneath the window, an inkwell and quill at the ready atop a neat stack of parchment.

Against another wall stood a tall carved wardrobe for her belongings. Next to it, a delicate vanity table bore a lace doily and a silver brush and comb set.

The room was elegant yet understated, lacking the brazen affluence she'd seen in London. As she began to unbutton her damp dress, Bridget allowed herself a small smile. Maybe, just maybe, this place would offer the respite she desperately needed.

She thought of the rolling hills of the Highlands, the scent of heather and peat fires, and the sound of Gaelic songs drifting through the air. Her heart ached for the rugged beauty of her homeland and the fierce pride that came with it. But that world felt impossibly far away just now, almost like a dream.

Before she could collect herself, a soft knock sounded at the door.

"Come in," she called.

The door creaked open, and a young woman carrying fresh linens stepped inside.

Bridget's eyes widened in astonishment. "Catriona? Is it truly you?"

The maid looked up. Recognition lit her face, followed by a warm, familiar smile. "Lady Bridget! I scarcely expected to find you here." Her Scottish accent wrapped around the words like a welcome shawl.

She had no idea Catriona had remained in England, let alone here. Bridget's feet moved before her thoughts caught up. In two steps, she crossed the room and embraced her. "It's so good to see you! I thought you had gone to Ontario with your family."

Catriona returned the hug with quiet warmth, then stepped back, her smile still bright. She set the linens on a nearby chair and crossed the hearth to prepare tea. "Aye, my family did go to Ontario. But I married Killian Bain, and we chose to remain. Your father made arrangements for us. We were introduced to Lord Alastair, who offered us positions here."

"Married Killian Bain, did you?" Bridget's eyes sparkled with intrigue. "Now, *that* is a story I must hear!"

Catriona leaned against the dressing table, a wistful smile playing on her lips as she recalled the moment. "Ah, Lady Bridget, you should've seen him. All that strength, all that confidence he carries around like an iron shield, and yet, when it came to asking for my hand, the man was a bundle of nerves."

Bridget, seated near the hearth, raised a brow. "Killian? Nervous? I find that hard to believe."

Catriona let out a laugh, shaking her head. "It's true! I swear it. The man who could face down a raging bull without flinching fumbled his words like a lad reciting his lessons."

She sat beside Bridget, eyes shining as she continued. "He'd planned it, you see. Had everything arranged just so. Took me for a walk along the river, the sun setting behind the hills like something out of a painting. He was unusually quiet. Far too quiet for a man who always has something to say."

Bridget smiled at the image, picturing Killian, so steady and sure in most things, suddenly rendered uncertain by love. "And what did he say when he finally found his words?"

Catriona pressed a hand to her chest, feigning deep emotion. "Och, my lady, it was the most poetic speech you've ever heard," she teased, then softened, her voice taking on a more affectionate lilt. "He told me he'd spent years shaping iron and steel, bending it to his will, but that I was the one thing in this world he couldn't shape, couldn't force. That he didn't want to, because he loved me exactly as I was."

Bridget's breath caught, just for a moment. The words settled in places she hadn't expected. The quiet corners where doubt and pride still lingered.

"That's..." She paused, then smiled faintly. "That's rather

beautiful." And she meant it. Even if she couldn't imagine anyone ever saying it to her.

"Aye, well, then he dropped the ring."

Bridget blinked. "He what?"

Catriona burst into laughter, shaking her head. "Right into the river, mind you! The poor man nearly threw himself in after it. He was sputtering, cursing himself for a fool, soaking wet up to his knees." She wiped a tear from the corner of her eye. "It was the most ridiculous, wonderful thing I'd ever seen."

Bridget laughed, unable to help herself. "Did he find it?"

"Oh, aye. And when he did, he got down on one knee, soaking wet and grinning like a madman, and asked me properly. What could I do but say yes?"

Bridget reached for her friend's hand and gave it a squeeze. "I can't imagine a better proposal."

Catriona sighed, a dreamy look settling on her face. "Neither can I. It wasn't perfect, but it was ours. And that, my lady, is what makes all the difference." Her smile deepened. "He went to your father first, of course. Said he couldn't ask for my hand until the clan chief gave us his blessing."

Catriona leaned back in her chair, a wistful smile playing on her lips as she recounted the memory. "You should have seen Killian that day. He was steady as a mountain, but I knew him well enough to see the tension in his jaw, the way his fingers curled just so, like he was bracing himself for the hardest forge he'd ever faced. Standing before your father, the clan chief himself, is not a task for the faint of heart."

Bridget chuckled. "My father doesn't make things easy."

"No, he doesn't," Catriona agreed, shaking her head. "He listened, silent as ever, while Killian made his case. Told him plain that he loved me, that he'd stand by me, provide for me, and give me a life of honor. And your father just watched him, like a hawk sizing up a man before the strike. It was the longest moment of my life."

Bridget arched a brow. "And what did my father say?"

A smile touched Catriona's lips. "He told Killian that a man who bends steel with his hands ought to know the strength of a promise. And then, just like that, he gave us his blessing." She let out a small laugh. "I nearly wept from relief, but Killian? He only nodded, like he'd known all along that he'd earn your father's respect."

Bridget smiled, warmth filling her chest at the thought of her father granting his approval. "And what of your own family? They had plans to go to Ontario."

Catriona's expression softened. "Aye, they wanted us to go with them. A new life, fresh land, all of it seemed full of promise. But Scotland is in our bones, Killian and I both knew it. We couldn't go that far away, not when our roots were here."

Bridget's voice dropped to something softer. "I'm glad you stayed."

Catriona squeezed her fingers in return. "So am I. And I suppose fate had its own plans. Your father, in his quiet way, was our guardian angel."

Bridget smiled fondly. "Father does relish playing the hero."

"He spoke on our behalf. He introduced us to Lord Alastair. Shortly afterward, Lord Alastair offered us both work," Catriona continued. "Killian at the forge, me helping run the household. It wasn't what we had imagined, but it's become home."

Bridget's gaze grew distant for a moment before she smiled. "Funny, isn't it, how life takes you where you're meant to be, even if you never saw the path ahead."

"We were both torn. We didn't want to go so far away, but with little work to be had, we thought our only choice was to leave. We have hopes of returning some day."

"Killian made his grand declaration just as you were about to depart?" Bridget laughed softly. "Did he whisk you off your feet?"

Catriona's eyes danced with amusement. "Hardly. He nearly knocked me over in his haste. Subtlety has never been his strong suit."

Bridget grinned. "Life with him must be anything but dull."

"Aye, that it is," Catriona agreed with a fond smile. "We have each other and that, my lady, makes all the difference."

Bridget's expression softened. "I'm sincerely glad you both are faring well."

Catriona glanced at her thoughtfully. "And you, my lady? How are you faring?"

Bridget paused, choosing her words carefully. "Oh, managing as always."

Catriona gave her a knowing look but chose not to press further. "If there is anything you need during your stay, please do not hesitate to ask."

"Thank you," Bridget replied genuinely. After a pause, she added, "I would enjoy hearing more about how you've settled here. Perhaps when you have a spare moment?"

"I should like that very much," Catriona smiled. "But first, let's see you out of those damp clothes. A hot bath is waiting for you."

As Catriona helped her undress, Bridget couldn't help but ask, "Do you ever miss home?"

For a moment, Catriona's hands faltered. "Every day," she admitted softly. "But I hold onto hope that things may yet change."

Bridget felt a pang in her heart. "As do I," she whispered. They shared a quiet moment. Scotswomen, hearts tied to a land that would not let them go.

"Thank you for your help. I can do the rest." Bridget said softly. "It's late, and I'm sure Killian is waiting for you."

Catriona shook her head lightly. "It's no trouble at all, my lady. I'm happy to assist you."

Bridget offered a gentle smile. "I appreciate your kindness, but I insist. You should get some rest. We can catch up more in the morning."

Catriona curtsied gracefully. "Good night."

As she moved toward the door, Bridget added, "And give my regards to Killian."

A soft blush touched Catriona's cheeks. "I shall. He'll be pleased to hear you're here."

With a final smile, Catriona slipped out of the room, closing the door quietly behind her. Bridget listened to the fading footsteps in the corridor before letting out a soft sigh.

As she slipped beneath the water's warmth, the ache in her limbs began to fade, but the tightness coiled in her chest did not. Lavender and rosemary curled in the steam, their soothing scent failing to quiet the unrest in her mind.

Catriona and Killian had built a life here, finding a way to survive even as the echoes of the Clearances followed them. She had done the same, hadn't she? Yet, as she stared at the flickering candlelight reflecting off the bathwater, she wasn't so sure.

Her fingers drifted absently across the surface, sending ripples cascading outward. Then, unbidden, another image surfaced, storming-blue eyes, steady hands, and a knowing smirk beneath the brim of a rain-soaked hat. The Englishman. An irritation. A curiosity. And, most troubling of all, a distraction she could not afford.

Bridget exhaled sharply, sinking lower into the water. She had come to England with a purpose. And she would do well to remember it. She remained in the bath until the water cooled and her limbs grew heavy with fatigue. Only then did she rise, wrapping herself in a towel and moving slowly, as if the air itself resisted her return to the world beyond the warmth.

She dressed in silence, donning a fresh linen nightdress and wrapping herself in a thick woolen shawl. The air had cooled since she'd arrived, and the warmth from the bath only lingered so long. She crossed to the window and pushed back the heavy drapes. Moonlight filtered through the mist, casting a soft glow across the gardens. Somewhere in the distance, an owl hooted, its cry both eerie and comforting in the stillness.

The night held its breath, the hush stretching long and wide, as if the world itself waited for what might come next.

Bridget pressed her fingers to the cold glass. So much depended on her success here, her family's hopes, her people's survival, her own heart's stubborn need to matter beyond titles and ties.

She would do her part. But she would not be molded.

She would not be traded. And she would not be silenced.

She let the curtain fall and turned back to the room. The fire had dwindled to embers, but it was enough. Tomorrow, the masks would rise. But tonight, for a little while longer, she could simply be herself.

Chapter Three

June 26, 1821
Alastair Court

THE FOLLOWING MORNING, Bridget rose and brushed aside the curtain, letting the sunlight spill into the room. She stood at the window, her gaze drifting over the estate's manicured lawns, trimmed hedges, and the fountain in the middle of the duck pond at the lower end of the garden.

It was all orderly. Sculpted into submission. Beautiful, yes. But not alive the way the Highlands were.

She admired it, even envied its stillness. But it was not hers, not truly. She closed her eyes, lifted her face to the sun, and drew in a slow, steady breath.

The breath steadied her… carried her home to a world where the land stretched wild and unbroken, where the loch gleamed like liquid silver under the early morning sun, and the heather-kissed moors rolled endlessly toward the horizon. Her world. Her Highlands. Her Home. A place where she belonged, not this world of clipped hedges and sculpted fountains, but where the wind ran free and unbound.

She straightened and stood taller. She was Lady Bridget McConnell, daughter of Laird Duncan McConnell of Glencross, Chief of Clan McConnell. She was Highland born, Highland bred, and there was no English drawing room that could make her forget it.

She opened her eyes, but instead of the sculpted gardens

below, her mind offered another image, the man on the road. Tall, steady, rain-soaked, and silent. His eyes had unsettled her, not for their intensity, but for what they seemed to see. She had dismissed him as English, irrelevant. And yet, in a single glance, he had pierced the armor she thought impenetrable. That alone made him dangerous.

"Excuse me, Lady Bridget," Catriona said softly as she entered the room, setting a breakfast tray on the table.

Bridget turned, the aroma of warm bread and fresh tea drawing her back to the present. "Ah." She smiled as Catriona poured her tea. "It smells divine. It looks to be a good day. There's not a cloud in the sky."

She sat at the table, lifted her cup, letting the warmth seep into her fingers. "I was thinking this morning how difficult it must have been for you, leaving Glencross, your family, everything familiar, to start a new life here. Not every woman would have that kind of strength."

Catriona set the sugar bowl down, her expression thoughtful. "Your father always said the strongest women make the best wives. I remember him telling Killian that when he asked him, the clan chieftain, for his blessing."

Bridget leaned forward slightly, interest lighting in her eyes. "I don't believe you told me the full story of your wedding last night."

Catriona's cheeks pinked as she set down the sugar bowl. "Oh, it wasn't grand, not like the weddings in London. It was just the way we wanted. Small, in the village chapel, surrounded by friends."

Bridget exhaled, setting down her cup. "I should have been there."

Catriona's expression softened. "You were, in a way. Your father gave us his blessing in your name. He even made a toast at the gathering afterward. Said something about how no man with sense would let a good woman slip away."

Bridget let out a small laugh, though it didn't quite reach her eyes. "That sounds like my father."

"It was a beautiful day," Catriona said with a wistful lilt. "The sun broke through the morning mist just as we left the chapel. The whole village came out, even old Mrs. MacTavish."

"Mrs. MacTavish! She hasn't left her house in years." Bridget laughed, the sound easing some of the heaviness she hadn't realized she carried.

"She was one of the first to start dancing." Catriona took a breath. "We danced until the stars came out. Killian nearly put his foot through the floorboards, trying to keep up."

Bridget smiled, but something inside her ached. Longing curled in her chest, unwelcome but insistent. She could picture it, the warmth of the firelight flickering against the stone walls, the scent of peat and heather thick in the air, the sound of fiddles and laughter ringing across the hills. She should have been there.

She took a slow sip of tea, forcing her voice to stay even. "And you? Were you nervous?"

Catriona chuckled. "Nervous? Aye, but not about the marriage. Only that I'd trip on my own skirts and make a fool of myself before I got to the altar, but the moment I saw Killian waiting for me, it didn't matter." She looked down for a moment, her voice gentling. "That's how you know. When the rest of the world fades, and there's only the two of you."

Bridget tried to swallow around the raw, hot knot in her throat. That kind of love, steady, certain, all-consuming, was something she dreamed of. But it had never seemed further out of reach than at this moment.

She wiped her lips with her napkin, pushing the thought aside. "I am glad, Catriona. Truly. If anyone deserves happiness, it's you."

Catriona pulled a day dress out of the wardrobe and laid it out across the bed. She turned back to Bridget, studying her for a moment before nodding. "And so do you, my lady. When the right man comes along."

Bridget huffed a small laugh. "If the right man comes along."

Catriona smirked knowingly. "Och, I wouldn't be so quick to doubt. Stranger things have happened."

"That remains to be seen." She set her cup down, straightened her shoulders, and pushed aside the emotions clawing at her. This was not a morning for wistful dreaming. It was a morning for duty. Her breakfast finished, she rose and put the napkin on the table. "Help me dress. I don't want to keep Lady Marjory waiting."

⇶⇷

BY THE TIME Bridget entered the drawing room, the scent of fresh ink and beeswax polish filled the air. Marjory paced before the writing desk, a note crumpled in her hand. Her husband, Mark Alastair, leaned against the mantel, arms crossed, watching his wife with a bemused expression.

"A dilemma?" Bridget teased as she approached. The tension in the air was palpable, though not the kind that heralded disaster, the kind that meant Marjory had a problem to solve and was determined to solve it perfectly.

Marjory let out a sharp breath and tossed the note onto the desk. "One of the gentlemen has sent his regrets at the last moment. The seating, the teams for the chase, even the numbers for dinner, it's all in disarray."

Alastair smirked. "It's hardly the end of the world, my dear."

Marjory shot him a glare. "Spoken like a man who has never had to manage a house party."

Bridget pressed her lips together to stifle a laugh.

"And now what?" Alastair asked, folding his arms. "Will the universe collapse because a chair is left empty?"

Marjory rubbed her temple. "You don't understand, Mark. It's not just a missing chair. It's the balance of the entire weekend."

He sighed and shook his head. "There are times I think you

create these problems simply to have something to fret over." He paused, his gaze lingering on her. "Or perhaps to keep yourself distracted."

Before Marjory could retort, the butler appeared at the doorway. "My lord, a Mr. Edgar Tresham has arrived to see you."

Alastair straightened, surprise flickering across his face before recognition dawned. "Tresham? The professor? I wasn't expecting him, but this is excellent."

Marjory arched a brow. "Who is Edgar Tresham?"

Her husband grinned. "A scholar and historian. He specializes in ancient texts and has been invaluable in helping me authenticate some of my rarer acquisitions."

Bridget noted Marjory's skeptical expression. "And why, precisely, is he here?"

Alastair shrugged. "I've no idea, but I'm eager to find out." He turned to the butler. "Have him wait for me in the library."

Marjory waved a distracted hand. "Go, then. Bury yourself in your old books while I sort this out."

"I do want our house party to be a memorable event. I'll return as soon as I see why the professor is visiting." He gently kissed the top of Marjory's head. "Try not to plot my demise while I'm away."

"No promises," Marjory called after him, though a glint of amusement had crept into her eyes.

Bridget watched the exchange with quiet fondness. Whatever tension lingered beneath the surface, Marjory and Alastair were still partners, tied to one another by habit, affection, and something older than titles and expectations.

ALASTAIR ENTERED THE library to find Tresham standing before the towering bookshelves, his fingers trailing reverently over the spines. The scholar was so engrossed that he did not immediately acknowledge Mark's presence. He looked as though he had stepped into a sanctuary.

"Good morning, Professor. Your visit is a pleasant surprise." Alastair walked toward his visitor to see which of his prized tomes interested the man.

"Impressive," Tresham murmured. "You've collected some remarkable works, Lord Alastair. I admit, I had not expected such dedication."

"Books are one of the few indulgences I allow myself." Alastair glanced lovingly at the shelves before his gaze returned to his guest. "And, as you know, I've been working diligently to restore this library."

The professor's gaze drifted back to the shelves, stopping on a particular volume. "A surviving edition of *De Secretis Naturae*," he murmured, his voice touched with reverence. "There are very few copies left intact. Many believe its contents to be mythical. It is said to contain knowledge on alchemy, processes lost to time."

Alastair smirked. "And do you believe in such lost wisdom?"

Tresham's lips quirked. "I believe that those in power have often sought to suppress what they do not understand and cannot control."

The professor returned to investigate the spines on the shelf. His fingers moved to another volume. "*Historia Regum Britanniae*, a text filled with myths interwoven into history. Geoffrey of Monmouth's account is more legend than fact, but it shaped the way many view Britain's past." He glanced at Alastair. "It is interesting that you have both of these works side by side. One speaks of power through knowledge, the other of power through narrative. Together, they shape history or erase it entirely."

Alastair studied him. "And which do you prefer?"

Tresham's lips twitched. "The truth, wherever it may lie."

A silence stretched between them, broken only by the distant chime of a clock.

"I am here to pay my respects to a fellow collector." He glanced at the shelves. "I am glad I did." Tresham hesitated. "I had planned to leave for London tomorrow, but seeing your collection, I find myself regretting that I hadn't arranged time with you."

Alastair regarded him thoughtfully, weighing the opportunity. Marjory had been fretting about the imbalance since the letter arrived that morning, Baron Linwood had taken ill, leaving them one gentleman short. She had already begun reshuffling seating arrangements, but a last-minute addition would certainly ease her concerns.

Yet it was not only Marjory's predicament that gave Alastair pause. He had long since learned that men like Professor Tresham did not speak idly. The regret in his tone was genuine, but there was something else beneath it, a hunger. It was the look of a man who had found something unexpected and wasn't ready to leave it behind.

Alastair let his gaze sweep the library, the warm glow of candlelight flickering over rows of priceless tomes. He had spent years amassing his collection, curating it with care and discretion. Only a handful of men could appreciate its worth, not merely in monetary value, but in historical significance. Tresham was one such man.

It was a risk, but also an opportunity.

He nodded at last. "We find ourselves short a guest for our weekend house party. Allow me to extend an invitation. You would be doing us a favor."

Tresham inclined his head, a thoughtful glint in his eye. "Are you certain? I do not want to impose."

"Not at all, Professor. Your presence will round out the event nicely."

Tresham tapped a finger against his chin, his gaze drifting once more to the shelves. "An unexpected turn of events, indeed." His hesitation was tinged more with calculation than reluctance. "I must admit, the opportunity is tempting."

Alastair grinned, sensing the scholar's interest lay less in the company and more in the tomes before him. "I shall send word for your belongings. You'll find Alastair Court accommodating in every way."

As he turned to leave, Alastair glanced back. "By the by, you do play Whist, don't you?"

Tresham hesitated before answering, but Alastair had already turned, his fingers tapping absently against his thigh, a restless habit Marjory had mentioned only days ago.

Tresham's attention snapped from the books to his lordship. "No, I do not."

Alastair hesitated only a fraction before waving off the concern. "Not an issue. We'll be playing here in the library. You'll be among us, even if not at the tables. Take your time with the books. Should anything pique your interest, I'd be glad to discuss it."

Tresham's lips quirked, his gaze sweeping the shelves once more. "I suspect there is more hidden in these pages than meets the eye, my lord."

Alastair chuckled. "Scholars and their secrets."

With that, he strode out, already anticipating Marjory's relief at his solution.

Chapter Four

MARJORY EXHALED. HER expression shifted from playful amusement to a trace of lingering frustration as her husband disappeared down the hall. "Men," she muttered with a sigh. "They always seem to think that with enough patience, every problem will sort itself out."

"We still have one more lady than gentleman for the weekend, and he's content to leave it to fate. I'd rather not begin the house party with an imbalance that sets tongues wagging."

Marjory took a deep breath and turned to Bridget as she lifted the teapot with practiced ease. "Did you sleep well? I know you had an awful experience last night." She poured the tea slowly, her movements composed and careful.

Bridget nodded. "Yes, thank you. I was warm and dry before I knew it." But her shoulders hadn't yet eased. The memory of the rain and the mud clung to her skin, no matter how she tried to forget it.

Marjory offered her the teacup. Steam rose in delicate curls, fragrant and comforting. Bridget inhaled it, but her thoughts had already begun to wander elsewhere.

The rain. The road. The captain with the steady blue eyes.

She had spent half the night trying to forget him and the other half wondering why she couldn't. It was foolish, she knew. He was likely no more than a soldier passing through, and yet the memory clung to her like damp wool.

"And thank you for sending breakfast up this morning." Bridget accepted the cup with a small, grateful smile. "It was a bit decadent, but I enjoyed the sunshine, and the view of the garden made it a delightful treat." She paused to savor the tea, adding, "And thank goodness for no rain."

Setting her cup aside, she glanced at the papers scattered before Marjory. "Now, where shall we begin?"

Marjory sighed and ran a hand over the guest list. "I thought I'd arranged everything perfectly, but with one less gentleman, the balance is thrown into disarray, assuming Mark's friend doesn't cancel as well." Her gaze drifted toward the door. "Mark may have a solution, though his mind has been elsewhere of late. I suppose we'll just have to plan around it."

"We can review what you have and see where we need to make adjustments," Bridget offered as she leaned in and studied the list.

Several heartbeats later, Bridget raised her head. "I hadn't realized Lord Byron Davenport was attending."

"Indeed, he was one of the first to respond." Marjory rolled her eyes. "He's quite the chatterbox, especially about horses."

Bridget smiled slyly. "Perhaps we should seat him next to Lady Carlisle. From what I recall from your soiree in London, they are two of a kind. Besides her fascination with horses, I'm not sure which one of them can out-chatter the other."

Marjory let out an unladylike snort and waved a hand at the list. "I'm not sure you've met everyone yet. Lord Barrington and his ever-gracious companion, Mrs. Bainbridge will be joining us. They never fail to brighten a room. Then there's my dear friend, Miss Penelope Hathaway, who has agreed to delight us with a few rousing tunes on the pianoforte. As for Miss Arabella Gray, she's a veritable butterfly, vivacious and flitting from one sparkling conversation to the next. And finally, there's Sir Frederick Townsend, a quiet, down-to-earth man with a keen mind. I daresay his company will be most engaging."

"It looks like Lord Blackwood and Lady Worthington complete your list," Bridget observed, lifting her head. "But it's a bit uneven, seven women and only five men. Besides the one gentleman who sent his regrets, who's the other missing mystery man?"

"A friend of Mark's," Marjory replied with a dismissive flick of her hand. "I prefer not to write him off until I get his response. Perhaps Mark can persuade him to bring a companion."

Bridget only half-listened. The house party was a world unto itself, intriguing, yes, but hardly what occupied her thoughts. Still, she conceded that the evening might pass quicker with good company, and after all, even the most meticulously arranged gatherings held their share of surprises.

Alastair returned to the drawing room with a casual, triumphant smile playing on his lips.

"That was rather quick. What was all that about?" Marjory asked.

He grinned, clearly pleased with himself. "Fortune has smiled upon us, my dear. We are no longer short a gentleman."

Marjory raised an eyebrow, skepticism lacing her tone. "Indeed? And who is to be our savior?"

Stepping closer, he poured himself a cup before answering. "Edgar Tresham, a historian of some renown, well-versed in rare texts. He came to discuss matters concerning my library."

Marjory's eyes narrowed slightly. "And you invited him to stay?"

"He showed great interest in the collection. It seemed only logical," he replied, looking quite proud of himself. "And as luck would have it, he was not opposed to an extended visit."

"A historian? Attending a house party?" Bridget mused.

Alastair chuckled. "Not every guest need be preoccupied with fashion and frivolity, or Whist for that matter. Besides, Lady Worthington might find him interesting. Her father, Lord Kerrington, was quite the scholar."

"Are we playing Whist?" Bridget glanced at Marjory.

"Indeed. Marjory firmly believes that a well-matched partnership brings out the best in both players. Two minds in concert make victories all the sweeter. Whoever heard of a solo triumph?" Alastair teased, glancing at his wife with playful amusement, though his smile didn't quite reach his eyes.

"Thank you for evening out our table, but that doesn't help me with the plans for the card room." Marjory returned to studying the guest list.

"I would enjoy being your partner. However, you will be darting about. I might as well be playing alone." Alastair let his words rest. "I shall see that Tresham participates in our other entertainments. Is that satisfactory?"

Marjory pursed her lips, then let out a slow breath. "I suppose it is better than enduring an uneven table."

Alastair reached for her hand, brushing a kiss over her knuckles. "You wound me, my love. A perfectly balanced guest list and not a hint of gratitude?"

Marjory sighed, though a mischievous twinkle softened her words. "You are insufferable."

"And yet, you married me."

Bridget smothered a laugh behind her hand as Marjory sighed with exaggerated suffering.

"Very well, then. I shall have a place set for Mr. Tresham."

He gave a satisfied nod. "Then all is settled."

Marjory turned to Bridget with a bemused expression. "A historian at our house party. What do you make of that?"

Bridget tapped her fingers thoughtfully against the rim of her teacup. "I think this party will be more intriguing than anyone expected."

"Let's hope the professor finds something to amuse him," Marjory said. "We wouldn't want him asking too many questions."

Bridget arched a brow. "Questions? What might he ask?"

"Only about old books and older stories. Now, if you will excuse me," Alastair said with a lazy smile as he moved toward the door.

"Bridget." Marjory put the papers aside. "I want to have one last look at the blooms. The hydrangeas and lavender will be a perfect addition to the vases for the dining room."

The invitation lightened the moment. Bridget followed as Marjory led her toward the garden. Along the winding path, manicured hedges gave way to bursts of color from the flowering bushes in full bloom.

Pausing before a particularly vibrant cluster of hydrangeas, Marjory gently brushed her fingertips over the petals. "These are stunning. Just imagine how they'll bring life to our table. I'll have the gardener bring some to Mrs. Simmons. We can add them to the floral arrangements."

They strolled quietly, enjoying the gentle breeze that carried the delicate scent of roses and honeysuckle. "You seem more at ease today," Marjory said to Bridget.

Bridget nodded thoughtfully. "There's a certain comfort in being useful. Keeping busy helps to take my mind off...things."

Marjory gave her a knowing look as they reached the garden wall. "I'm grateful for your help." She glanced toward the house. "Come along. There is still much to prepare. I had the staff bring the vases into the drawing room to finish the arrangements."

Bridget followed her back through the garden. "You've planned the perfect weekend," she said with a small approving smile.

"Planned, yes," Marjory said, though her smile faltered as they entered the drawing room. "Yet Mark has been... preoccupied lately." She smoothed an invisible crease on her skirt.

"Excuse me, my lady." Drummund, the footman, approached with a slight bow, a silver tray in hand.

Marjory glanced at her writing desk, where an array of open invitations and neatly penned responses lay in careful order. She accepted the morning post with a quiet nod, sorting through the letters briefly, until Drummond, handed her a final sealed missive.

She paused, then took it from Drummund with a quiet, "Thank you."

Bridget, seated nearby, sipped her tea, observing with mild amusement as Marjory methodically sorted through the correspondence, the rhythm of her movements precise and practiced. House parties required an artful balance of matching personalities, avoiding known feuds, and ensuring that no guest felt slighted in their placement. It was a task Marjory handled with remarkable skill, though even she could not mask the occasional flicker of exasperation when dealing with the more demanding guests.

Marjory broke the wax seal of the latest letter, her eyes scanning the contents before a satisfied smile curved her lips. Setting it aside, she reached for her quill and adjusted the seating arrangements yet again.

"Well," she said at last, her tone tinged with amusement as she placed her pen down. "I believe we've accommodated everyone's preferences and peculiarities. No small feat, I assure you." She folded the final guest list with an air of triumph. "We've added the esteemed professor, and as for the other missing gentleman, here is his confirmation." She paused for effect, glancing at Bridget with a knowing glint in her eye. "Thomas Grenville has confirmed his attendance."

Bridget raised an eyebrow. "Alastair's friend, I presume?"

"Yes. They met in Spain, in an antique shop of all places. He has been working on restoring Grenville Hall to its former beauty. At the time, Mark was searching for books that were once owned by his family. That's what led to his obsession with old books."

"And he met Grenville while he searched for antiques?"

"Actually, they met at a booth outside the antique shop. Mark was thumbing through a book written in a foreign language. Mark knows five or six languages, but this one escaped him. Grenville heard him struggling with Old Gaelic and stepped in."

Bridget stared at Marjory for several heartbeats. "Grenville can read Old Gaelic?"

Marjory lifted her brow at Bridget's tone. "Don't look so

surprised. Grenville is an outstanding man, even for an Englishman." She stirred her tea leisurely, clearly enjoying Bridget's reaction. "He spent years abroad, and only recently returned to England to restore his family's estate. He is, by all accounts, well-read, well-traveled, and, if the rumors are to be believed, quite the mystery."

Bridget chuckled softly as she folded her arms, and considered this new piece of information. "And you've invited him here."

Marjory tilted her head, mischief flickering in her eyes. "Naturally. A gentleman of intelligence, charm, and intrigue? How could I not?"

Bridget shook her head, suppressing a smile. She had a feeling Marjory was quite enjoying the challenge of orchestrating this particular gathering.

Marjory laughed lightly. "Well, I look forward to seeing if Mr. Grenville lives up to the legend. They say he's gathered a wealth of experiences from his travels. Some even whisper that he's not the same man who left England all those years ago, though no one can quite say why."

Bridget offered a soft laugh. "People do tend to embellish when it involves someone's dramatic return."

"Perhaps," Marjory conceded, "but there's something about a man with a few unanswered questions that makes him... intriguing, don't you think?"

Bridget shook her head lightly. "You know me, I've little interest in chasing after shadows and secrets."

Marjory chuckled. "Maybe so, but a touch of uncertainty adds a bit of thrill to a house party. Grenville might prove to be a refreshing addition to our gathering."

"We shall see," Bridget replied, a subtle smile playing on her lips.

Marjory gestured toward the row of boots lined neatly near the hearth. "At least the weather has improved. I daresay we won't be stepping through puddles today."

Bridget's gaze lingered on the worn leather boots near the

hearth, a pair clearly left by Mark. They were scuffed at the toes and softened by use, an everyday sight in an English country home. But to her, they were a symbol of how easily men could remain grounded in comfort, in their world of familiar rules and solid expectations. A quiet envy stirred, of their certainty, their simplicity. She drew a breath, reminding herself why she had come.

A weekend house party required preparation, and esteemed guests would soon be arriving. She must set her thoughts in order.

Marjory couldn't resist. "You know, with all these eligible gentlemen arriving, perhaps one will catch your eye."

Bridget smirked. "I came to enjoy your gardens and good company, not to parade about for suitors."

She paused, then softened. "But if I find a friend, someone worth knowing, well, we'll see what develops."

Her tone was light, but the words carried. She didn't fear men, but English gentlemen often viewed spirited women as projects to tame, not equals to admire.

"Can't it be both?" Marjory teased.

"Not when the suitors in question are more interested in their own reflections than meaningful conversation."

Marjory shook her head, laughing softly. "One day, Bridget, someone will surprise you."

"Perhaps, but I won't hold my breath," Bridget replied.

"Excuse me, my lady." They both turned to Mrs. Simmons, a basket of flowers in her hand. "The gardener brought in lavender and hydrangeas to add to the floral arrangements you approved earlier."

Bridget sighed, eyeing the flowers warily. "Lavender and hydrangeas, so we're aiming for elegance with a hint of 'don't cross me'?"

Marjory laughed. "Precisely. Nothing says refined hospitality like flowers that could double as a warning."

"Allow me to finish the arrangements for you," Bridget offered. "I'll come and get you when I'm done."

"That would be a big help. Now that we have our final guest list, Mrs. Simmons and I can meet with Cook, finalize the menu and sleeping arrangements for the weekend. I want everything in place before our guests arrive today. Are you sure you don't mind?"

"I'm in need of some activity." Bridget took the basket from Mrs. Simmons. "You go ahead. I'll have them all done by the time you return."

⊱⊱⊱✦⊰⊰⊰

GRENVILLE RODE UP the gravel path leading to Alastair Court, the estate as impressive as he remembered. It was hard to believe it had been five years since he'd been here. He dismounted and handed Valor's reins to a waiting stable boy.

Alastair hurried down the steps, a knowing smirk in place. "Grenville! I was beginning to think you'd abandoned us altogether."

Grenville shook his friend's hand. "Not for lack of trying. The roads are conspiring against me."

Alastair chuckled. "Some things never change. Come inside before my wife puts you straight to work."

As they walked through the grand foyer, Alastair glanced at Grenville. "Brace yourself. Marjory has assembled quite the gathering, and I suspect you'll be drawn into the intrigue before long."

"I'll do my best," Grenville said dryly.

"Good man. Oh, and you must meet Marjory's friend. She's sharp-witted, fiercely independent. I suspect you'll find her... intriguing."

Grenville nodded politely, though his mind was already sifting through what little he had been told. A woman described as *sharp-witted and fiercely independent* piqued his curiosity more than he cared to admit.

The women he had encountered at such gatherings typically fell into predictable categories. They were charming yet conventional, or intelligent but bound by propriety. Few possessed both qualities with any real force. If Alastair saw fit to offer a warning, however lightly spoken, then perhaps Marjory's friend was worth noting. He had met many intriguing people on his travels, but intrigue was not always a comfort. Still, something in Alastair's tone lingered, half warning, half invitation, and Grenville found himself unexpectedly alert.

"I look forward to it." He kept his tone carefully neutral.

"Now, go into the drawing room and pour yourself a drink. I'll join you shortly."

Chapter Five

B RIDGET ADDED THE last of the hydrangeas and lavender to the arrangements. Lost in thought, she didn't hear footsteps approaching. As she stepped back to admire her work, she collided with a solid figure.

"I beg your pardon," she exclaimed, regaining her balance.

"No, the fault is mine entirely," came a familiar voice.

Bridget looked up, her gaze locking onto a pair of striking blue eyes, ones she had tried and failed to forget.

"You?" they blurted out together.

Bridget's fingers curled into her skirts. A scowl formed, not from irritation alone, though that was part of it. Recognition struck, clean and immediate. The man from the road. The Baron of Bother, in the very flesh.

She drew a slow breath and smothered the impulse to step back. *No,* she told herself. *Not again.*

"What unfortunate twist of fate brought you here?" she asked, her tone edged with irritation.

Grenville arched a brow and smiled… maddeningly slow, as if he savored her displeasure. "Perhaps fate determined you required further instruction in gracious acceptance."

Bridget huffed, crossing her arms. "And you imagine yourself qualified for the task."

His smirk deepened. He dipped his head in a manner just polite enough to vex her. "It appears our paths cross once more, Miss…"

"McConnell," she said, her pulse still catching on recognition. She broadened her smile. "Lady McConnell."

"Captain Thomas Grenville, Baron of Bother, at your service," he said with an amused bow.

His playfulness broke through her reserve. *Baron of Bother.* She gently shook her head. "So, you're the elusive Captain Grenville everyone's been anticipating." She arched an eyebrow.

"I wasn't aware I was the subject of such discussion." A mischievous, playful smile tugged at his lips, one he failed to suppress.

"Oh, modesty doesn't suit you." She bit the inside of her cheek to keep from smiling. "But it does make for entertaining company."

He chuckled softly. "I'll take that as a compliment. And may I say, it's a pleasure to formally make your acquaintance, without the hindrance of torrential rain."

"Agreed. Though the mud did add a certain charm to our initial meeting." A playful glint touched her eyes.

"A charm I'd rather not repeat," he replied.

There was a moment of comfortable silence before Bridget gestured to the flowers. "I should return to these arrangements."

"Of course." He gave her a nod. "Perhaps we'll have the opportunity to speak again during the weekend."

"Perhaps," she echoed with a slight smile.

He gave a sufficient bow and left the room.

Bridget turned back to the flowers, her hands moving with deliberate precision. *He's just a man,* she told herself, *just a persistent, infuriatingly composed man with an annoyingly impeccable memory of their last encounter."*

He had steadied her with ease, without assumption, without condescension. That memory lingered, uninvited, unwelcome, yet not entirely unpleasant.

She tugged at a stem harder than necessary. No, not thinking about him at all. This is ridiculous," she murmured.

"May I assist you, my lady?"

Bridget raised her head quickly and stared at one of the footmen watching her. She drew a steadying breath.

"Thank you, but no. The hydrangeas seem to have a mind of their own today. But I am undaunted. They will bend to my will."

The young man nodded and left while she turned back to the flowers, which were more than compliant to her demands.

"There you are." Marjory swept into the room. She glanced around and then turned to Bridget. "I just spoke to the footman. Drummond mentioned that the hydrangeas presented a problem, something about not cooperating." She glanced at the vases on the table. "You must be a hard taskmaster. You have them standing up and saluting." Marjory's eyes twinkled.

"I didn't know you had spies about." Bridget focused on primping the flowers, although she was finished with them.

Marjory looked stunned but quickly recovered. "There are times when I do not know when you are teasing." She shook her head. "Now, let's see," she continued. "We need to put down the place cards. I thought to seat Lady Worthington to the right of Lord Blackwood. They always have such interesting conversations." Marjory picked up the place cards and began to arrange them.

Bridget didn't comment. She continued to tug at the lavender, her mind obviously elsewhere.

Marjory paused and stared at her guest for a moment or two. "We could seat Lady Worthington next to the giraffe," she mused. "I hear he's quite the conversationalist."

"Hmm? Oh, yes, that sounds fine."

"Perfect, and when the elephant arrives with the dessert, we can have him parade through the garden before serving."

"Of course, that sounds lovely," Bridget murmured, still lost in thought.

Marjory raised an eyebrow, a mischievous grin spreading across her face. "And perhaps we should invite Mark's pet tiger to lead the first dance?"

"If you like." Bridget's mind remained fixated elsewhere.

Marjory chuckled to herself. "You're not listening to me, are you, Bridget?"

Bridget blinked, finally pulling her attention back to the present. "I'm sorry, what did you say?"

Marjory laughed. "Oh, nothing important, just planning a royal circus for our guests."

Bridget smiled sheepishly. "My mind was elsewhere."

"On the flowers? Or perhaps on a certain captain who arrived?" Marjory's tone was teasing.

Bridget met her gaze with feigned innocence. "Surely, you're imagining things."

"Oh, I think you know exactly what I mean," Marjory said, a glint of mischief in her eye. "I saw you speaking with Captain Grenville a few minutes ago before he left the room almost whistling."

Bridget gave a dismissive wave. "Mere pleasantries after an unfortunate incident. Nothing to inspire gossip, I assure you." She busied herself with the nearest vase, pretending the arrangement required more attention than it did.

"Is that so?" Marjory leaned closer. "Because it seemed to me there was a spark of recognition between you two."

Bridget hesitated, then sighed. "We met briefly on the road yesterday. He assisted me when my carriage was stuck in the mud."

"In all that rain? And you failed to mention this?" Marjory feigned offense.

"It slipped my mind amidst wanting to get out of my wet clothes," Bridget said dismissively.

"Hmm, I doubt that." Marjory tried to suppress her smile but failed miserably. "We've done enough here. We have time for tea before we need to get ready. You can tell me all about your brief encounter with Grenville. Mrs. Simmons mentions she'd like us to sample tomorrow's dessert."

"You will be sorely disappointed. A wheel got stuck in the

mud, we fixed it, and I promptly forgot about it, until now, thanks to you."

She avoided the mention of his hands on her waist, or the brief, unsettling moment when she felt safe, just for a breath. That was the part she wanted to forget.

"The two of you? You? And the mud?" Marjory grabbed her by the hand and tugged. "Come with me. Now, you must tell me what happened."

Chapter Six

L ATE AFTERNOON SETTLED over the estate, dimming the day's sharper moments. Bridget's encounter with Captain Grenville and her quiet conversation with Marjory still lingered, unresolved and unsettled. But as the manor filled with warm voices and the rustle of evening preparations, the gentle murmur of the guests offered a welcome reprieve.

Bridget stood near the tall windows draped in rich velvet, her fingers lightly resting on the stem of a crystal wine glass. The soft murmur of conversation flowed around her like a gentle breeze. She gazed out into the twilight, where the last traces of daylight lingered over the gardens. Despite the gathering crowd, she felt oddly adrift, the memory of the Captain's gaze, searching and stubborn, still prickling at the edge of her thoughts.

Marjory approached with a warm smile, accompanied by a young woman with chestnut curls and lively eyes.

"Bridget, I'd like to introduce you to Miss Arabella Gray," She gestured to the young woman at her side. "Miss Gray, meet Lady Bridget McConnell."

Miss Gray curtsied gracefully. "Lady Bridget, it's a pleasure to make your acquaintance. I've heard much about you."

Bridget offered a warm smile. "The pleasure is mine, Miss Gray. I hope you've heard only favorable things."

"Indeed," Miss Gray replied with a light laugh. "Marjory speaks highly of your wit and spirit."

Marjory hesitated for a heartbeat, her smile faltering before she recovered. Whatever thought crossed her mind, she kept it to herself. "If you will excuse me, Lady Carlisle requires my attention." She turned back to them with a knowing smile. "Lord Blackwood is eager to meet you. I'm sure he will seek you out shortly."

Before Bridget could respond, Marjory slipped away into the crowd. Miss Gray watched her depart, then turned back to Bridget with an amused expression.

"Marjory does enjoy arranging introductions," Miss Gray remarked.

"She is ever the attentive hostess," Bridget agreed, a hint of irony.

"I suspect she delights in orchestrating more than social niceties." Miss Gray's eyes gleamed with mischief.

Bridget arched an eyebrow. "Are you suggesting she has ulterior motives?"

"Not at all," Miss Gray protested. "Only that she has an eye for potential friendships." She paused, her gaze thoughtful. "Lord Blackwood is a notable figure, charming and well-regarded."

"Do you know him well?" Bridget hoped Marjory wasn't playing matchmaker.

"We have crossed paths at various gatherings," Miss Gray replied. "He is a man of agreeable company."

A voice interrupted, smooth and unmistakably confident. "Miss Gray, spreading your charm as ever."

They turned to find Lord Cedric Blackwood bowing with polished ease.

Miss Gray greeted with a polite nod. "Lord Blackwood, may I introduce Lady Bridget McConnell?"

Blackwood inclined his head with a charming smile. "A pleasure, Lady Bridget. Lady Alastair mentioned your recent arrival from Scotland."

Bridget's gaze lingered on him for a moment. His smile was practiced. His manner was smooth, altogether too smooth. Her wariness was stirred, not by fear, but from instinct, honed by too many encounters with English charm that hid something less honorable.

Bridget studied him briefly before responding. She had met enough men like him to recognize the easy charm for what it was, a mask worn smooth with use. Still, she returned the courtesy with a slight nod. "Yes. I find Sommer-by-the-Sea possesses its own charm."

"Indeed," he agreed. "Though I confess, nothing quite compares to the rugged beauty of the Highlands."

Bridget's interest piqued. It was rare for an Englishman to speak of Scotland with more than a passing remark about the unpredictable weather or wild landscape. Her gaze sharpened slightly. "You are familiar with Scotland?"

A flicker of something unreadable crossed his expression before he answered. "My family has ancestral ties to the region," he explained. "Though circumstances have kept me away for some time."

There was a careful neutrality in his words, a vagueness that pricked at Bridget's instincts. Men who spoke fondly of Scotland usually did so with passion or nostalgia, but Blackwood's tone carried neither.

"It's refreshing to meet someone who shares an appreciation for my homeland," she said warmly, though she kept her curiosity close. "Few speak of it with such awareness."

Blackwood's smile held, but there was the slightest pause before he replied. "One never truly forgets the land that shaped them."

With amusement, Miss Gray gave a knowing smile and stepped back. "I shall leave you both to discuss the merits of the north. If you will excuse me."

Bridget barely registered her departure. Alone with Lord Blackwood, her wariness sharpened. It was instinct, honed by years of watching charm wielded like a polished blade. He was articulate, refined, and just ambiguous enough to stir the caution her father warned her never to ignore.

Something about his words lingered, like a thread left dangling. She had spent her life learning to hear what was left unsaid. And Lord Blackwood, for all his elegance, was choosing his words with care.

Careful men often had something to hide.

"Miss Gray is a delightful companion," Blackwood observed.

"Yes, she is."

Blackwood's gaze was thoughtful. "Tell me, Lady Bridget, what do you miss most about Scotland? Aside from your family, of course."

She considered his question for a moment. "The vast landscapes, the sense of freedom. There is a spirit in the air that one does not find elsewhere."

He nodded appreciatively. "Very true. The heather-covered hills and the mist over the lochs hold a certain magic."

Bridget smiled softly. "You speak as one who knows them well."

"I have spent sufficient time there to understand their allure," he replied.

"Do you plan to return soon?" she asked.

He gave a slight shrug. "Duty often dictates one's movements. But I hope to revisit when the opportunity allows."

Before Bridget could respond, the butler's voice carried across the room. "Lord Barrington and Captain Thomas Grenville."

Her gaze swept toward the entrance at Mr. Simmon's announcement. Of course it was *him*, the infuriating Englishman who had not only pulled her carriage from the mud but also managed to wedge himself stubbornly into her thoughts. Tall and composed, he surveyed the room with the ease of a man accustomed to command.

Lord Barrington stood next to him, poised yet undeniably imposing. Candlelight played upon his sharp features, casting shadows that accentuated the strong line of his jaw.

Her eyes met the captain's, and for a fleeting moment, something unspoken crackled between them, a flicker of annoyance, she assured herself.

"You appear most displeased, Lady Bridget," Blackwood observed, his gaze shifting between her and Grenville. "I take it you know him?"

"Our paths have crossed," Bridget replied tersely. She resisted the urge to fidget with her skirts, instead lifting her chin ever so slightly.

"A man of distinguished service," Blackwood remarked. "Though perhaps a tad stern."

"Is that what you English call arrogance?" she muttered, not bothering to mask the disdain in her voice.

Blackwood arched an amused brow. "Such conviction, Lady Bridget."

She exhaled, her fingers tightening around her glass. "Experience is a cruel tutor. Particularly when one is confronted with a man who believes charm an adequate substitute for humility."

"Ah, I forget your sentiments about our southern neighbors," Blackwood said lightly. "Though not all Englishmen deserve such anger."

"Don't they?" Bridget retorted, finally tearing her eyes away from Grenville to look at him. "Tell me, Lord Blackwood, have you not seen the effects of their so-called progress? The Clearances have left scars that run deep."

Blackwood's expression remained unreadable. "I have, indeed. But time has a way of reshaping wounds into history. And history is often kinder to those who adapt."

"Easy to say when it's not your family being uprooted," she replied, the bitterness evident in her tone.

He inclined his head. "Touché."

Bridget stole another glance at Grenville. He had stepped aside with Lord Barrington near a table with crystal decanters. Their heads were inclined toward one another, the soft murmur of their conversation lost amidst the background chatter.

⫸⫷

Lord Barrington handed Grenville a glass of claret, his gaze sweeping over the elegantly attired guests. "A proper evening of leisure. There are no pressing matters, no looming urgency. Refreshing, wouldn't you agree?"

Grenville accepted the glass with a slight nod. "A rare indulgence, perhaps, but not unwelcome."

He let the claret settle on his tongue a moment longer than necessary. "Though I confess, the token you sent didn't suggest leisure."

Barrington's smile was mild. "No, I suppose it didn't." He took a sip of his own, adding after a heartbeat, "But your arrival was necessary all the same."

Barrington swirled his wine, his expression laced with quiet amusement. "It occurs to me you may have forgotten how to enjoy an evening without purpose."

Grenville huffed a quiet laugh. "I suppose old habits are difficult to break."

Barrington followed his line of sight, his eyes settled briefly on Bridget, who was engaged in an animated discussion with Blackwood. "Lady Alastair has gathered quite the collection of personalities. Some more intriguing than others."

Grenville took a measured sip of his wine. "Intriguing, indeed."

Barrington arched a brow. "And yet your attention seems drawn to one in particular."

Grenville raised an eyebrow in return. "Observant, as always."

"Years of practice." Barrington's lips quirked. "Though I'd wager you've had little practice in dealing with a woman of Lady Bridget's caliber."

Grenville exhaled, tilting his glass slightly. "Our acquaintance is... complex."

Barrington smirked knowingly. "Most worthwhile things are. Perhaps it's time you considered challenges of a different nature."

Grenville cast him a wry glance. "You sound perilously close to matchmaking, Barrington."

"Perish the thought," Barrington said, eyes twinkling. "Though I do believe the game is already afoot."

The dinner bell rang.

"Come now," Barrington said, gesturing toward the dining room. "Lady Alastair has gone to great lengths to arrange this evening, and I, for one, am eager to see how the players position themselves at the table."

Before Grenville could respond, a familiar voice, rich with amusement, joined them.

"Ah, discussing the evening's entertainment, are we?" Mrs. Honoria Bainbridge appeared at Barrington's side, a knowing twinkle in her eye. "Or are you both scheming something far more intriguing?"

Barrington chuckled. "Merely an observation or two. You know how I enjoy studying the field before play begins."

Honoria's gaze flitted briefly to Bridget, then back to Grenville. "Indeed. And I suspect tonight's field will be quite the spectacle."

Grenville sighed, already suspecting he was the subject of some private jest between the two. "You are both incorrigible."

Honoria smiled as she patted Barrington's arm. "Come, gentlemen. We mustn't keep our hostess waiting. Besides, I, for one, am eager to see how our players handle the game before them."

⇻⟫⟩⟨⟨⟨⇺

"ARE YOU QUITE certain you don't wish to acknowledge Grenville, Lady Bridget?" Blackwood teased.

Bridget replied coolly, "I prefer managing without another lecture on unsolicited help."

Blackwood smiled. "A story for another time, then."

Grenville approached, his stride purposeful. Bridget felt her spine stiffen instinctively.

"Lady Bridget, Lord Blackwood," he greeted, his tone polite but distant.

"Captain Grenville," Blackwood replied. "We were just discussing the merits of chance encounters."

"Is that so?" Grenville's gaze flickered to Bridget. "I trust your day was less eventful than our last meeting, Lady Bridget."

She met his eyes coolly. "Quite uneventful, thank you. A most welcome change."

Grenville smirked. "And no call for heroics? How disappointing."

Bridget lifted her glass, her tone dry. "I assure you, Captain, I managed to endure the day without catastrophe."

"It seems my title, 'Baron of Bother,' is here to stay."

"As long as you keep 'Bonnie Battler' confined to whispers, we shall manage."

Blackwood glanced between them, a hint of curiosity in his expression. "It seems there's a story here after all."

"Nothing of consequence," Bridget said dismissively. "Simply a misunderstanding during a storm."

"Misunderstanding or not, I'm pleased to see you've arrived safely," Grenville said.

"Especially when certain individuals insist upon interfering," she retorted, lifting her chin slightly.

His eyes hardened almost imperceptibly. "A gentleman cannot, in good conscience, leave a lady in distress."

"I was not in distress," she countered. "Merely delayed."

"Semantics," he replied smoothly. "In any case, I meant no offense."

Bridget felt a flush rising in her cheeks, not from embarrassment but from the familiar irritation that he seemed so adept at provoking. "Offense or not, I prefer to handle my affairs independently."

"An admirable quality," Blackwood interjected, casting a sidelong glance at Grenville. "Though sometimes, collaboration yields better results."

Bridget's lips pressed into a firm line. "Collaboration requires mutual agreement," she countered, her tone measured but unwavering.

Grenville exhaled slowly, his gaze assessing. "Perhaps, then, we can at least agree the matter is settled," he said, his tone cooling further.

"Agreed," she said curtly, turning her attention back to Blackwood. "Lord Blackwood, you mentioned earlier your interest in shaping one's own destiny."

"Indeed," he replied, seizing the opportunity to steer the conversation away from the tense exchange. "I find that taking action is preferable to waiting upon fate."

"An interesting philosophy," Grenville remarked. "Though fate has a way of intervening regardless of our intentions."

"Only if we allow it," Bridget snapped, her frustration spilling over. "Some of us prefer to forge our own paths without unwanted interference."

Grenville's gaze narrowed slightly. "A noble endeavor, but sometimes circumstances necessitate adaptation."

"Adapting to circumstances is one thing," she countered. "Uninvited meddling is quite another."

Before the conversation could escalate further, Grenville let out a measured breath, his expression shifting. "Still, I'm pleased you've arrived safely."

Blackwood chuckled, clearly sensing the tension between them. "A fortuitous arrival indeed, especially since you are seated beside one another."

Bridget's eyes narrowed slightly. "How… delightful."

"It seems fate possesses a wry sense of humor," Grenville remarked dryly.

"Or perhaps our hostess has a twisted sense of humor," Bridget retorted.

Marjory appeared at Bridget's side, her eyes sparkling mischievously. "Is everyone ready for a splendid evening?"

"Absolutely," Blackwood affirmed, offering his arm to Bridget. "Shall we?"

Before she could respond, Grenville stepped forward. "I believe, given the seating arrangements, the honor is mine."

Bridget glanced between the two men, suppressing a sigh. "There's no need for ceremony. I can find my seat just fine."

"Nonsense," Marjory interjected with a smile. "Tradition must be upheld."

Resigned, Bridget accepted Grenville's offered arm. The fabric of his coat was warm beneath her gloved fingers, his presence solid beside her.

As they moved toward the dining room, she held her back straight, determined to ignore the disconcerting nearness that threatened to stir her feelings.

Grenville tilted his head just enough to meet her gaze. "I assure you, Lady Bridget, I am merely adhering to propriety."

She glared at him, her lips curving in a faint, almost reluctant smile. "Propriety," she echoed dryly. "How commendable."

Chapter Seven

B RIDGET'S STOMACH GAVE a small twist as she reached the table. She had not been assigned this seat. She was certain of it. Her place card had been beside Lord Davenport's when she and Marjory were reviewing the dining room earlier. And yet, here it was, resting beside Captain Grenville's as if it had always belonged there. Her eyes narrowed, just for a moment. Marjory. It had her mark all over it.

"Lady Bridget," Grenville said, his voice low and precise as he pulled out her chair with deliberate care. "Allow me."

"Thank you," she murmured, sliding into her seat with practiced ease. He settled beside her, far too close for comfort, or perhaps too close for indifference. The scent of sandalwood lingered, frustratingly familiar. She focused on the polished gleam of the silver or the careful arrangement of the place setting, anything to avoid glancing his way. Around them, conversation rose and fell in gentle waves, but it might as well have been silence for how acutely aware she was of *him*.

The first course arrived, a parade of delicately arranged hors d'oeuvres and steaming bowls of consommé amid muted laughter. Guests, familiar with each other from many previous gatherings, conversed easily, their voices blending into a comfortable hum.

Yet Bridget's attention was riveted on her plate, determined to suppress the unsettling emotions stirred by Grenville's presence.

After a few measured bites, Grenville leaned forward, his eyes searching hers for any hint of uncertainty. "Are you familiar with the area, Lady Bridget?"

Her eyes stayed fixed on her meal as she replied curtly, "Not much. My visits to England have been... brief. Mostly to London."

A soft smile played across his lips. "Perhaps tonight might tempt you to linger longer."

Bridget's green eyes flashed calm defiance as she met his gaze for a fraction of a second. "Highly improbable. I never found English company all that tempting."

He paused as if choosing his next words carefully, finally adding with a playful lilt, "Then I suppose persistence must be part of our English charm."

Before their conversation could deepen further, Captain Grenville smoothly interjected. "Lady Alastair, I must compliment you on the arrangement of tonight's seating. It seems you have an instinct for placing the most... spirited of guests together."

Marjory, ever the gracious hostess, smiled as she set down her glass. "A happy coincidence, I assure you, Captain."

Grenville chuckled. "A fortunate one, indeed. There is nothing quite so dull as an evening where all are in perfect agreement." His gaze flicked briefly toward Bridget, his meaning clear.

Bridget merely lifted her glass, taking a slow sip before responding. "How fortunate, then, that I have no inclination to provide dull company."

A knowing gleam flickered in Grenville's eye, but he did not press further. Still, Bridget's earlier retort lingered like a quiet challenge in the charged space between them.

Later, as Marjory introduced her "Confessions and Challenges" game, a series of revelations and light-hearted dares that set the table abuzz with laughter and hushed confidences, Bridget's mind kept returning to that initial exchange with Grenville.

"What, no game of chance?" a shocked Lady Worthington asked from across the table. "I don't know when I've been to one of your parties when you haven't challenged us with a game of cards."

Marjory glanced at her guest with a smile that didn't reach her eyes. "Evelina, of course, I have a card game planned for after dinner. I wouldn't want to disappoint you. But now we're playing Confessions and Challenges." She glanced at Mark, who appeared less than pleased.

Bridget turned to Blackwood. "I would think that a game of Vingt-et-un is non-threatening. The person closest to twenty-one wins the hand."

The smug, knowing smile on Blackwood's face told Bridget there was more to this game. "Is there something special about Marjory's card games?"

He pursed his lips and leaned toward her so only she could hear. "Card games are very revealing. I doubt Marjory has Vingt-et-un in mind. No, she wants a game with partners. Whist, I suppose." He paused. "And she will choose who partners with whom."

"Lady Bridget," Miss Hathaway called from across the table, her eyes bright with anticipation. "Have you played any of Marjory's games before?"

"Yes, I have," Bridget said, her gaze remaining on Marjory. "In London, she organized a memory game with various objects. "Och, we were in kinks wi' laughter," Bridget admitted with a grin. "Though I fear my partner nearly needed a brandy to recover."

Grenville, who had been watching her, let a slow smirk creep onto his lips. "And did you, my lady, grant him mercy in the end?"

Bridget drummed her fingers on the tabletop, feigning great thought. "Mercy? Ah, but where's the fun in that?"

A brief silence followed, subtle but present. Bridget felt it, an almost imperceptible shift. She had spoken without thinking, the lilt of her childhood sneaking past her carefully measured tone. Her spine stiffened, her fingers pressing lightly against the stem of her glass. Did they notice?

Beside her, Grenville did.

He didn't react outwardly, but she caught the flicker of something in his gaze, curiosity, perhaps amusement. His thumb traced the rim of his wineglass, a contemplative gesture, but he said nothing.

"Of course, we all agree, Lady Marjory," Davenport chimed in. "Your games are renowned for getting us laughing. What do you have in store for us this evening?"

Marjory turned toward the butler and gave a subtle nod. Moments later, a discreet footman presented a silver tray with elegantly folded cards.

"I'll go first," Marjory said.

She drew a folded card from the tray and opened it. "Truth," she said. "What inspired you to host this gathering?"

She paused, then answered her own question with warmth. "Truth be told," she smiled warmly. "I've missed the joy of good company filling these halls. After such tumultuous times, I wanted to create an occasion where friends, old and new, could find relief and enjoy one another. I daresay that seeing all your faces here tonight has already made it worthwhile."

As she spoke, Bridget noticed a fleeting shadow pass over Marjory's features, a hint of melancholy that she quickly masked.

At the head of the table, Mark Alastair shifted subtly. His gaze focused intently on his wife, a trace of weariness in his eyes.

Marjory's eyes briefly met Bridget's, then moved to Blackwood and Grenville.

The first few rounds passed in a blur of laughter and lighthearted confessions. Lady Carlisle admitted a fondness for collecting seashells, while Lord Davenport humorously reenacted a clumsy dance from his youth, much to everyone's amusement.

When it was Bridget's turn, she drew a card that read: "Describe a moment when you defied expectations."

"I suppose traveling unaccompanied from Scotland to England might count." She gave a mischievous glint. "But more so, I once engaged in a debate on philosophy with a professor at Edinburgh University." She cast a sidelong glance at Professor Tresham. "Much to his astonishment. It seems some believe a lady's mind is best kept confined to embroidery and etiquette."

"Ah." Blackwood raised an elegant eyebrow. "The lady reveals her intellect and independent spirit."

Bridget tilted her head, her smile deepening. "Alas, it didnae go weel," she said, her Scottish burr thickening as she relaxed into her words. "Ye'd ha' thought I'd challenged him to a duel! Mony a man, whether here or there, cannae handle a lass who wields words sharper than a saber."

For a heartbeat, the room was silent before erupting into hearty laughter.

Lord Davenport chuckled, shaking his head. "A duel of wits, indeed! I daresay the poor professor didn't stand a chance."

Lady Worthington pressed a gloved hand to her chest, eyes glinting with amusement. "Oh, Lady Bridget, you are a delight! I can only imagine his astonishment."

The admiration around the table was undeniable. Bridget had won the moment, but when she glanced toward Grenville, he was the only one who wasn't laughing. His expression remained contemplative rather than amused, his gaze lingering on her. It wasn't disapproving, but discerning, as if he were assessing what lay beneath the clever words.

He sees me. The thought flickered through Bridget's mind, unbidden and unsettling.

As the laughter subsided, Blackwood caught her eye and he raised his glass. "You must have been a formidable opponent. Perhaps the professor learned a valuable lesson that day."

She inclined her head with a playful smile. "One can only hope, Lord Blackwood. Education should be a two-way street, after all."

Marjory, her eyes dancing with delight, chimed in. "Well said,

Bridget. Now, shall we continue?"

When it was Captain Grenville's turn, he drew his card and read aloud, "Recite a favorite poem or verse that holds personal meaning."

"Very well." Grenville paused thoughtfully, placing the card down on the table with deliberate care. The dancing shadows caused by the soft candlelight accentuated the sharp lines of his face. His fingers drummed on the table, and for a few heartbeats, he seemed to withdraw into himself.

Finally, he lifted his gaze slowly, settling it not on the guests but somewhere distant. His eyes reflected a quiet intensity, a hint of melancholy flickering beneath the surface. He sat with his hands clasped lightly before him as though grounding himself, took a breath, and began. He recited Blake's verse with deliberate intensity.

"To see a World in a Grain of Sand,

And a Heaven in a Wild flower,

Hold Infinity in the palm of your hand

And Eternity in an hour."

When he finished, silence clung to the air like a held breath. Grenville exhaled, his gaze shifting, as if returning from somewhere distant. "William Blake's words remind me that even the smallest moments hold infinite meaning."

Bridget's fingers curled around her glass. Unexpected. Unsettling. His voice carried a quiet reverence that made her question, just for a moment, whether he was truly the man she had judged him to be.

For an instant, his gaze found hers. Something passed between them, something graver than she cared to name. Recognition? Understanding? Whatever it was, it unsettled her. Then, as if aware of the moment's significance, he looked away, his expression unreadable. There was, perhaps, the faintest hint of color touching his cheeks, though whether from the warmth of the wine or something more, it was impossible to tell.

It was Blackwood's turn. He drew the truth card. "Have you ever kept a secret that could alter someone's perception of you?"

He paused, brushing his fingers over the card before he lifted his gaze. "Perhaps," he said at last. "But don't we all have our own secrets to keep?"

As the game continued, Lady Worthington chose a dare card to share a piece of advice she had once been given. With a twinkle in her eye, she proclaimed, "Never underestimate the art of listening. A well-timed ear gathers the best gossip."

An uproar of laughter filled the room, lightening the mood of the room.

As the conversation shifted to lighter topics, anticipation of the following day's equestrian chase, playful jabs about Marjory's penchant for card games, and the odd humor of the gathering, the focus gradually drifted back to the broader group.

Marjory's announcement that the ladies would soon join her on the terrace temporarily dispersed the lingering tension. Stepping outside, Blackwood remarked quietly as Bridget and he moved to a quieter corner, "You handle him well."

Bridget's lips tightened in a half-smile. "I'm not handling anything, just enduring."

Blackwood chuckled softly. "Perhaps tomorrow's chase will offer a welcome distraction."

Her reply was gentle, almost wistful, "One can only hope." Yet, even amid the light chatter and clinking glasses, Bridget's thoughts repeatedly returned to that intense moment during Grenville's recitation, the openness in his eyes, the vulnerability that betrayed a hidden side of him. She wondered, against her better judgment, if that glimpse might hint at something more than mere English arrogance.

Outside, on the terrace beneath the stars, Bridget leaned against the cool stone balustrade. The night air carried the sweet scents of roses and night-blooming jasmine, mingling with the distant strains of laughter drifting through the open door.

Miss Gray joined her, her smile gentle and perceptive. "You were quiet after the game, Bridget. Not your usual lively self."

Bridget exhaled slowly, her gaze drifting over the darkened gardens. "Some truths have a way of lingering after the laughter fades."

Miss Gray's eyes twinkled. "Perhaps that's the charm of these nights, mystery in every shadow."

Before Bridget could offer a reply, Marjory called out. "Ladies, to the library for our card game!"

"Coming," Miss Gray replied, then turned back to Bridget. "Are you joining us?"

"In a moment," Bridget said. "I just need a bit more air."

"Don't stay out too long," Miss Gray advised with a wink. "Who knows what secrets the night might reveal, and you don't want to miss any."

As Miss Gray returned inside, the soft sounds of laughter and clinking teacups drifted from the open doors. She closed her eyes briefly, inhaling the mingled scents of roses and night-blooming jasmine.

Try as she might, she couldn't banish the memory of his voice, the quiet reverence, the fleeting hesitation, the way his gaze slipped into something distant, something untouchable.

It unsettled her. She had known men who used words as weapons, who twisted sentiment into advantage. Was he any different? It was as if, for the span of a few lines, he had allowed a glimpse into a guarded heart.

Why should it matter? she chastised herself. *He's still the same man who embodies everything I distrust.*

And yet, the disquiet remained.

With a determined breath, she straightened her shoulders. Tomorrow would bring the equestrian chase and, with any luck, a distraction from these unsettling thoughts. She resolved to focus on the tasks at hand, supporting Marjory, keeping Blackwood's amiable company, and, most importantly, maintaining her guard against unwanted entanglements.

With one last glance at the moonlit gardens, Bridget turned. She did not see the shadow lingering beyond the doorway, nor feel the watchful eyes that traced her every step as she disappeared inside.

Chapter Eight

THE LIBRARY WAS a grand, imposing room. The towering oak shelves were in various states of restoration. They were partially filled or hauntingly bare, reluctant to reclaim their past. The scent of parchment and candlewax mingled with something more elusive. A faint, almost herbal trace, as though the parchment had absorbed whispers of old remedies and ink-stained secrets.

A long central table stretched before the hearth, polished to a deep sheen, its edges worn and smoothed by time. At one time, it might have served as a place of scholarly pursuit or hushed conversation, but for this evening, the library had been transformed into a lively gaming hall, the scent of brandy and cigars mingling with the traces of ink, parchment, and leather. Several smaller tables that were throughout the room had been cleared of books and scrolls and transformed into a battlefield of cards and calculation.

Bridget hesitated at the entrance and scanned the room. There was a charged expectancy in the air. It wasn't from the game, but from the players. She recognized it well. The kind of subtle tension that lived between rivals, conspirators... or strangers with too much to lose.

From his position near the hearth, Grenville seemed detached from the cheerfulness around him, his focus drifting not to the game but to the shadows cast by the firelight. There was a distance in his eyes, as if he were present but holding something back. Marjory moved through the chamber with ease, pouring wine and gesturing for the guests to take their seats. Lady Worthington examined the shelves with mild interest, trailing her fingers along the spines of the old editions.

Marjory stood in front of the large fireplace, tapping a delicate silver spoon against her wine glass. The murmurs of conversation softened, and all eyes turned toward their hostess. Her eyes swept over the gathered guests, and the playful glint in her gaze hinted at mischief yet to come.

"My friends," she began with a warm smile, "as promised, the evening would not be complete without a touch of friendly competition. Tonight, we shall play Whist, a game of skill, strategy, and, of course, partnership."

Knowing glances passed around the room. Marjory's games were never quite as simple as they seemed.

"To keep things lively, I've arranged the partners myself. A little strategy in the pairing makes for a more entertaining game, wouldn't you agree?" She gestured to the footman, who stepped forward with a small tray of elegantly folded cards. "These will reveal your pairings."

One by one, the guests selected their cards, revealing their designated partners.

"Lady Bridget, you shall partner with Captain Grenville."

Bridget schooled her expression. Though she suspected Marjory's matchmaking tendencies were at work. Across the room, the captain inclined his head slightly. There was no sign of surprise in his eyes. Only the faintest flicker of tension that he quickly masked.

"Mark, you will be partnered with Lady Worthington."

A faint flicker of something unreadable crossed his features before he offered a polite nod to his partner. Lady Worthington smiled, obviously pleased by the arrangement.

"Lord Barrington and Mrs. Bainbridge, a most experienced duo."

Barrington shared an amused glance with his longtime friend.

"A wise pairing, indeed," he remarked, earning a mischievous smile from Mrs. Bainbridge.

"Lord Davenport, you shall play alongside Lady Carlisle."

Lady Carlisle beamed. "An excellent choice, Marjory. Though I must warn you, Lord Davenport, I intend to win."

Davenport chuckled, shaking his head. "I suppose I shall have to keep my wits about me."

"Lord Blackwood, you will partner with Miss Hathaway."

Blackwood inclined his head toward Miss Hathaway, who studied him with quiet curiosity. The reserved woman would make for an interesting match with the charismatic but unreadable lord.

"And finally, Sir Townsend, you are with Miss Gray."

Miss Gray's eyes gleamed with mischief as she cast an appraising look at her partner. "A man who is reserved but deliberate, how fascinating. Let's see if you're as sharp at cards as you are at observation, Sir Townsend."

Townsend offered a mild smile. "I shall do my best to keep up, Miss Gray."

Marjory's eyes twinkled as she surveyed the group. "Now that our teams are set, let the game begin. May the best partners win."

She made her way to one of the tables.

"Strange, isn't it?" Blackwood let out a low chuckle as he shuffled the deck of cards with a practiced hand. "It makes one wonder what was so dangerous that every book and map in this library had to be removed."

Bridget glanced at him. "Emptied? Why? What happened?"

He shrugged. "Only whispers. It's said the Alastair ancestor who last used this room wasn't merely a scholar but a man of, shall we say, unconventional pursuits." He gave a knowing smile. "Alchemy, if you believe the legends."

"Alchemy?" Bridget repeated, intrigued despite herself.

A murmur of intrigue passed between them. Bridget's eyes narrowed slightly as she pressed, "There must be more to that tale."

Blackwood placed a card down, his expression carefully neutral. "And that, dear lady, is why history claims he was burned for witchcraft."

"Ah, Lady Bridget," Grenville's voice cut through the hum of conversation, a hint of amusement playing at his lips as he took a seat opposite her at the table. "Are you ready to try your luck?"

"Luck rarely determines the outcome, Captain," she countered, her smile cool.

"Though I imagine it's rather useful for those who lack skill." His brow arched. "Ah, but luck favors the bold. Shall we see which of us it chooses tonight?"

She met his gaze, the challenge unmistakable. "It would be my pleasure."

She'd meant to study him. Now, she wasn't sure who was watching whom.

She looked across at her partner, Captain Grenville, and their opponents, Blackwood and Lady Worthington. A footman arrived with a fresh decanter of wine, pouring generous servings as coins and small promissory notes were placed upon the table.

The first round began in earnest. Grenville played conservatively, studying his opponents rather than pressing his advantage. Bridget, on the other hand, played aggressively, pushing the stakes higher with every calculated move.

"Marjory always arranges the partnerships," Lady Worthington noted, absently swirling her wine. "It's one of her little traditions, you see. She believes the game reveals things about people."

Bridget arched a brow. "And does it?"

Blackwood smirked. "Oh, most certainly. If you pay attention."

"A dangerous strategy," Grenville murmured as Bridget raised the bet once again.

"Only if one lacks confidence," Bridget countered, her eyes gleaming.

Across the table, Blackwood chuckled, the sound low and deliberate. "Confidence can be a double-edged sword, Lady Bridget. But I admire the courage."

Bridget met his gaze. He played with precision, but he withheld something, as if every card he laid down was meant to distract from the ones he never showed.

Marjory moved among the tables, offering a well-practiced smile as she observed the play, but there was something off. Her fingers tapped rhythmically against the back of a chair, a nervous habit Bridget had never noticed before. She laughed at something Barrington said, but the sound was a touch too light, too controlled.

Barrington caught Grenville's eye across the room. There was a brief exchange, a silent nod, perhaps a confirmation. It was quick, almost imperceptible, but Bridget saw it. She remembered now. Barrington had summoned Grenville. But why? And what hadn't they said aloud?

Grenville gave the faintest nod in return. He still wasn't sure why Barrington had summoned him, only that it hadn't been for cards or conversation. Whatever this was, it ran deeper than a house party.

At Davenport's table, the dealer revealed the next set of cards, and a murmur of appreciation passed through the players. Yet Marjory's gaze flickered toward her husband as if watching for something…waiting.

"A fine hand, Lady Bridget," Blackwood remarked. "Perhaps the fates favor you tonight."

As the evening's card game continued, laughter and conversation filled the room. The dealers dealt the next hand. The players exchanged knowing glances as they placed their bets. The energy in the room shifted subtly, some eager for a victory, others already resigned to their losses.

Alastair played with an almost unnatural precision tonight, his focus shifting between his cards and his wife with a deliberateness that felt out of character.

Bridget wasn't the only one who took note of it. Grenville watched the game with an air of quiet amusement.

As the game reached a natural pause, the door to the library opened, and Mr. Simmons entered, followed by several footmen carrying silver trays laden with an assortment of desserts, delicate pastries, fresh fruit, and rich puddings. The warm, spiced aroma of baked apples and cinnamon filled the air as they carefully spread out a cloth and arranged the dishes on the large library table.

Marjory rose with a graceful smile. "Ladies and gentlemen, a brief respite before we continue. I daresay a bit of nourishment is in order, after all, strategy is best served with a touch of indulgence. Do help yourselves to something sweet before we return to our game."

A murmur of approval rippled through the room as guests stood and made their way toward the refreshments.

Bridget hesitated, taking the moment to study the other guests. Blackwood leaned in slightly as he exchanged a few words with Davenport, who looked less than pleased. Nearby, Grenville's gaze flickered toward her before he turned his attention back to Barrington and Mrs. Bainbridge, engaged in an amicable discussion.

Bridget glanced up from her seat as Miss Gray wandered toward the towering bookshelves, her fingers lightly brushing over the leather-bound spines. The younger woman hesitated, plucking a book free and flipping through its pages. Her brows knitted together in thought before she snapped the volume shut and tucked it under her arm.

Bridget's pulse quickened as she recalled the odd script, a secret almost whispered through the pages. 'There's more to this manor than meets the eye,' she thought, determined to uncover its hidden past. Unable to resist the pull of the mystery, Bridget stepped closer. "Have you found something interesting?"

Miss Gray startled slightly before offering a quick smile. "I'm not sure." She hesitated, then tilted the book in Bridget's direction. "This one caught my eye. It's filled with odd script, part English, part something else. You know old languages, don't you?"

Bridget turned, brow arching. "A few. Why?"

Miss Gray hesitated before passing her the book. "This passage, it reads like something meant to be forgotten."

Bridget tilted the book toward the candlelight. Her eyes narrowed at a faded margin note, written in Gaelic. She murmured aloud, translating: *"Guard what must be buried. Speak only in shadow."*

A chill passed through her. She glanced at Miss Gray. "I think this is more than a forgotten manuscript."

A shiver traced down Bridget's spine. "This… this isn't just any old book. Someone meant to hide it."

Miss Gray hugged her arms. "It felt different when I picked it up. As if it was waiting to be found." She let out a breathy laugh, shaking her head. "That sounds ridiculous, doesn't it?"

Bridget didn't answer right away. Her fingers traced the edge of several torn pages, her thoughts swirling. "Not necessarily." She met Miss Gray's gaze, studying the uncertainty in her expression. "Where did you find this?"

"Just there," Miss Gray gestured to the shelf. "Tucked behind a row of estate records. Almost as if someone had hidden it."

Bridget frowned as she wondered who tried to conceal it. Alastair?

She handed the book back, her mind racing. "Perhaps it would be worth looking through properly later."

Her father's warnings echoed in her mind, half-formed phrases, odd silences, letters that had never made sense until now. Could this be tied to what he feared? What he tried to protect her from?

Miss Gray nodded, pressing the volume to her chest. "I think I will."

Bridget watched her retreat, the uneasy feeling lingering.

"Professor," Davenport called out, eyeing the vacant seat, "it seems Miss Gray has had her fill of cards for the evening. Would you mind taking her place?"

Tresham hesitated before he reluctantly lowered himself into the chair.

"Our hostess mentioned you don't play Whist," Davenport remarked as he shuffled the deck with practiced ease.

"Well," Tresham exhaled slowly. "I do play. I simply choose not to."

"Are you trying to tell us you don't know how to play at all?" Sir Townsend asked. He gave Davenport a curious glance.

The professor let out a slow breath as if summoning patience for one of his students. "I know the game well enough, Sir Townsend. In fact, I played often at the university."

The competitive banter eased as the game began. With the first hand played, a hush settled over the table. Tresham laid down his cards with deliberate precision, claiming the win.

Davenport huffed and shifted in his chair. "Luck," he muttered, already dealing the next round.

That refrain was repeated after the next hand. And the next.

By the fourth consecutive win, Davenport groaned, tossing his cards onto the table. "I thought you didn't know how to play."

Tresham met his gaze with mild amusement. "I never said that. I said I played at university. And then I stopped."

Townsend arched a brow. "Stopped? Why?"

Tresham's lips quirked faintly. "Because I was the undefeated Whist champion for four years. It became rather difficult to find a game where anyone wished to sit across from me."

Davenport pushed back his chair, brandy swirling in his glass. "I believe that's enough cards for one night. Some of us have an early morning." His tone was clipped but not enough to cause a scene.

Marjory's gaze followed him as he left. "Well," she said lightly, turning back to the group. "That was a most enlightening evening. Shall we call it a night?"

Bridget nodded. Lord Blackwood had been correct. There was much to be learned at the Whist table. The overly aggressive way Alastair had played. The tension in Marjory's shoulders. Bridget's gaze lingered on Miss Gray, the book now tucked discreetly against her side, as if it had chosen her, not the other way around.

Bridget gathered her winnings, but her focus remained on Marjory, who had suddenly left the room. Lady Worthington's gaze lingered on Marjory's retreating form, her fingers tightening briefly around her glass before she turned back to the others.

"A curious evening indeed, wouldn't you say?" Blackwood murmured, watching the last of the guests depart.

Chapter Nine

IN THE MORNING, the scent of fresh bread and strong tea lingered in the air, mingling with the earthy dampness that still clung to the manor's walls from the previous night's rain. Though the skies had cleared, the ground remained sodden, making an outdoor breakfast impractical. Instead, the household had arranged for a more informal setting inside the east-facing breakfast room, where the morning sunlight poured through the windows and glinted off polished silver and porcelain.

Clusters of guests gathered around small, elegantly laid tables, some helping themselves to warm scones and fresh fruit while others lingered near the sideboard where steaming pots of tea and coffee awaited. There was no assigned seating arrangement this morning, only casual mingling and light chatter. Some engaged in lively conversation, while others were still fatigued from the late night.

Bridget stood near the hearth, a delicate china cup cradled in her hands, surveying the room. The quiet hum of morning chatter soon gave way to lively debates about last night's game, signaling that the day's events were far from over.

From her place near the hearth, Bridget observed the room. Marjory, seated beside Lady Worthington, seemed distracted, stirring her tea absently as she nodded at something the older woman was saying.

Alastair had yet to make an appearance, which was unusual, considering his tendency to be an early riser. A flicker of unease crossed Marjory's face before she quickly masked it behind a polite smile.

"Lady Marjory," Mrs. Bainbridge began as she buttered her toast. "I thought your sister might be joining us for the weekend."

"Alas, Miss Ellington prefers quieter gatherings." Marjory leaned toward Mrs. Bainbridge with a conspiratorial smile. "Which translates to, Betsy doesn't care for my games."

A ripple of amusement passed around the tables.

"A shame, truly," Lady Worthington remarked, setting down her teacup with a flourish. "Your games are half the reason we all agreed to come."

Blackwood smirked over the rim of his glass. "A pity. One must have a talent for intrigue to appreciate such diversions."

Mrs. Bainbridge chuckled, dabbing her napkin to her lips. "Not everyone enjoys mischief, I suppose."

From the far end of the room, Lord Davenport and Sir Townsend were deep in conversation. "Quite the game last night," Davenport noted, taking a sip of coffee. "Some hands were most revealing."

Townsend chuckled. "Indeed. A game of Whist does more than reveal skill. It exposes a player's disposition. Some take risks, others remain cautious."

"And some," Blackwood interjected with a smirk, "are far too aware of their own cleverness."

The remark hung in the air briefly, drawing a ripple of knowing laughter from those nearby. "A subtle jab, Lord Blackwood?" Grenville's voice held an amused lilt as he approached, a plate in hand. "Or an admission that you lost more than you anticipated?"

"Hardly," Blackwood replied, shaking his head. "I merely observe that certain individuals play their cards as they do their lives, with careful intent."

Bridget arched a brow. "And what, precisely, does that say about you, Captain?"

"That I always know when to hold back and let the trick decide," he answered smoothly, lifting his teacup in a mock toast.

A murmur of laughter spread around the table, but the exchange had done its job, setting an undercurrent of intrigue. The card game had not been merely entertainment. For some, it had been an exercise in calculation and control.

Across the room, Miss Gray returned the borrowed book to a side table with a slight frown. She hesitated before turning back to Miss Hathaway. "I took this from the library last night, something about the old manor and its first inhabitants. It was an intriguing read, though it left me unsettled."

Miss Hathaway glanced at the tome. "Unsettled? How so?"

Miss Gray lowered her voice, aware of the curiosity sparking in those nearby. "It detailed the life of Alastair Court's first master, a Druid scholar whose studies delved into alchemy and transformations, practices that some believed strayed dangerously close to sorcery."

Bridget's attention sharpened. "What became of him?" Bridget asked, her interest piqued.

"Executed," Miss Gray said grimly. "Though, according to the book, his work wasn't destroyed. Some believe pieces of his records were hidden or possibly passed down in secret."

"Perhaps there's more to Alastair Court's history than its foundation stones," Miss Gray murmured as she set the book down.

The table fell into a moment of thoughtful silence before Blackwood smirked. "Perhaps Alastair's sudden interest in antiquities is more than simple restoration, then? Could he be searching for how to turn lead to gold?"

The door opened, and Alastair entered, wearing his usual easy smile. "A fascinating theory, Lord Blackwood. But I assure you, my interest in the past is purely academic."

Bridget studied Alastair as he spoke, recalling how he'd played with such boldness at the card table the night before. Was it mere bravado or something else?

Lady Worthington observed the exchange with quiet interest, though she said nothing. Instead, she turned her attention to

Bridget. "Will you be joining the chase, Lady Bridget?"

Bridget nodded. "I wouldn't miss it."

Lady Worthington smiled, though there was something calculating in her expression. "I find such outings tend to reveal things about people, who leads, who follows, and who knows when to sprint to the finish line."

The Captain, who had resumed his meal, let out a quiet chuckle. He tilted his head slightly, his eyes narrowing in quiet observation, as though committing her to memory. "And which do you suspect Lady Bridget to be?"

"That remains to be seen," Lady Worthington mused, dabbing her lips with a napkin before setting it down. "But I suspect she is one to act when the moment calls for action."

Bridget met her gaze evenly. "Hesitation rarely serves anyone well."

Marjory abruptly set down her spoon, the gentle clink against the china oddly loud in the lull of conversation. "Perhaps we should all take caution today. The grounds are still damp, and the course is not without its risks."

Alastair exhaled sharply, rubbing a hand over his jaw. "We've had worse conditions, Marjory. There's no need for concern."

"Perhaps not," she replied, but her fingers tightened subtly around her napkin.

Bridget glanced between the two, a quiet tension pressing in around Marjory's words.

She caught Grenville's eye, and though he said nothing, there was a shared understanding in the look they exchanged. Marjory's unease ran deeper than the weather. But whatever stirred beneath it, they would have to wait to learn more.

Across the room, Blackwood clapped his hands together. "Enough with the serious discussions! A good chase is exactly what we need after last night's revelry. And I, for one, intend to enjoy it."

"Spoken like a man who lost more than he'd care to admit," Davenport teased.

"And yet," Blackwood countered, lifting his cup in another toast, his gaze flickering across the table, "I remain unscathed. Can the same be said of all present?"

Laughter rippled through the gathering, shifting the mood effortlessly, anticipation replacing the earlier tension as the guests began to disperse to prepare for the chase. A new energy stirred, one charged with anticipation and the unspoken. Revelations would come, perhaps on the heels of galloping hooves. But for now, the secrets remained tucked behind smiles and morning pleasantries.

Miss Gray's words stirred curiosity among the guests. Lady Worthington pursed her lips thoughtfully, then added, "It is not the first time such tales have been whispered about old estates. There are always rumors of ghosts, lost knowledge, hidden secrets, even hidden treasures."

Davenport, setting down his coffee cup, mused, "Stories like these often hold a grain of truth. And considering Alastair's recent acquisitions, well, I'd wager some of those relics have more than just sentimental value."

As the guests began to disperse to ready themselves, the captain lingered at the doorway, watching Bridget.

He caught the barest flicker of amusement in her gaze, defiant, self-assured, and altogether too intriguing.

"Lady Bridget," he said at last, "try not to fall behind."

Her answering smile was quick, teasing. "I'd be more concerned about whether you can catch me."

He felt a flicker of amusement himself as he tipped his head. "I look forward to it."

And with that, the morning's preparations for the chase were fully underway.

THE MORNING AIR carried the night's lingering chill, crisp yet mild, as Grenville joined the others. He could almost taste the promise of a new day beginning in the cool dampness, each step echoing the uncertainty of a day reborn after storm and suspense. Beneath his boots, the ground remained slick from the relentless downpour of the past three days. Overhead, the sky stretched in crimson and gold, dawn breaking as if the storm had been nothing more than a distant memory. He could almost taste the promise of a fresh start in that cool, damp air.

The guests began to mount their horses on the wide drive by the front lawn, chattering with excitement while the horses, held by the stable boys, snorted and stamped, eager to begin the equestrian chase.

Alastair lingered near the edge of the group, absently tightening the leather strap on his glove, then loosening it again. His gaze kept drifting toward the tree line. Marjory, standing beside Bridget, let out a quiet sigh. "He's been like this all morning."

"Distracted?" Bridget asked.

"Restless," Marjory murmured, adjusting her reins. "As if waiting for something, though neither he nor any of us can say what that might be."

At the head of the group, Davenport, dressed in a blue morning coat and tan breeches, sat astride a roan mare like a hunt master leading his company. At Alastair's request, he issued the last-minute instructions, his voice carrying easily over the commotion.

"Hear ye, hear ye!" Davenport called, raising a hand for silence. "Before we set off, let me remind you of a few important details regarding today's course."

The group quieted, their attention fixed on him.

"As you all know," he continued, "the heavy rainstorm has rendered certain areas of the grounds treacherous. Hazardous sections have been marked with red ribbons, while the yellow flags, uniquely chosen for today, indicate the proper route to follow.

He paused, letting his authoritative tone settle over the gathered riders. "And one last reminder. Beyond the east hedge lies a stretch of land that is waterlogged and deceptive. Do not test your luck there." His meaning was unmistakable.

Grenville swung into the saddle, feeling the familiar comfort of Valor beneath him. His gaze swept the gathered riders before pausing on Bridget. Clad in a deep green riding habit, she sat astride a chestnut mare, adjusting her reins with practiced ease.

There was a spark in her eyes that caught him off guard. It was defiant, amusing, and far too intriguing for comfort.

Her focused, unyielding expression stirred something unfamiliar in him. Was it mere admiration for her spirit or something altogether more troublesome?

As the riders took their positions, Blackwood's voice cut through the murmur. "Ready for the chase, Captain?" he taunted lightly.

Grenville adjusted his gloves, casting a sidelong glance. "The chase is hardly the challenge."

Overhearing their exchange, Bridget shot him a sharp look. "Do you make a habit of underestimating your competition, Captain?"

Their eyes met briefly, and in that shared glance was a tension neither named, one part rivalry, one part reluctant fascination. Whatever unsettled Marjory, it wasn't only the weather.

A slow smile tugged at Grenville's lips. "Only when they insist on proving me wrong."

Bridget's fingers tightened briefly on the reins. "A most welcome reprieve, Captain. No treacherous waters, no inclement weather, and most importantly, no gallant interference from unexpected quarters."

His expression didn't change, but there was something watchful behind it. It was as if he heard more in her words than she had meant to reveal.

"And yet, here we are, crossing paths once more," he said.

She lifted her chin. "An unfortunate coincidence, I assure

you."

Before they could continue, Blackwood nudged his horse closer, speaking just loud enough for the surrounding riders to hear.

"Seems a shame to avoid the most interesting parts of the land," he mused. "A true rider doesn't fear a bit of mud."

Bridget shot him a sharp glance. "A true rider knows the difference between bravery and recklessness."

Blackwood smirked. "Recklessness? Or an opportunity for a true challenge?"

Bridget caught the tension in Grenville's jaw before he replied.

"Some challenges aren't worth the cost."

A knowing gleam sparked in Blackwood's eyes. "Ah, but the thrill of the chase is in its uncertainty, is it not? One never knows where the course might lead."

Davenport cleared his throat. "Let's not test our luck before we even begin, shall we?"

"Indeed," Lady Worthington added with a sharp look. "Youth and arrogance are often a fatal combination."

Blackwood merely grinned, tipping his hat. "Experience must start somewhere, my lady."

Miss Gray laughed, guiding her horse between them. "I, for one, am quite content to leave reckless heroics to others."

Bridget smirked. "Sensible advice."

The horn sounded, cutting off further conversation, and the riders surged forward. The rhythmic pounding of hooves, the rush of wind, tore through the morning air.

Grenville kept his mount steady, scanning the course ahead, marked by fluttering yellow flags. He spotted Bridget leaning low over her mare's neck, her form tight and poised. There was something fiercely alive in her, a wild joy that flashed like sunlight through storm clouds.

One of the flags twisted in the breeze, and he caught the brief tension in her posture, subtle but unmistakable.

Grenville urged Valor forward, and the formation tightened. As they advanced, the crowd's chatter faded into the pounding of hooves and the thrill of the pursuit.

A flicker of motion to his left, Bridget. Her mare surged forward, nimble and unyielding, matching the stallion's pace with surprising determination.

Grenville adjusted his hold on the reins, noting the way she moved in rhythm with the animal, her posture sure, eyes fixed ahead. She rode as though the wind answered to her will.

He closed the distance, his voice cutting through the rush of wind. "You ride well for someone who claims not to enjoy competition."

Grenville glanced at Bridget, her bonnet nearly torn loose by the wind as she turned to glare at him. "And you pursue me with entirely too much enthusiasm for a man who claims to be a gentleman."

He grinned, leaning closer in the saddle. "A gentleman knows when to let a lady win. I'm afraid I haven't decided yet if you deserve such courtesy."

She scoffed, flicking her reins. "How magnanimous of you, Captain."

THE TERRAIN SHIFTED beneath them, the path narrowing as they approached a dense thicket. Twigs snapped beneath the pounding hooves, and branches clawed at Bridget's sleeves as she forced her horse forward. She stole a glance over her shoulder, others were falling behind, some veering toward another path, others struggling to maintain control on the uneven ground. But not Grenville. He remained beside her, matching her stride for stride, his expression one of amusement and unwavering focus.

Ahead, the course split. Bridget's eyes flicked toward the yellow flag haphazardly planted in the ground, marking the path set that morning.

She veered right, remaining on the trail. Her mare surged forward with renewed vigor, the ground undulating beneath them, treacherous roots and hidden dips threatening disaster. Bridget gritted her teeth, as she navigated every twist and dip with precision.

Behind her, Grenville's dark stallion matched her pace and cleared a downed log, landing with an impressive display of control. He shot her a dark look. "You're reckless," Grenville called out as he pulled alongside her for a brief moment.

"You're predictable," she countered, a triumphant smirk playing on her lips.

Thomas didn't push her further. Instead, he hung back, watching as she urged her mare onward with fierce determination. He wasn't going to intervene, not yet. She could do this. She would prove she could.

Bridget's focus remained ahead, the rapid beat of her horse's hooves syncing with the hammering in her chest. She was nearly through the worst of it when—

A branch snapped.

Her horse reared violently. She gripped the reins tighter, fighting for control. She barely had time to react before another sound reached her—

A distant, unmistakable cry echoed through the trees.

Before she could process what she heard, an obstacle appeared, a jagged rock, half-hidden in the underbrush. She jerked the reins, but the abrupt movement unbalanced her. She clung on, breathless, heart pounding as her mare steadied. Grenville was still behind her, watching, waiting.

She gritted her teeth. She didn't need saving.

Then the cry came again, sharp, pained, and close by.

Bridget jerked her head toward the noise, her stomach twisting. The other riders were still navigating the divide, unaware of the sudden disturbance.

She yanked the reins, steering her horse toward the sound.

Her pulse thundered in her ears as she broke into the clearing, pulling up sharply. Her mare danced beneath her, sensing her rider's alarm, but Bridget barely registered the movement.

Grenville surged past her, his focus locked on the fallen rider. "Stay back!" he ordered.

Bridget ignored him, kicking her mare forward.

Grenville reached Alastair first, swinging down from his horse in one swift motion. His boots hit the ground hard as he crouched beside the unmoving figure, fingers pressing against his neck. He held his breath for a moment. Then he released it in a slow, controlled exhale.

Bridget's stomach clenched. She swung down from her saddle, boots sinking into the damp earth as she rushed to his side.

Grenville's lips pressed into a firm, unreadable expression as he checked again, first the wrist, then the chest. Nothing. His fingers lingered for a fraction of a second longer before he let out another breath, his gaze locked on the lifeless form before him.

"He's gone."

Bridget's throat tightened. Her gaze dropped to Alastair's fingers, where dark moisture gleamed against his pale skin, red, wet, and spreading.

"Good God," Grenville muttered, his voice edged with something between shock and fury. His eyes met Bridget's, now dark with alarm and questions he hadn't yet voiced. He understood something. Something she hadn't yet grasped.

The wind stirred through the trees, a stark contrast to the stillness before them. The chase had begun as sport, a harmless diversion.

Now, it had become something else entirely.

Bridget scanned the area, her pulse still racing. The scene before her stirred a memory. "I remember the shadows that moved through the mist," she said quietly. "Bodies left behind along with the helpless cries of those who had no chance to fight back. The Highland Clearances taught me what it meant to be powerless. I won't stand idly by now."

A muscle twitched in Grenville's cheek. Bridget recognized the look. She had seen enough men fall in battle to know when death was unexpected. She watched as he ran his hands carefully along Alastair's coat, methodically searching for signs of injury beyond what a simple fall could cause. His fingers paused over a dark stain that had already begun to seep through the fabric. Instead of pulling it back, he leaned closer, his expression tightening.

"The blood's not pooling at the base," he murmured. "It's deeper… too clean. A wound like this. It was made with precision, not force."

Bridget crouched beside him, her expression tightened. A sharp, bitter scent hit her nose, herbal, metallic, unsettling. She flinched, recognizing it instantly. "That smell. My mother used a plant to relieve pain and for fevers," she hesitated. Her eyes flicking to Grenville. "It reminds me of wolfsbane."

Grenville's gaze snapped to hers. "Poison?"

She swallowed. "Aye. In the Highlands, hunters once laced blades with it. The wounds looked clean until the man collapsed." Her voice turned grim. "This wasn't a fall."

Grenville gave a slow nod, the weight of her words sinking in. "It's beginning to look that way."

Her throat tightened as she spoke, her voice steady despite the turmoil inside. "Alastair helped Catriona and Killian escape Scotland when no one else would. If it weren't for him, they would have been another casualty. I owe Alastair for that. I need to know what happened to him and why." She glanced at him. "You wouldn't understand."

He studied her face, searching for something, but she didn't know what. Was he judging her determination or his own?

Finally, he let out a deep breath. "I understand more than you think."

Bridget looked away from him. How could he understand?

He reached for her arm, grounding her with his touch. "Whatever drove someone to do this, Mark Alastair didn't deserve it. I will do all that is in my power to bring them to justice. Are you with me on this?"

She blinked, visibly startled. She looked at him as if seeing him for the first time. The man before her wasn't just a soldier, or outsider, but a man willing to stand with her. For Lord Alastair. For justice.

"You're asking me… You want my help?"

Grenville held her gaze. "I need someone with your tenacity, someone who won't let this be brushed aside. You see things others miss, you trust your instincts, and you don't back down when the truth is hard to hear. You know the Highlands, the old ways, things I don't. And you can move through these circles and ask the right questions without raising suspicion. I need you. No, Alastair needs you. Will you work with me to bring him justice?"

Chapter Ten

GRENVILLE'S GAZE SWEPT over the scene, his practiced eye catching something off. It wasn't just the sight of his lifeless friend. It was the position of Lord Alastair's body. It was too deliberate, too…arranged. Someone wanted this to be found.

He took a step back, taking stock of the irregularities. His coat was bunched oddly at the side. His boots were streaked with mud in uneven patterns, drag marks. Alastair hadn't fallen. He'd been placed here.

Grenville crouched, pressing his gloved fingers against the disturbed ground. "No. He didn't fall," he murmured.

A quiet rustle at his side caught his attention. Bridget was already at Alastair's horse, her movements careful, methodical. He watched her examine the animal and noted her steadiness. That, at least, he could count on.

"The horse is too calm," she called softly. "A horse that had thrown its rider or witnessed violence should still be agitated, but this one had settled, suggesting the incident had occurred some time ago."

She ran her fingers along the animal's flank, feeling for any abnormalities. The horse twitched beneath her touch, flinching slightly when she pressed just behind the saddle. Frowning, she traced the outline of what looked to be a deep bruise forming along its side. "This isn't from the ride," she called to Grenville. "This looks like… he was thrown over the saddle…carried."

Grenville straightened. "Carried?"

Bridget nodded and pointed. "Blood pooled on the leather, not spattered. He was already injured when he was put up here."

Grenville's jaw tightened. "Then he was killed elsewhere and brought here. That means whoever did this wanted us to find him, but not where it happened."

Bridget's voice wavered. "The scream?"

Grenville's eyes narrowed. "A man's scream, not from pain, but intent. A lure."

"Lord Blackwood," she murmured.

Grenville didn't answer her immediately. He didn't want to leap to conclusions, yet. Though the thought of Blackwood's involvement had already taken root. Instead, he bent again over the body, trying to keep emotion at bay. He needed facts. He needed control. It was the only way he'd get through this.

"Marjory," Bridget murmured, her voice trembling. Her voice pierced the stillness. "They were riding together. Where is she?"

That struck harder than it should have. Grenville rose swiftly, scanning the woods. He hadn't seen her, not once, on the course. "She can't be far. We'll find her."

Grenville turned from the body, whipping his hands clean on a cloth. *Focus*, he told himself. Emotions clouded judgment, and he'd been trained to override those. But Alastair had been a friend. And Marjory... her absence added another layer of urgency.

Bridget's breath hitched as her gaze fell to Alastair's hand. His fingers were curled tightly, gripping something, a scrap of paper, barely visible between the mud-streaked knuckles.

Bridget moved to Alastair's hand. Grenville watched as she carefully pried it open. He noted the stiffness, the way her fingers hesitated. There was something there. A scrap of parchment. His eyes followed it, and for a moment, he meant to speak to her about it. But at the sound of hoofbeats, her fingers closed around it, and she slipped it into her pocket.

Grenville's instincts flared. He shifted closer to the body, his hand brushing near the hilt of his knife.

Davenport arrived, pale and stammering. Grenville barely acknowledged him beyond a clipped, "We found him like this."

Another set of hoofbeats approached, slower this time, more measured. Barrington rode into the clearing. Grenville watched him take in the scene with that unreadable expression of his. But his gaze lingered on Alastair and the mud splattered along his coat. Without a word, he dismounted and stood still, scanning the ground before taking a careful step forward.

As Barrington and the others spoke of Alastair's position, the scream, the red ribbons, Grenville's eyes remained fixed, but his attention had already fractured. Yes, details registered, but they skated across the surface of his thoughts. Beneath it ran something deeper. Alastair, his close friend, was dead, and his concern for Marjory gnawed at him. He glanced at Bridget; her calm, her persistence, kept slipping past his defenses in ways he hadn't yet named.

"I heard the scream just as I cleared the far hedge," Davenport offered. "I rode this way as quickly as I could." He paused, visibly rattled, his fingers tightening and loosening around his reins. "I caught a glimpse of Alastair earlier. He wasn't with the main group. He rode ahead alone. Odd, but I assumed he knew where he was going."

Grenville watched as Barrington crouched near the body. He pressed his boot lightly into the mud, noting how it resisted, then flicked his gaze toward Alastair's outstretched hand. Was he drawn, as Bridget had been, to the way his fingers were curled? He didn't say anything.

"We need to ensure nothing is disturbed until we've had time to assess," Barrington said smoothly.

"Did you see anyone else?" Barrington asked, his voice low and edged with authority.

"No," Davenport replied, shaking his head. "The path was clear, though the red ribbons were…odd. I pulled one off a tree." He held it up. "Look at it. They were tied in a crude knot, the fabric frayed. These weren't placed by my men."

"What about Marjory?" Bridget asked, her voice breaking slightly. "She was riding with him. Have you seen her?"

Davenport shook his head, looking genuinely distressed. "No, my lady. We haven't seen a trace of her." He looked at Grenville with a pained expression. "The ribbons…"

"We'll address that later. We need to spread out and search. Lady Alastair can't have gone far," Barrington insisted.

"Do you think she might…be hurt?" Davenport asked, confusion etched in his tone. "Or worse?"

"We won't know until we find her," Barrington said sharply.

Barrington issued orders. Grenville nodded, accepting the silent responsibility passed to him. Find the girl. Bring her back.

He turned away, meant to go alone. That would have been simpler. Cleaner. But something about Bridget, her refusal to flinch, the steadiness in her voice when others stammered, cut through the old instincts. She wasn't acting out of panic. She was choosing courage.

And damn him, but he recognized it.

He turned back to her. "Come with me. We'll lead the horses."

Barrington's gaze flicked to Davenport. "Mrs. Bainbridge went back to the manor to alert them that someone was hurt. Get word to Mr. Simmons to have someone come here and stand watch over Alastair's body. I'll remain here and make sure no one disturbs the scene."

Davenport, still shaken, turned and mounted his horse.

Barrington's gaze flicked to Bridget, assessing. "Are you hurt?"

"No," she said. "Only…shaken. I'll be alright with the captain."

Barrington nodded, and Grenville and Bridget headed for their horses. "I thought you would leave me with Alastair." It wasn't a statement or an acknowledgment. It was said with gratitude.

"Not taking action, even if it comes to nothing, would have eaten you alive," Grenville said softly. "She is your friend, and friends don't abandon each other, especially in the face of danger."

She reached out and gently touched his arm.

Startled, he glanced at her hand and then at her face.

"Thank you, Captain." She withdrew her hand. "For understanding."

He said nothing. He helped her into her saddle and mounted his horse. He leaned in toward her. His voice was quiet but firm. "Marjory needs you. And whether you admit it or not, you need to be here, too."

They moved through the trees with purpose, the damp earth muffling their approach as the tension deepened with each stride.

"She must be somewhere nearby," Bridget insisted, her voice taut with urgency. "Marjory would never leave Alastair, not willingly."

Grenville cast her a sidelong glance. "Let's hope you're right. We need to be prepared if she's hurt...or worse."

He watched as Bridget moved ahead, each step deliberate, her breath tight in her throat. The oppressive silence stretched between them until she froze. He followed where she was staring and saw a glimpse of fabric through the tangled ferns.

"Captain!" she gasped, pointing toward the base of a tree.

"Captain! Over there!" she called again.

He hurried toward the crumpled figure lying near the tree's base, partially hidden by a tangle of ferns.

"Marjory?" he said urgently.

A weak groan. Marjory stirred, her bonnet askew, her riding habit muddied. One hand clutched her side while the other fumbled at the damp earth as if trying to push herself upright.

Grenville dropped to one knee beside her, his voice low and steady. "Marjory, it's Grenville. You're safe now."

Bridget dropped to her knees beside her friend, helping her sit up. Marjory's head shifted against Bridget's shoulder as her lashes fluttered open. Her eyes were unfocused, her expression caught between confusion and grief.

Bridget smoothed the damp curls from her forehead. "Marjory, you're safe now. Can you tell us what happened?"

Marjory's lips moved, barely forming words. "He…he was looking for it…"

Bridget exchanged a quick look with Grenville. Whatever happened, it was more than a fall.

Marjory's breath came in shallow bursts, her gaze darting between them as though searching for an anchor. "We were riding together. He said he needed to check something… told me to stay on the path." Her voice wavered, her fingers trembling against Bridget's arm. "I waited, but he didn't come back."

Grenville's stance remained steady, his voice measured yet firm. "You didn't see him after that?"

Marjory shook her head. "I called for him. I thought I heard something, but the wind, it was loud." She swallowed hard, her brows knitting together as she fought to recall. "I didn't think…I didn't know…"

Grenville watched as Marjory faltered, her words thinning. It was hesitation, not from fear, but from knowing more than she could bring herself to say. Grenville exhaled and lowered his voice. "Marjory… we found Mark."

The words hung in the air like a slow-falling weight. Marjory's breath hitched. "Where?" she whispered, her fingers curling into Bridget's sleeve.

Bridget hesitated, glancing at Grenville. He met Marjory's gaze evenly, his expression grave. "Near the clearing. I'm sorry."

Marjory's lips parted, her breath stuttering as if the truth hadn't fully taken shape. For a moment, disbelief flickered in her eyes, a desperate hope that she had misheard, that the meaning could be reshaped into something less final.

Her grip on Bridget's arm tightened. "No—he can't be—he was just—" Her voice cracked, a sharp sob breaking free before she clamped a hand over her mouth.

Bridget pulled her into a firm embrace, steadying her as the tremors overtook her. "I'm so sorry," she murmured, her voice barely above a whisper.

Marjory clung to her, the weight of reality sinking in, though part of her still seemed to war against it. "I should have gone after him," she rasped. "I should have—"

Grenville's voice cut through gently, though with a firmness that brooked no blame. "You couldn't have known."

Marjory squeezed her eyes shut, pressing her forehead against Bridget's shoulder as silent tears spilled down her cheeks.

Grenville glanced at Bridget, his jaw tightening. "We need to get her back to the house. She's in no state to be out here."

A low rustle in the underbrush snapped Grenville's attention to the tree line. His fingers hovered near his knife. It was too slow for an animal and too quiet for an approach by chance.

Bridget stiffened beside him.

A moment later, branches swayed, and Blackwood stepped into view. His expression was composed, too composed. His gaze flicked over the scene, lingering a fraction too long on Marjory's disheveled state.

"So," Blackwood said, his voice light but measured. "She was here all along." His gaze flicked over Marjory, assessing rather than concerned. "I heard the scream, but by the time I reached this part of the course, it had gone quiet. I've been looking everywhere."

"She'll be fine," Grenville said shortly. His voice rang colder than he intended, but the control steadied him. It always had. Control, discipline. These were the rules he lived by. But standing in the woods with a grieving woman, a silent partner who kept pace with him, and a man he no longer trusted, he felt the fault lines shift beneath those rules.

Grenville's gaze sharpened as he took a measured step toward Blackwood. His posture stiffened, his shoulders squared, tension radiating from him like a drawn bowstring. "Where were you, Blackwood?"

The other man raised a brow, his calm demeanor unwavering. "Following the course, like everyone else. It seems we've all been thrown off track."

Bridget bristled, but Grenville silenced her with a look. "Let's get back to the house," he said, his voice low.

Grenville exhaled sharply. He cast a glance toward Bridget. "She's in no state to ride alone."

Bridget nodded, already shifting to help. "She'll ride with me."

Grenville didn't argue. Instead, he stepped forward, scooped Marjory up with practiced ease. She gave a faint protest, but her limbs lacked the strength to resist. He lifted her onto Bridget's horse, settling her carefully in the saddle. Bridget swung up behind, wrapping an arm around her friend to keep her steady.

"Keep her talking," he murmured, passing the reins into Bridget's hands. "Don't let her slip under."

Bridget tightened her grip around Marjory. "I won't."

Once Grenville and Blackwood mounted their own horses, the group turned toward the house, moving swiftly but carefully through the dense wood.

Side by side, they made their way back to the manor house. Grenville cast a glance at Bridget, half-expecting her to challenge him, to press for more answers. But she didn't. Instead, her expression matched his own, focused and determined.

As they pressed on, Grenville felt a shift, not just in the investigation but in something deeper, in her. Bridget rode with composure, sharp and ready, her eyes always forward. He had expected resistance or questions. Instead, she met the moment with determination. And for the first time, he didn't just tolerate her presence, he counted on it.

He didn't trust easily. But she'd earned it, not with words, but with how she moved through fire. And in this, perhaps, they were more alike than he'd dared admit.

Chapter Eleven

EVEN BEFORE THEY reached Alastair Court, the air had grown heavy. The manor stood silent against the grey sky, its windows dark, its walls steeped in the hush that follows a blow. Hooves struck the damp earth in a solemn rhythm, but no one spoke. The cheerfulness of the weekend had died with Alastair, and they rode toward something colder than grief—uncertainty, as he relayed the update: the icehouse was being prepared. The words settled over them like a shroud. No one argued or questioned it. Death had a way of silencing even the most obstinate.

Barrington gave the footman quiet instructions before turning toward Blackwood. They exchanged a brief look before mounting up and making their way toward the manor without exchanging a word.

Grenville glanced over. Bridget hadn't dismounted. She sat rigid in the saddle, her fingers curled tightly around the reins. Her mind refused to be still. Every detail of the past hour replayed in relentless succession. Alastair's unnatural stillness, the way his hand had frozen in its final grasp, the lifelessness that had settled into his once expressive features. And the parchment. The slip of paper now hidden inside her pocket, an unspoken whisper demanding her attention. The sensation of it, thin, fragile, yet heavy with meaning, sent an unsettling prickle up her spine.

She had yet to examine it. Every time she even thought of unfolding it, another pair of eyes lingered too long, and another question was asked. No. Not here. Not yet.

Grenville rode beside her, his silence a shield, his expression carefully schooled. But Bridget knew better. She recognized the way his jaw set when his thoughts ran ahead of him, when his mind was already pulling apart the puzzle piece by piece. He was calculating, assessing, and already forming the next step. It was an odd comfort, knowing she wasn't alone in this unraveling mystery.

Marjory remained quiet, cradled between Bridget's arms, her posture stiff with shock. Her hands clutched at the saddle, knuckles pale against the leather. She had not spoken since they left the clearing. The grief on her face was raw, unguarded. Every so often, her breath hitched, as though she were swallowing back a sob, unwilling to break before so many watchful eyes. The wind tugged at her riding cloak, but she hardly seemed to notice. She only stared ahead, unseeing, as if the weight of the world had settled upon her and she did not yet know how to carry it.

The others also bore the weight of the moment. The ease of camaraderie that had existed only hours before was now fractured, replaced with unease. Lord Davenport, who had insisted on accompanying them back, wore his emotions more plainly than the others. His brows were furrowed, his lips pressed into a tight line.

"It's an outrage," Davenport muttered at last, the first to break the tense quiet. His voice carried an edge of anger, whether at the situation itself or at the disruption of his weekend. "A damnable thing to happen here, of all places."

"Here?" Bridget asked sharply, her head snapping toward him. "As opposed to anywhere else?"

Davenport's jaw clenched. "I simply meant that Alastair was a well-respected man. Who would wish him harm?"

No one answered immediately. The question hung between them, thick and suffocating.

"Not a stranger," Barrington finally said, his tone measured, his gaze fixed ahead. "Not with how quickly it happened. Not with where it happened."

Davenport frowned, turning toward him. "What are you suggesting?"

Grenville's fingers flexed around the reins, his voice even. "That whoever did this knew the estate."

A sharp glance passed between some of the guests. That suggestion unsettled them far more than the idea of a passing thief. A stranger was easy to fear, easy to blame, but the notion that Alastair's murderer had walked among them? That was something else entirely.

The weight of it settled into their bones as the estate loomed before them, its tall windows glowing against the encroaching night. The laughter and music from the evening before had vanished, replaced by a silence that carried only one certainty.

No one in Alastair Court would sleep soundly tonight.

When they reached the manor, they found Barrington waiting for them at the entrance. He turned to Marjory, who stood rigid with the footman, her eyes shadowed with grief. "You should rest."

"I will do no such thing." Her voice was hoarse but steady as they walked into the entranceway. "Mark is, was, my husband. I will not be sent away like some fragile thing."

Bridget stepped closer, her fingers briefly squeezing Marjory's hand. There were no words for a loss like this, no comfort that could be offered when the wound was so fresh.

"Then you should at least sit," Barrington amended, gesturing toward the drawing room.

Marjory did not resist, though her steps were mechanical as she crossed the threshold. Bridget followed, her mind still whirling.

Blackwood entered the hall, his gaze sharp, as if he had already heard whispers of what had transpired. "Word is already spreading among the staff."

Barrington swore under his breath. "That was inevitable. The key is ensuring speculation doesn't overtake fact." He spoke to

Grenville, Bridget, and Davenport quietly. "Not a word about Alastair's wounds or where they are."

They all agreed.

Bridget listened but found her focus slipping. The investigation could wait for now. There was only one person who mattered.

⤞⤝

MARJORY SAT IN the drawing room, Bridget and Grenville across from her. The elegant surroundings offered her little comfort, as the memories of the chase, and the unbearable knowledge of Mark's death, replayed in her mind. Her gaze, unfocused and distant, lingered on the patterned rug as if searching for clarity in the midst of Mark's death. Each shudder that passed through her seemed to echo the chaos of the morning and the harsh reality of loss still fresh in her bones.

A short time later, Mrs. Simmons entered, her footsteps soft and her voice gentle. "My lady." She paused by Marjory's side, "you mustn't remain in these muddy clothes. Please, come with me. You'll feel better once you've changed into something dry."

Despite the deep sorrow etched on her face, a flicker of gratitude warmed Marjory's eyes. With a reluctant sigh, she rose and, with Mrs. Simmons's guidance, climbed the stairs.

⤞⤝

BRIDGET STARTED SLIGHTLY as Grenville's fingers closed around hers, a silent reassurance she hadn't known she needed. She turned to him with a smile. "It seems whenever we're together, we wind up in the mud."

His face broke out with a smile that, even amid the gloom, took her breath away. "You go on. I need to clean up as well." A playful note softened his tone, a brief spark of levity in an otherwise depressing morning.

She went up the stairs and when she entered her room, found Catriona already at work. The woman was selecting a fresh day dress from the wardrobe. Bridget's heart lifted at the sight of her fellow clanswoman.

"Catriona, I'm glad you're here." Bridget's voice was low as she stepped forward.

"Stay where you are, and I'll get those clothes off you." Catriona was already moving to help her.

As Catriona worked, Bridget ventured carefully. "You've heard about Lord Alastair, haven't you?"

Catriona's expression darkened as she adjusted the dress. "Aye. It was a shock. Everyone below stairs is unsettled. They don't know which way to turn. Drummond said you and the captain found his lordship and Lady Marjory. Do you have any idea what happened?"

Bridget's heart ached at the thought of stirring gossip, yet silence would serve no one. "Nothing conclusive. It looks as though Alastair fell from his horse."

"And her ladyship?" Catriona's voice softened as she helped Bridget into the fresh dress. "How is she holding up?"

Bridget paused, her gaze flickering with both sorrow and steely determination. "She is utterly taken aback, devastated." The words were difficult to say as she tried to steady her racing heart.

Catriona sighed deeply, her eyes reflecting a shared grief. "Aye, my lady, it is a bitter pill indeed. But we must keep our tongues in check. Rumors have a way of igniting fires where they ought not to burn. There, you're all done."

Bridget offered a smile of gratitude before nodding. She left the room and returned downstairs.

She found Marjory in the conservatory, seated on a chaise with her knees drawn up and her arms wrapped tightly around them. The faint scent of lilies filled the room, and sunlight streamed through the tall windows. Marjory looked up as Bridget approached, her face pale and drawn, but her lips tightened in something that wasn't quite a smile.

"Bridget." Her voice was a hoarse whisper. "You've come to scold me for running away, haven't you?"

"Not at all," Bridget replied gently, taking the chair opposite her. "I've come because I'm worried about you."

Marjory let out a soft, bitter laugh. "Worried about me? Of all the people here, I'm the least deserving of anyone's concern."

Bridget leaned forward, resting her hands lightly on her knees. "That isn't true, Marjory, and you know it. Please, talk to me. I'm here to listen, and I'll believe whatever you're willing to tell me."

For a long moment, Marjory stared at the delicate patterns on the carpet beneath her feet. Finally, she sighed and leaned back against the chaise. "Mark and I rode together earlier," she began, her voice barely above a whisper. "Something was on his mind. I could feel it, but he wouldn't share."

"Did he mention meeting someone?"

Marjory opened her mouth, then closed it again, her fingers twisting in her lap. Finally, she exhaled. "Mark... he wasn't himself these last few weeks. I thought it was just a passing distraction, but..." She trailed off, shaking her head. "I should have asked him more questions."

"He changed, Bridget," she said softly. "At first, I thought it was just excitement over some discovery. But then he started waking in the middle of the night, poring over that book. He wasn't just interested, he was obsessed with it."

Bridget frowned. "Did he ever tell you why?"

Marjory swallowed hard. "I asked him." She hesitated and swallowed hard. "He said, '*Some things are better left buried*'."

"Did he tell you anything else? Even something small?" Bridget asked softly.

Marjory's eyes glistened as she shook her head. "He said he needed to meet someone, 'someone important.' I thought it might have been Lord Barrington. He'd been spending more time in Mark's company of late."

"Yes," Bridget said, her heart sinking as the pieces began to align. "Did he seem frightened?"

"Not frightened," Marjory said after a moment's thought. "More… determined. As if he had made up his mind about something. But there was an edge to it. I told him he should take care, but he dismissed me. Said it wasn't my concern." She bit her lip, her shoulders trembling. "I thought he was angry with me. So I rode ahead. I didn't want to fight anymore. When I turned back to look for him, he was gone. Just gone."

Bridget reached over and took Marjory's hand, holding it tightly. The warmth of her friend's fingers was a stark contrast to the cold fear curling in her stomach. "Marjory, when you rode ahead, did you see anyone else on the course? Even in the distance?"

Marjory frowned, her gaze growing distant as she tried to recall. "There was someone," she said slowly. "I didn't see their face, but… there was a sound."

"What kind of sound?" Bridget pressed gently.

Marjory swallowed. "A metallic click. Or at least, I think it was. I thought it was tack or a loose stirrup, but now…" She shivered, shaking her head. "I don't know. I keep replaying it in my head, but maybe I imagined it. Maybe it was nothing."

Bridget nodded, her heart aching for her friend even as her mind raced. A metallic click. A sound so small, so easily dismissed, yet it had stayed with Marjory. A warning? A weapon? Or something else entirely? "Marjory, you've been so brave to tell me this. Alastair was a dear friend to my family, and I promise you, we will find out what happened."

Marjory's grip on Bridget's hand tightened briefly before she let go, leaning back against the chaise with a weary sigh. "Just tell me one thing, Bridget." Her voice was barely audible. "Did he suffer?"

Bridget swallowed hard, willing her voice to remain steady. "I don't believe so. It would have been quick."

Marjory closed her eyes, a single tear slipping down her cheek. "Thank you."

Bridget rose, more determined than ever, as she left the conservatory. Alastair had been silenced, and the key to uncovering the truth now lay in the shadows of his final moments. Whatever secrets he had been carrying, they would not remain hidden for long.

She turned toward the hall, her fingers curling around the parchment that she hid in her pocket. The paper was rough against her skin, a stark reminder of the man's grasp. He had fought to keep this. She would fight to understand why. Whatever message he had died trying to deliver, she knew she could not unravel it alone.

Her steps quickened. There was only one person she could trust with this, only one who would take it as seriously as she did.

Bridget found the captain in the dimly lit corridor, his brow furrowed in thought. The death of a friend was never easy. At the sight of her, his expression shifted, concern flickering in his gaze.

"Bridget," he greeted, his voice low. "Is Marjory—?"

"She's holding on," Bridget said. Then, without preamble, she reached into her dress and pulled free the scrap of parchment, holding it out to him. "I found this."

His eyes sharpened as he took the crumpled fragment, carefully smoothing it between his fingers. His thumb skimmed over the faint markings, his jaw tightening. The ink had bled in places, but a few letters still remained: *'gton.'* A place? A name? A chill skated down her spine. For a fraction of a second, something flickered in his gaze. Recognition? Disbelief? But it was gone before she could place it. Though worn and stained, the faint outline of something, a sigil? A crest? lingered on the surface.

"Where did you find this?"

Bridget stared at him. "Alastair was holding it. Tightly. As if he wanted someone to find it."

He stared at her.

Bridget lifted her chin slightly. For a moment, she hesitated, the vulnerability of trust pressing against her ribs. But she did trust him. "Help me understand what it means."

For a long moment, he said nothing. Then, with a quiet nod, he folded the parchment. "May I keep this?"

She nodded at once.

He tucked it into the inner pocket of his coat. "Then let's find out what he means."

The distant chime of the clock reminded them both of the lateness of the afternoon. Bridget exhaled, only then realizing how close they stood. She inhaled again, steeling herself.

"We should return to the scene," she murmured. "We must bring Alastair home."

He studied her for a beat before nodding. "Barrington will also want to go over everything before we move him."

Bridget forced herself to suppress a shiver. They weren't just retracing Alastair's final steps. They were stepping into the unknown, into something far more dangerous than they had anticipated. They would return to the clearing in the woods, to the place where Alastair had drawn his last breath. And perhaps, this time, the dark would not let them walk away empty-handed. Not if she had anything to say about it.

Chapter Twelve

A S THEY LEFT the manor and followed the familiar wooded path, the gentle rustle of leaves and quiet crunch of underbrush slowly replaced the hum of estate life. In the subdued light of the late afternoon, Grenville and Bridget exchanged a brief, knowing glance. They would find the answers and give Alastair justice.

As they stepped into the clearing, a young footman straightened from where he had been leaning against a tree. His face was pale but composed, and he quickly adjusted his coat as they drew closer.

"All's been calm here, Captain," the footman said, addressing Grenville with a faint bow. "No visitors, no animals. Just as Lord Barrington ordered." He hesitated, glancing toward the body. "It's been a grim watch, my lord, but no one's disturbed the site."

Grenville nodded curtly, his tone clipped. "You've done well. Lord Barrington and Mr. Townsend will be here shortly. Stay close and make certain no one bothers us."

The footman took a step back, the tight line of his shoulders easing slightly, though his gaze lingered on the covered body. "Thank you, sir," he murmured, his voice betraying his exhaustion and unease. "Didn't want to leave him alone."

Grenville gave a curt nod, his gaze flicking toward the shrouded form on the ground. "You did right in staying as long as you could," he said, his voice steady. "But he's not alone. Not now."

The footman exhaled, some of the tension in his stance releasing at Grenville's reassurance.

Grenville stood with his arms crossed and his expression dark. He barely noticed Bridget pacing until her voice broke the silence.

"I spoke with Marjory," she said softly, stopping a few steps away.

Grenville turned, his sharp gaze meeting hers. "What did she say?"

"Alastair was supposed to meet someone," Bridget continued, moving closer. "She thought it might be Barrington. He had been secretive, and she saw someone, a rider, through the trees just before she rode ahead."

Grenville frowned, processing her words. "Did she say who it was?"

"No," Bridget admitted. "She couldn't see clearly. But she mentioned Alastair seemed… determined. Like he'd already made up his mind about something."

Grenville exhaled slowly, his gaze sweeping the clearing. "If he was meeting someone, why here? Why not at the house? Whatever it was, he didn't want anyone else to overhear or know about it."

Bridget followed his gaze to the spot where Mark's body lay. Her stomach churned at the memory. "We assumed he had nothing with him. But what if we were wrong? What if there was something we overlooked, something the killer never found?"

Grenville gave a grim nod. "Then we look again."

They crouched near the disturbed ground, and Grenville carefully pulled down the blanket covering Mark's body. The sight made Bridget avert her eyes for a moment, but she steeled herself, determined to help.

The sound of hoofbeats cut through the silence, the rhythm steady and purposeful. Grenville rose instinctively, turning toward the approaching riders.

Barrington and Townsend emerged from the trees, their expressions taut. Barrington swung off his horse, his sharp gaze sweeping the clearing before settling on Alastair's body.

"What is it?" he asked, his voice low.

Grenville motioned to Bridget, who was still crouching near the body. "We were just about to examine him further."

Barrington nodded, stepping forward, scanning the ground with a practiced eye. Townsend, meanwhile, dismounted more slowly, his gaze lingering on the surrounding trees as if assessing the space for hidden dangers.

"No signs of a struggle?" Townsend observed. "He didn't have time to fight back."

Grenville shook his head. "Whoever did this was swift and precise."

Bridget's breath caught as she leaned in. There was something, something wrong. A smudge of dirt, a shadow? No... not just dirt. It was deliberate. Her pulse quickened. "Captain." Her voice broke through, low and urgent.

Grenville followed her gaze, his expression tensing as he noticed the same thing. He reached for his handkerchief before carefully tilting Mark's head. A sliver of parchment protruded between the man's lips.

His breath caught as he drew it free. "What the hell is this?"

Barrington, now kneeling on Alastair's other side, also leaned in, his eyes sharp. "There's a symbol drawn on the parchment. Faint, but deliberate."

Bridget's stomach churned. "It looks similar to something I saw earlier."

Using the handkerchief, Grenville carefully wiped away more of the grime, revealing the symbol in full.

The ink caught the light, uneven, deliberate, and Bridget's stomach turned.

"That's no accident," Townsend murmured. "That symbol. It's a message."

Barrington exchanged a look with Grenville. "They left it on purpose. Someone wanted us to find it."

Grenville's jaw tightened. "Whoever he was meeting was

afraid of what he was about to share."

Bridget stared at the symbol, her mind racing. "Alastair must have known he was in danger. That's why he was so secretive. But why now? Why during the chase?"

"To scatter everyone," Grenville said. "It was the perfect opportunity to isolate him and leave a message."

The symbol was small, no larger than a coin, inked with care. A stylized raven perched on a branch with its wings partially spread, as if caught midturn. Beneath it, a single word had been scrawled in tight, slanted letters: *Watch*.

Barrington stood slowly, his face grim. "We need to move the body back to Alastair Court. But we also need to find out what this marking means."

Townsend exhaled sharply. "If it's what I suspect... we're dealing with something far more calculated than a mere rivalry or personal grudge."

Bridget swallowed hard, her resolve hardening. "Then we need to figure out who he was meeting, and why this message was meant for us."

Grenville met her gaze, his expression grim but determined. "We will. But we have to tread carefully. Whoever did this isn't finished yet."

With grim efficiency, they set to work, wrapping Mark's body for moving. The footman stepped forward hesitantly, his face tight with unease as he assisted. No one spoke as they lifted him onto a makeshift stretcher. The scent of damp earth and blood clung to the air, thick and unshakable.

Bridget swallowed hard, her fingers clenching around the reins as they prepared to ride. The silence stretched between them, heavy with unspoken thoughts. As the party turned toward Alastair Court, the rhythmic thud of hooves against the softened ground carried them forward in a silence no one dared break.

Chapter Thirteen

T HE LIBRARY AT Alastair Court was quiet. The tension was unmistakable. Professor Tresham sat among the ancient books, but even he could not concentrate. Barrington stood by the desk, his expression unreadable as he held the note delicately between his fingers. Townsend looked over his shoulder, his eyes narrowing as he studied the scrawled words. Grenville and Bridget stood nearby.

Barrington carefully unfolded the parchment that he'd taken out of Alastair's mouth. His eyes narrowed as he read the inscription: *"For those who betray the Shadows, silence is eternal."* He exhaled slowly, recognition crossing his face.

"This is no idle threat," he said grimly. "It bears the Order of Shadow's seal, meant to silence and intimidate. I've seen it before." He angled the parchment toward the firelight, revealing a faint symbol, a raven with wings spread wide inside a diamond. "They want us to know exactly who is responsible."

Grenville crossed his arms, his jaw tight. "They didn't just kill him. They made an example of him. The question is, why now?"

Townsend tapped his chin thoughtfully. "If Alastair was meeting someone to share something, the timing was deliberate. The Order of Shadows didn't want to risk him talking."

Bridget stepped closer, her gaze fixed on the symbol. "The Order of Shadows?"

Barrington nodded. "They're not a legend. The Order of Shadows is a centuries-old syndicate that manipulates power behind the scenes of the aristocracy, politics, and commerce. Most never hear of them. That's how they operate. Until now." He met Grenville's eye. "Which is why I sent for you."

Grenville glanced at Bridget before speaking. "I suspected it was more than a courtesy visit," he said quietly. "But I didn't expect… this." His voice lowered, shaded with something darker. "Not the Order."

Bridget's fingers tightened around the edge of her sleeve. This Order wasn't some whispered threat. Alastair was dead because of them. Justice, not fear, pushed her forward. She couldn't let his death be swept into silence. Not when the truth was close enough to touch.

A hush settled again, heavy with shared understanding.

The door creaked open, breaking the stillness. Marjory stepped inside, pale but composed, her gaze scanning the room before settling on Barrington.

"I thought I might find you here," she said quietly. "Have you discovered anything?"

Barrington's expression remained neutral. "We found this," Barrington said, showing her the note. "It was on Alastair. Do you know anything about the Order?"

"Not at all." Marjory's eyes widened as she read the message, her hand flying to her mouth. "That handwriting…" She swallowed hard. "I—I've seen it before." She looked at them, her eyes full of pain. "I don't recall where." Her voice was a whisper.

"Don't worry. It will come to you," Townsend said smoothly, his gaze sharp as he observed her reaction. "Was Alastair involved in anything… unusual?"

Marjory shook her head vehemently. "No. At least, not that he told me. But he—" She hesitated, glancing away. "He'd been distant lately. No, distracted. He'd been asking strange questions about my family, people long dead, ancestors I barely remember hearing about. I thought it was just another one of his scholarly pursuits." Her voice dropped, and her cheeks flushed. "But I never imagined… this."

Bridget's expression softened. "Did he say anything to you about being blackmailed? Or mention anyone suspicious?"

Marjory shook her head again, her voice trembling. "No. I thought he was trying to protect me from something, but I don't know what it was. If he was being blackmailed, he never told me."

No one spoke. Her meaning had been clear enough.

"We'll figure this out," Barrington said firmly. "Alastair may have taken secrets to his grave, but we'll uncover the truth."

Marjory nodded, her eyes glistening with unshed tears. "Thank you. Please… let me know if you find anything else."

She left the room quietly. The moment the door clicked shut, Townsend exhaled. "She may not know what Alastair was involved in, but she's hiding something. Or someone."

Barrington paced the length of the room.

Grenville crossed his arms, his expression unreadable. "You believe Alastair uncovered something specific?"

Barrington turned toward the bookshelves, his eyes sharpening with understanding. "In his search for the past, Alastair must have found something. Something about the Order of Shadows." He reached for the nearest shelf, his fingers skimming the spines of the carefully arranged volumes. "If he discovered information they wanted hidden, that could explain why he was silenced."

Bridget studied the vast collection before them. "But what exactly was he looking for?"

Barrington exhaled. "That's what we need to find out." He turned to the others gathered in the room, his tone shifting to one of command. "The books need to be searched. If there's a record, a letter, anything tucked between these pages, we must find it before it disappears." His gaze landed on Professor Tresham. "You may have some idea where to start looking."

Tresham, who had been silent until now, straightened slightly, his curiosity piqued despite the grim circumstances. "Alastair's collection is extensive. But if he had found something particularly valuable, something that threatened the Order, it wouldn't be among his usual acquisitions. We should begin with any books he kept separate, any volumes he recently obtained or studied in private."

Barrington nodded. "Good. We need to search here as well as question everyone carefully. Someone in this house knows more than they are saying." His voice dropped slightly, the tension in the room thickening. "And I have no intention of waiting for them to come forward on their own."

A charged silence followed, each person exchanging wary glances. They all understood that this was no longer just about Alastair's death. It was about what he had uncovered, and what it might cost them to reveal it.

⫸⫷

THE LATE AFTERNOON light filtered through the tall library windows. Grenville and Bridget searched the library drawers. They unrolled ancient parchments, scanning them for any references to the Order.

Grenville pulled open a drawer, every movement controlled, but a current ran beneath his skin. He wasn't calm. He was concentrating, holding back the surge of something bigger. Something that had started when Bridget touched that note.

Even amid the grim task of unraveling Alastair's secrets, Bridget couldn't help but note how Grenville's steady presence anchored her, a quiet comfort that she dared not yet name.

"Marjory said Alastair kept things to himself," Bridget said as she looked through a library drawer. "But everyone has a habit, a place where they believe their secrets are safe."

Grenville arched a brow at her. "Speaking from experience?"

Bridget shot him a cynical glance. "Observation." She crouched and inspected the small cabinet beside the desk.

Minutes passed as they worked in silence. Grenville sifted through a stack of papers, searching each one before setting it aside. Bridget ran her fingers along the underside of the desk drawer, searching for a hidden compartment.

She paused, her fingertips froze on an uneven edge. "Captain," she whispered, sharper than a summons, more like a warning or a victory. Grenville's head snapped up. He was already crossing to her as she carefully pulled out a folded sheaf of parchment tucked against the back of the drawer. The parchment was aged, the ink faded, the letters deliberate but frustratingly faint. A shiver ran down her spine as she studied the markings.

"This… this is the same as the scrap of parchment I gave you," she whispered, not quite trusting her voice. "Alastair didn't just tear it. He meant to protect it."

She looked at him then, not just for confirmation, but connection. And it hit him, how deeply she'd believed they'd find this. How fiercely she'd fought to follow the truth.

Grenville pulled the scrap from his coat pocket, the one Bridget had taken from Alastair's grasp. Carefully, he aligned the edges. The two pieces fit seamlessly together.

Bridget pressed her lips into a thin line. "Alastair didn't just tear this out to keep it." She exhaled. "He wanted to make sure no one else did."

Grenville studied the reunited parchment, his brow furrowing. The ink was too faint in certain places, the letters smudged with age. Some words were clear, but others, especially the crucial ones at the seam where the paper had been torn, were nearly illegible.

Bridget frowned. "Some of this script… it's Old Scots."

Grenville's expression darkened. "I've seen this language before." His voice was low, edged with recognition. "Alastair bought that odd book outside the antique shop in Spain. I remember because he couldn't read it, but he was certain it was important."

He stepped to the bookshelf, scanning the titles before pulling out a worn, leather-bound volume. He set it down before Bridget, flipping through the brittle pages.

Bridget ran her fingers over the worn parchment. "This is the book Miss Gray read Friday evening. She said it was disturbing."

Together, they paged through the book. The script was painstakingly written, archaic in style, the meaning just out of reach. Then they stopped. Several pages had been violently torn from the binding, leaving ragged edges where words had once been recorded.

Bridget inhaled sharply. "Whatever he found in here," she murmured, "he believed it was worth risking everything."

Grenville studied the missing pages, his brow furrowed. "And whoever wants it back will kill again if necessary."

Bridget let out a sharp breath. A sound that carried shock, fury, and wild exhilaration. "We were right," she said, her eyes blazing. "We bloody well—" She struck the desk with her open palm, her energy sparking into motion. "He left a trail, and we found it. We did."

Her voice rose with conviction, and Grenville turned toward her, staring not at the parchment now, but at her.

It wasn't just the Order. It wasn't just danger. It was the way she stood before him, fierce and unyielding, her voice still ringing in his ears. It was the way she *believed*. The way she *knew*.

She was the fire that made the storm make sense. And suddenly, Grenville didn't want sense at all. He wanted her.

The Order. The threat. The choice Alastair had made and what it had cost him. But also, Bridget.

Her voice. Her fire. Her belief in this moment. In *him*.

Grenville's control, so carefully kept, *broke*. Not violently. Not wildly. But with *absolute clarity*.

He reached for her, one hand catching her waist, the other rising to her cheek. His lips captured hers in a kiss. It was fierce and breath-stealing, born of too many held-back thoughts and the pounding rush of truth finally seen. Her breath caught, then melted into his, her fingers gripping the front of his coat.

When they broke apart, just long enough for air, Grenville saw her, truly saw her. Flushed. Her green eyes were wide, flickering from surprise to something deeper. Certain. She reached for him, fingers fisting his coat, and kissed him back.

This time it was slower. Richer. A question asked and answered without a word.

When they finally parted again, the silence that followed was no longer heavy. It vibrated with something new. Something neither of them had dared name until now.

The room hadn't changed. But everything else had.

Bridget drew in a shaky breath, and Grenville watched her chest rise, the color still high in her cheeks. Her fingers had curled slightly at her sides, as if part of her wasn't ready to let go.

Neither was he.

His thoughts reeled, but one truth shone through like fire-light. He hadn't meant to kiss her. Not yet. Not now. But *holding back had become impossible.*

The heat of her lingered on his lips, and behind his ribs, something kicked to life, something too unruly to name. Not just desire. Not just relief. But *recognition.* As if something in him had been waiting for this, *for her,* without realizing it until that very moment.

She stood before him, flushed, breath unsteady, and utterly unafraid. And Grenville felt... undone. Not weakened. Not distracted. Just... honest, in a way he hadn't been in years.

He opened his mouth, searching for the words that might make sense of what they'd just done. But there were none.

"I didn't plan—" he started. Then stopped. His voice wasn't steady enough.

Bridget's lips curved into the barest smile, soft and knowing. "I know."

The silence that followed held no regret. But he recognized it was something new, something fragile, *just born.*

Without thinking, he reached for her hand. Not to pull her close again. Just... to feel her warmth, the proof that she was real, and so was their kiss.

Bridget didn't flinch. She didn't step away. Her fingers curved around his, not tightly, not possessively, but deliberately. As if anchoring them both.

It lasted only a second. Then the moment shifted, and the room came back into focus with the books, the torn pages, and the truth still waiting in the shadows.

But Grenville would remember that second. The way her hand felt in his. The fire behind her eyes. The kiss that had stopped time.

⟫⟫⟫⟪⟪⟪

MRS. BAINBRIDGE WALKED briskly alongside Townsend, their steps echoing softly against the polished floors. The air in the corridor was cool, the scent of aged wood and wax lingering from the morning's tidying. She kept her voice low as she glanced up at her companion.

"Barrington wants us to speak to Dr. Manning and have him come here immediately," she murmured, urgency tightening her tone.

Townsend gave a crisp nod. The esteemed physician was known not only for his medical expertise but for his unflinching manner when dealing with matters of an unsettling nature. He would know what to make of the situation.

"I'll speak to Judge Scofield," Townsend added. "He, too, must be informed."

Mrs. Bainbridge agreed, though a chill of apprehension crept into her spine. A death under mysterious circumstances, especially that of a respected gentleman, was no small matter. How swiftly would the law intervene?

As they disappeared down the corridor on their errand, the manor remained charged with uncertainty.

In the quiet of the drawing room, hushed voices and subdued conversation wove through the area, the guests restless but unwilling to break the fragile calm.

Near the mantel, Davenport and Tresham stood locked in discussion, their low voices a murmur of speculation. Their brows were drawn, their expressions grave, piecing together the morning's grim discovery.

Across the room, Blackwood kept himself occupied with the *Sommer Sentinel*, though his occasional scoff at the thinly written columns betrayed his disdain. "Not quite *The London Gazette*," he had grumbled earlier, "but I suppose it will suffice."

A few feet away, Miss Hathaway and Miss Gray exchanged a fleeting glance, subtle but telling. They had not spoken much, yet their eyes carried an understanding, a quiet acknowledgement of the morning's turn.

By the window, Lady Worthington sat with the poise of a woman unaffected by such grim affairs. Her embroidery hoop rested in her hands, the rhythmic whisper of her needle piercing the fabric the only consistent sound in the room. The sapphire on the top of her bodkin case caught the fading light, a glint of steel against her measured composure.

No one spoke loudly. No one dared shatter the stillness.

The manor had settled into an uneasy calm, each guest lost in their own thoughts, the gravity of the morning lingering like a storm on the horizon.

Chapter Fourteen

THE STEADY CLIP of hooves on gravel announced their arrival before the footman had even reached the door. Dr. Manning and Judge Scofield stepped down from the carriage, their expressions already set with grim understanding. Townsend and Mrs. Bainbridge, having secured their assistance, led them through the entrance hall, where the hush of the household had thickened into something near suffocating.

Dr. Manning, a man of precise movements and keen observation, wasted no time. "Where is he?" he asked, adjusting the cuffs of his coat.

"This way," Barrington said, his tone clipped, leading them toward the icehouse.

The scent of damp stone and lingering cold met them as they stepped inside. Alastair's still form lay undisturbed, death turning his once-vibrant features into something unfamiliar. Dr. Manning efficiently moved beside the body while the others watched in tense silence.

Judge Scofield, normally a man of unwavering authority, stood near the entrance, his face drawn. He had known Alastair since he was a babe. He had watched him grow into a man of standing and respect. Now, he was tasked with ensuring justice for him.

Dr. Manning placed his hands on Alastair's limbs, pressing along the joints, feeling for fractures. He lifted one of Alastair's eyelids, studying the dull, clouded iris before pausing.

His brow furrowed. He leaned in slightly, adjusting his spectacles, then examined the other eye.

"What is it?" Barrington asked, watching the doctor's sharp focus.

Dr. Manning didn't immediately answer. He pressed two fingers against Alastair's jaw, tilting his head slightly before exhaling.

"His pupils," he murmured, "They are…unnaturally dilated."

Bridget, standing just behind Grenville, felt a prickle of unease. "What does that mean?"

Dr. Manning glanced at her, then returned his focus to the body. "The eyes do not respond to light after death, but such pronounced dilation suggests something more." He hesitated, then sniffed the air subtly before lowering his nose toward the wound near Alastair's ribs. His face hardened.

A slow tension rippled through the gathered onlookers.

Grenville took a step forward. "Doctor?"

Dr. Manning straightened, rubbing his chin in thought. "The wound is small, precise. Not a deep cut but placed with intent." He leaned down again, inhaling briefly before his expression turned grim. "And there is… a smell."

Barrington frowned. "A smell?"

Dr. Manning gave a sharp nod. "It is faint, but unmistakable. Belladonna."

A hush fell over the room.

Judge Scofield, who had been silent until now, stiffened. "Belladonna? Are you saying he was poisoned?"

Dr. Manning exhaled slowly, his voice firm. "Yes. But not in the way you might expect." He turned to the others. "A blade, dipped in belladonna, delivered the fatal dose directly into his bloodstream. The poison would have acted swiftly, his pupils show classic signs of belladonna poisoning." He gestured toward the slight rigidity in Alastair's fingers. "Muscle paralysis would have set in almost instantly. He wouldn't even have time to cry out."

"The magistrate at Bamburgh Castle should be notified," Scofield said. "I'll leave at once." Without waiting for a reply, he turned and strode briskly from the icehouse, the door creaking shut behind him.

Bridget's stomach twisted. A stab wound alone could have killed him, but this? This was something else. This was deliberate, insidious.

Grenville's voice was quiet but cold. "He was lost the moment the blade struck."

Dr. Manning nodded. "Precisely." He stepped back from the body, glancing between them. "Whoever did this was skilled. They knew that even a small wound, if laced with the right poison, would be just as deadly as a sword to the heart."

"Then the fall was a ruse," Townsend restated. "Whoever did this wanted us to believe it was an accident."

Grenville exhaled slowly. "And they nearly succeeded."

Bridget stared down at Alastair's still face, a deep unease settling within her. She found it all difficult to believe. The wound, the poison, the deception, this was no crime of passion or momentary rage. This had been planned. Carefully. Methodically.

She turned to Grenville. "I had hoped we were wrong. This was more than murder. It was an execution. What do we do?"

Grenville briefly met her gaze, and for once, he did not argue. "We find his executioner."

Bridget inhaled, steadying herself. "And whoever did this… is still here."

The gravity of her words settled over them like a storm rolling in.

Dr. Manning turned back to his grim work, his voice low as he spoke to Judge Scofield. The conversation drifted beyond Bridget's awareness, a steady hum of duty and procedure, necessary, but not something she could bear to hear.

The walls of the icehouse seemed to close in, the air too heavy, too thick with the scent of cold stone and death. She had seen enough.

Bridget stepped back. "If you'll excuse me," she murmured, though no one stopped her.

Slipping out, she moved through the dim corridors of the manor, each step precise, though her thoughts raced ahead. The hush of the house was deafening, thick with uncertainty and suspicion. Each guest was now a potential killer.

Scofield had already departed for Bamburgh Castle. His absence, though reasonable, left the household in an uneasy limbo, and not everyone believed it was wise.

At last, she reached the quiet sanctuary of her room. The moment the door shut behind her, she released a slow breath and crossed to the window.

Now, she sat staring out over the estate, the landscape stretching before her in eerie stillness.

The chase had been for sport. But the real hunt had only just begun.

CATRIONA STOOD BY the wardrobe, carefully folding one of Bridget's shawls. The mood was subdued, but the silence was overwhelming.

"What's the gossip below stairs?" Bridget asked lightly.

Catriona turned with a small smile, her shoulders relaxing slightly. "Oh, the usual sort. The scullery maid's got her eye on the new footman, but he's too green to notice. And everyone's fretting over Lady Marjory. They say she hasn't been eating much."

Bridget nodded thoughtfully. "Poor Marjory. I suppose it's to be expected after such a shock."

Catriona hesitated, her expression faltering. "There is… something else, my lady."

Bridget looked up from the fire. "Go on."

"Well," Catriona began, glancing toward the door, "Killian

heard from his lordship's valet that the staff are uneasy. They think there's no closure, not for Lady Marjory, and not for themselves. They're wondering whether they should prepare for the funeral."

"A funeral," Bridget repeated softly, her gaze distant. "Yes… it would provide some solace."

Catriona nodded. "The valet also said his lordship was meeting someone the morning of the chase. That's why he was near the lowlands and that he was told to stay behind, which wasn't like him at all."

Bridget frowned. "Did the valet know who Alastair was meeting?"

Catriona shook her head. "No, but he said Lord Alastair seemed nervous. Almost as if he knew something was wrong."

Bridget tapped her fingers against the arm of her chair, her mind racing. "And Killian? Did he hear anything?"

Catriona nodded. "The stable lads mentioned a visitor, a man none of them recognized, came by a few days ago. He and Lord Alastair spoke privately in the stables. It was brief, but it left everyone wondering. The visitor didn't stay long."

Bridget leaned back, her thoughts churning. "Thank you, Catriona. This is helpful. If you or Killian hear anything else, no matter how small, tell me immediately."

"Of course, my lady." Catriona hesitated, then added softly, "It's troubling, isn't it? To think someone might have meant him harm."

"It is," Bridget agreed quietly. "But we'll get to the truth."

As Catriona left the room, Bridget stared into the empty hearth. The scullery maid's infatuation and Marjory's grief were harmless enough, but the rest? A secret meeting, a mysterious visitor, and Alastair's unusual behavior painted a much darker picture. One that she knew she couldn't solve alone.

The drawing room hummed with quiet conversation as the guests gathered for lunch. Miss Hathaway, seated near the hearth, gestured for attention.

"I believe it's time we address the matter on everyone's mind," she began, her voice gentle but resolute. "The staff are understandably shaken, and Lady Marjory... well, she hasn't made a decision yet, but surely a funeral would provide a sense of closure for everyone."

The room fell silent as the weight of her words settled over the group. Davenport, his usual cheer subdued, nodded. "It would. But has anyone spoken with the magistrate? I assume Judge Scofield would need to approve arrangements."

Barrington, seated near the window, cleared his throat. "I spoke with Scofield earlier. He's asked that everyone remain here until the investigation is concluded. However, a funeral might be permissible, provided it does not interfere with the inquiry."

Miss Hathaway glanced toward the hallway where Marjory had last been seen. "Someone should speak to her. Perhaps broach the subject."

Bridget exchanged a glance with Grenville, a silent question passing between them. Grenville inclined his head slightly, deferring to her.

"I'll speak to her," Bridget said, her voice steady. "If she's amenable, the staff can begin planning."

Miss Hathaway offered a small smile. "Thank you, Lady Bridget. I'm sure it will bring her comfort."

Bridget left the room and followed the quiet sound of footsteps down the corridor. In a secluded corner near a carved oak door, she found Marjory seated alone, staring out at the gardens. The recent events seemed to take their toll. Bridget gently cleared her throat.

"Marjory," Bridget began softly, "there's talk of planning the funeral. They say it might bring some measure of comfort."

Marjory turned slowly, her eyes reflecting a deep, unspoken grief. "I... I've been avoiding that subject," she admitted, her voice barely above a whisper. "The thought of laying him to rest feels so final, like sealing away the last hope of understanding."

Bridget reached out, resting a reassuring hand on Marjory's

arm. "Perhaps, honoring his memory properly, we'd be preserving the dignity he deserves. It allows us to share our grief, make it easier to bear if only for a short while."

Marjory's gaze dropped for a moment before meeting Bridget's steady eyes. "You're right, of course. I only wish I were stronger in facing it all." A faint, rueful smile touched her lips, and she added, "And yet, I suppose we must begin. For his sake as well as our own."

Bridget offered a gentle nod. "Then I'll help you every step of the way."

⊱⟫⟪⊰

THE FOLLOWING DAY, the sky remained a dull, oppressive gray, as if the heavens themselves mourned with those gathered near the Alastair family gravesite. Though it was June, a brisk coastal breeze swept through the churchyard, rustling the black mourning veils and carrying with it the scent of damp earth. The air held a lingering chill, one that clung to the skin despite the season.

Mark Alastair had been laid to rest in his finest, dressed as a man of his standing deserved. His coffin, adorned with a simple yet elegant engraving of the family crest, rested beneath a solemn canopy of yew trees, their branches swaying gently in the morning wind.

Bridget stood toward the back, pulling her shawl closer around her shoulders. She had not expected to feel cold, but grief had a way of seeping into the bones.

The clergyman's voice droned on, steady and practiced, his words meant to comfort the living, though little could ease their grief.

Marjory stood beside the grave, poised yet fragile, her black mourning gown a stark contrast against the pale stone markers of those who had come before. The loss was a suffocating stillness that settled between them.

Even the household staff, many of whom had served Alastair for years, stood among the gentry, their faces drawn and solemn. The stable boys had been permitted to linger at the edges of the gathering, caps in hand, their usual restlessness subdued. They, too, had lost a man they respected.

Marjory had not wept before the others. She carried herself with the quiet dignity expected of a woman of her station, her back straight, her chin lifted. But Bridget saw the tremor in her shoulders, the way her fingers twisted and untwisted the handkerchief she clutched. The grief was there, beneath the carefully controlled exterior, simmering just below the surface.

Grenville stood to Bridget's right, his expression unreadable, hands clasped firmly before him. Barrington, just beyond, kept his gaze fixed on the grave, his usual air of command tempered by unspoken respect. Even Blackwood, so often a man of practiced charm, stood in rigid silence, his gloved hands flexing slightly at his sides.

When the final prayers were spoken, and the first shovel of earth fell upon the coffin, a finality settled over them all. One by one, the mourners turned to depart, their murmured condolences barely breaking the still air.

Yet Marjory did not move.

Bridget hesitated, watching as the others drifted back toward the manor, their voices low, their steps slow. But Marjory lingered, her gaze fixed upon the fresh mound of earth.

Bridget stepped forward, quietly, carefully, until she stood beside her friend. For a long moment, Marjory said nothing. Then, in a voice barely above a whisper, "He hated being cold."

The words were so soft Bridget almost thought she imagined them.

Marjory exhaled a slow, unsteady breath, her grip on the handkerchief tightening. "Even in the dead of summer, he'd complain of a chill." Her lips pressed together, as if willing herself not to say more, not to let grief pull her under.

Bridget reached out, her gloved fingers gently brushing Marjory's forearm in quiet support.

Marjory swallowed hard. "They took him from me." The words trembled on the air, raw, pained. "And I cannot even weep."

Bridget's heart clenched. "You are not alone," she murmured.

Marjory turned her face away, blinking fiercely against the sting of unshed tears. Her grief was a cruel thing, and the expectations placed upon a grieving widow even crueler.

Bridget would stay with her. For as long as Marjory needed. She let out a slow breath, forcing her hands to remain at her sides. This was not her loss to grieve, but she understood it. More than that, she understood the need for closure. And she would make certain Marjory had it.

Marjory's gaze remained fixed on the headstone as her fingers brushed over the folds of her gown, a slight frown crossing her face.

"He kept notes on everything, you know. Every deal, every meeting. Even things I told him in confidence." Her lips pressed into a thin line. "But he never trusted a single place to hold them. He'd jot things down on scraps of paper. He used to slip them into books or tuck them away where no one would think to look. I always teased him about it, how he couldn't let a single thought slip away unnoticed. He didn't stop until he couldn't find what he was looking for."

"Did he keep his notes somewhere specific?" Bridget asked.

Marjory blinked, her gaze distant. "Yes. There was a book, a battered old volume with a cracked spine. It wasn't valuable, at least not to anyone but him. He used it to store things, slipped pages inside, pressed between the covers. He wouldn't go anywhere without it." Her brow furrowed. "I thought I'd find the book in his desk, but it wasn't there."

"What did he write on the papers? Things about his day?" Bridget pressed.

When Marjory looked at her, she noticed she swallowed

hard. "He wasn't writing about himself. He was writing names." Marjory's eyes grew heavy, and she shifted uncomfortably in her seat. "I'm simply too tired to think right now," she murmured, her voice barely audible.

Seeing the strain etched on her friend's face, Bridget gently reached for Marjory's arm. "Come with me. Let's get you back to the house so you can rest." Reluctantly, Marjory allowed herself to be led away, her footsteps slow as the reality of the day hit her.

Once Marjory was safely tucked away in the quiet of her private room, Bridget took a deep breath. She needed to speak with Grenville immediately.

But before she could take another step, raised voices drifted from the drawing room.

Frowning, she followed the sound, stopping just outside the threshold as Judge Scofield stood at the center of the room. Everyone was there, including the staff.

The air was thick with subdued conversation and clinking glassware, the guests attempting to return to some semblance of normalcy after the burial. The tension remained, but there was an unspoken expectation that the worst had passed.

"I will not keep you long. But there are matters that must be addressed."

The murmurs stilled.

Barrington's gaze swept the room, landing on each guest in turn. When he spoke again, his voice was clear and authoritative.

"Dr. Manning has confirmed what was previously surmised. He determined that Lord Alastair's death was no accident."

The reaction was immediate. Several guests stiffened, and others exchanged nervous glances. Lady Worthington inhaled sharply. Lord Davenport's brows knit together in concern. Even Blackwood's grip on his glass tightened, his expression unreadable.

"Make no mistake, this was a crime. And until the person responsible is identified, this house remains under investigation." He paused. "For that reason, no one may leave Alastair Court until further notice."

The room erupted. Protests burst forth in overlapping waves, voices rising in disbelief, outrage, and fear. Chairs scraped against the floor. The refined calm of the drawing room dissolved into a cacophony of objections.

Lord Davenport exhaled sharply. "Surely that is unnecessary?"

Barrington's gaze did not waver. "So is murder, Lord Davenport."

A tense silence followed. Barrington let it settle before delivering the next blow.

"To ensure order is maintained," Barrington continued. "Judge Scofield has gone to Bamburgh Castle to make arrangements for the militia. Until he returns, your full cooperation is expected. The magistrate's office will oversee proceedings here, and I strongly advise against interfering with this investigation."

Lady Worthington visibly blanched. "The militia?" she repeated, her voice strained.

"You mean to bring soldiers into a house of nobility?" Lady Carlisle muttered.

Barrington's expression hardened. "A man was murdered. I will not risk another."

Another pause. Some of the guests looked away, others stared at Scofield in open discomfort.

Only one man seemed wholly unbothered by the declaration.

Lord Blackwood tilted his head, his voice laced with mild curiosity.

"I assume, Barrington, that you are overseeing things in Scofield's absence."

The question hung in the air, drawing every gaze to Barrington.

Instead of answering directly, Barrington let the question remain unanswered.

"I expect this house to conduct itself accordingly," he said instead.

The silence that followed was deafening.

Blackwood's gaze flickered toward Barrington, suspicion sparking in his eyes. He let out a quiet exhale, a smirk just ghosting his lips.

"Convenient," he murmured, barely loud enough for those nearest to hear.

"Until Scofield returns, I suggest you all make yourselves comfortable."

With that, Barrington turned and left the room, leaving behind an even more unsettled household.

As the guests began to murmur among themselves, Barrington's words settled over them like a shroud. No one moved to leave the house, but there was an unspoken restlessness, a lingering unease that made them hesitant to remain where they stood.

Bridget knew this was her opportunity. While others remained distracted, she quietly made her way from the drawing room, slipping through the dimly lit corridor toward the library.

She found Grenville standing by a window, his face set in a determined expression.

Approaching him, she spoke in a hushed yet firm tone, "Captain, we must act quickly. The scraps, Alastair wasn't merely writing notes. He was leaving us clues. If what Barrington told us about the Order is true, they will stop at nothing to keep their secrets hidden."

He turned at the sound of her voice, the tightness around his eyes easing slightly. "We've come too far to falter now."

He met her gaze. "I understand. We'll leave no stone unturned."

Bridget nodded once, but her mind was already racing. There wouldn't be another chance like this. If they didn't find Alastair's notes soon, the truth might vanish along with whoever wanted it buried.

Chapter Fifteen

THAT EVENING, AS the manor's corridors settled into a quieter pace, the tension of the day began to ease. With Marjory safely retired for the night, the other guests sought the privacy of their own chambers. Bridget found herself alone with Grenville in the library.

The pressing urgency of their investigation gave way to a gentler atmosphere, a shared, unspoken understanding that provided a slight reprieve from the grief and duty that had defined the day. They both studied the scattered papers on the table that they had been reviewing. The silence between them was heavy, not with tension, but with something unspoken.

"You've been quiet," Grenville observed, his gaze shifting to her.

Bridget hesitated. "The day has been a full one."

"You are rather generous in your phrasing," he replied with a cynical tone.

Lost in thought, she slowly rose from her seat and moved toward the window. She drew the curtain aside, looking at the moonlight that spilled over the manicured garden. As she gazed out, her eyes wandered over the estate, and for a few fleeting moments, the day was like any other, without any mystery, death, or grief. After a moment, she turned back to the captain.

She exhaled, crossing her arms. "Alastair was killed because of something he knew, something he tried to hide. And the Order… they're biding their time."

Grenville studied her quietly. The firelight danced across his features as he seemed to be waiting for something.

For a heartbeat, the air between them seemed to hold its breath. They exchanged a look filled with unspoken understanding, a silent acknowledgment of a bond forged through shared trials. In that charged pause, Bridget's heart pounded with both longing and apprehension and the promise of his closeness.

Then, without a word, he stepped forward. His hand reached up, brushing a loose curl from her cheek. The simple touch anchored them. Then his lips found hers, not in haste, but with a slow, deliberate tenderness that ignited a long-simmering flame. His hands found her waist, drawing her flush against him.

The warmth of his body seeped through the layers between them. Every touch, every gentle press, felt like a quiet rebellion against the day's sorrow. Her breath hitched as his hand spanned the hollow just above her hips, fingers pressing lightly, possessively, as if grounding her in that fleeting moment of intimacy.

Her fingers fisted in the front of his coat, holding him as much for balance as for the need to keep him close. The world beyond them blurred, every thought reduced to the pressure of his lips, the steady rise and fall of his chest against hers.

She met his kiss with equal fervor, neither shrinking from the moment nor hesitating in her intent. She had never feared taking what she wanted, and in this, she wanted him.

A low sound rumbled in his throat as she pressed closer, and his arm tightened, his grip certain. She could taste the heat of him, the quiet restraint in the way he kissed her, as if she had undone him as surely as he had undone her.

His hand skimmed up her back, fingers threading into her hair. He shifted the angle, deepening the kiss until the ache of it settled low in her stomach.

A small table pressed into her back, but she barely registered it. His breath was warm against her cheek as he broke the kiss only to return, softer this time, lingering as if memorizing her.

It was too much. It was not enough.

The silence that followed was thick with the weight of what had passed between them. When at last they parted, their breaths mingling, her hands still clung to his coat, her body still leaning into his. He rested his forehead against hers, his thumb grazing the delicate curve of her cheek.

She swallowed, her pulse erratic. "Tell me you regret it, and I will walk away."

His hand tightened at her waist, his breath uneven. "I regret nothing where you are concerned."

A slow, knowing smile curved her lips. She had her answer. Her fingers curled into the front of his coat, keeping him close. She licked her lips and reached up to kiss him.

This time, he answered with more certainty. His lips moved against hers, deep and sure, as if marking a truth they could no longer ignore. Her fingers traced the fine fabric of his coat, feeling the taut muscle beneath, the steady, restrained strength that held her as if he might never let go.

The rumble in his chest deepened. His arm banded around her, anchoring them together, no hesitation left in his grip.

Her hands slipped to his shoulders, fingers tightening against the firm breadth of them. She had never shied from what she wanted, never allowed doubt to rule her, and she would not start now.

The forgotten papers on the small table scattered to the floor, as his palm splayed against the small of her back, drawing her impossibly closer. He broke the kiss briefly, brushing his lips along her jaw before returning to her mouth, slower now. Reverent. Savoring. As if he were learning her in pieces and treasuring every one.

He inclined his head, but his gaze never left hers. A sigh escaped her, and his grip tightened, deepening the kiss with a hunger that had long simmered between them.

It was not a moment of restraint nor one of hesitation. It was a claiming, an admission neither was ready to voice aloud.

The world beyond them ceased to matter, time thinning to

the rapid beat of her pulse and the steady rise and fall of his chest.

When at last they separated, her hands still rested on his chest.

His eyes darkened, but he did not step away. She was breathless when they pulled apart, staring at him in disbelief. His hand lingered at her waist before he pulled back entirely, his jaw tight.

"We shouldn't—" he started.

"No," she agreed, though the word rang hollow. The line they'd promised not to cross was already behind them.

Chapter Sixteen

B RIDGET AND GRENVILLE stood before Alastair's large oak desk, the atmosphere unnervingly still. The room had been undisturbed since his passing, yet something was amiss. The room was too pristine as if someone had meticulously erased every trace of Alastair's presence. There was no hint of leather, tobacco, or even the faint scent of his lingering cologne.

Grenville ran a hand over the desktop as he scanned the room. "If he kept his notes close, they should be here. The question is, who got to them first?" He hesitated, then shook his head. "Or perhaps they were never meant to be found."

Bridget's eyes narrowed. "Alastair knew he was in danger. If the notes were here, he wouldn't have left them exposed. He would have hidden them."

Grenville nodded slowly. "Unless he was forced to show them as proof."

"Or perhaps," she quipped, "he gave them something else instead."

His gaze darkened as he stared at the desk. "That would explain the parchment in his mouth. It wasn't a message to others, but his punishment."

Bridget's thoughts raced. "Whoever took his notes must have planned this carefully. They left behind only these fragments as a grim signature."

Bridget turned toward the bookshelves, stepping closer to inspect the volumes. Some were coated in dust while others bore fresh smudges, evidence that someone had been here, sorting and searching. "What better place to hide pages of notes than between the pages of books?" she mused under her breath.

The quiet between them pulsed with purpose. Standing side by side in the hushed library, Bridget felt the remnants of last night's closeness settle over her like a familiar, comforting shawl.

"Captain," she said softly, breaking the silence, "I find that despite all this darkness, I'm grateful to have you by my side."

Grenville stilled, his gaze settling on hers, the weight of her words sinking in. The past day had been filled with loss, suspicion, and uncertainty, yet here she stood, acknowledging not just their shared burdens but the quiet solace they had found in one another.

His lips curved slightly, though something unreadable flickered in his eyes. "Captain?" he echoed, stepping closer, his voice gentler now. "I think we're beyond that. Thomas will do nicely."

Bridget tilted her head, studying him, as if considering the shift between them. The use of his given name felt like crossing an unseen threshold, one they had been inching toward without fully acknowledging.

A smile, soft but knowing, touched the corners of her lips. "If that is the case, then you must call me Bridget."

A subtle warmth passed between them, a silent acknowledgment of the intimacy the moment carried.

"Very well… Bridget," he murmured, her name sounding like a prayer.

They lingered in the quiet that followed, a breath between before and after. For all the uncertainty that lay ahead, this, this was certain.

The search continued as they moved to Alastair's desk drawer. Bridget carefully pulled it open, noting the scratches along the edges, evidence of a hurried, forceful search.

Thomas ran his fingers along the bottom, brushing against something rough.

She paused, watching the crease in his brow and the way his

jaw tightened in concentration, a look reminiscent of their earlier battles of wit.

Bridget lent her hand and discovered a torn piece of fabric caught in the splintered wood, dark and delicate like the lining of a coat. "Someone was in a hurry. And they were careless," she murmured.

Thomas's expression was grim. "If Alastair hid his notes, why leave them where anyone could find them?"

Before they could probe further, the sound of footsteps in the corridor caused them to turn. Blackwood loomed in the doorway, his expression controlled yet unreadable. With a subtle shift, Thomas stepped in front of Bridget, an instinctive move that made her heart flutter, though she masked her reaction.

"Turning over the dead man's belongings already? How unseemly," Blackwood remarked, eyeing the papers in Thomas's hand. His gaze flickered briefly to the open drawer before returning to them.

Bridget stepped forward, meeting his steady eyes. "Then tell me, my lord, what exactly are we to be looking for?"

Blackwood hesitated, his fingers flexing almost imperceptibly. "I know where it was," he said finally, shrugging as if the answer were trivial. "But where it is now depends on how thoroughly you search."

Bridget's pulse quickened. "Who took it?"

Blackwood's smirk returned, dark and knowing. "Be careful, Lady Bridget. Sometimes, when you dig for secrets, you find things best left buried."

His parting words sent a ripple of unease through her, confirming that he knew more than he revealed.

"Thomas, why would Blackwood admit he knows where Alastair's notes were, yet refuse to tell us?" Bridget asked, her tone laced with equal parts frustration and curiosity.

His gaze darkened as he considered the question. "I suspect he seeks to hold that knowledge as leverage, testing if we're resourceful enough to uncover the truth on our own. Perhaps he is conflicted by his own loyalties, or simply put, protecting interests that run deeper than our investigation. In this dangerous game, he believes it's wiser to keep such vital information hidden until he's certain the consequences won't fall on him, or on any of us."

After Bridget's pointed remark, Thomas reached out and gently squeezed her hand in silent reassurance. "Let's not allow his evasiveness to slow us," he murmured. "We must resume our search. There are hidden compartments and neglected drawers in this room that might still contain Alastair's secrets."

Bridget nodded, swallowing her frustration. With renewed determination, they returned to their search. Methodically, they began examining every detail, the dusty ledgers, the false bottoms of drawers, even the spines of books lining the shelves that might shelter forgotten pages.

Together, they moved with quiet urgency, each discovery a small victory in their quest to piece together Alastair's final message before the Order could silence it forever.

Chapter Seventeen

B RIDGET STEPPED OUTSIDE, letting the crisp morning air cool the restless thoughts swirling in her mind. She found Catriona near the flower beds, her basket already half-filled with fresh blooms. The scent of rosemary and lavender lingered in the air as she clipped another sprig and placed it carefully among the others.

Catriona glanced up, offering a faint smile. "You look deep in thought, my lady."

Bridget exhaled. "There is much to think about." She gestured toward the basket. "Are those for Marjory?"

Catriona shook her head. "For you, actually. I thought some fresh flowers might make your room feel less…" She trailed off, searching for the right word.

Bridget gave a small smile. "Less like a house in mourning?"

Catriona nodded, the corners of her mouth tightening. "Everything feels different now. The household is working hard to keep things running as usual, but it's difficult. Mrs. Simmons met with us and told us nothing has changed at Alastair Court, but we all know it will never be the same." She hesitated, then added quietly, "Many of them have been here for years. Lord Alastair took care of them. They worry whether Lady Marjory will go to London or decide to stay here."

Bridget's chest tightened at the thought. She sat on the stone bench next to Catriona. "And Marjory herself?"

Catriona's fingers stilled on the flower stem she had been

about to cut. "She barely eats. She speaks when necessary, but it's as if she's moving through a fog. She hasn't spoken much about anything."

Bridget sighed, glancing toward the house. "That's understandable. Losing a husband is—" She stopped herself. "She must feel as if everything has shifted beneath her feet."

Catriona hesitated, then cut the stem and laid it in the basket. "If it were only grief, I could understand it, but I think something is troubling her. More than losing him, I mean."

Bridget frowned. "What makes you say that?"

Catriona shifted, adjusting her basket before answering in a quiet voice. "She hasn't spoken much, but the household staff have noticed. And there's something else… something I hesitate to mention."

Bridget's gaze softened, her voice quiet but steady. "Whatever it is, you can tell me." She didn't rush Catriona. She simply waited, her hands loosely clasped.

Catriona bit her lip. "Killian saw Lord Alastair on the course that morning. He said his horse was tethered. He got the impression he was waiting for someone. Lord Alastair had been looking forward to the equestrian chase for weeks. He wouldn't make an appointment in the middle of the race.

She tucked a loose strand of hair behind her ear. "He stopped to ask if everything was well, but his lordship handed him a package and told him to keep it at the barn. Said he'd retrieve it when he returned."

Bridget's breath caught. "Did Killian say what was in the package?"

Catriona shook her head. "No. He didn't ask. But his lordship was serious when he gave it to him. As if it was important."

Bridget hesitated, about to thank her, but another thought surfaced. "Do you know what time this was?"

Catriona frowned slightly. "Not exactly. Killian didn't say."

Bridget nodded, thoughtful. "And… did he hear anything afterward? A commotion, a shout—?"

Catriona shook her head. "No, my lady. He didn't hear anything at all. He only learned what happened much later."

Bridget rose to her feet and dusted off her skirt, but her mind was already working. A package. Left in the barn. Alastair had told Killian he would retrieve it after the race, but he never got the chance.

She met Catriona's gaze, offering a small but grateful smile. "Thank you. I need to speak with Killian."

Catriona stood as well, watching her carefully. "You're going to ask him about it, aren't you?"

Bridget nodded, determination sharpening her features. "If Killian had seen Alastair just before his death, and if Alastair had entrusted him with something, then Alastair must have suspected he was in danger. He had taken steps to protect something, something important. Knowing what the package contains could lead us to his murderer."

She turned toward the house and broke into a near run.

Bridget moved quickly through the halls and found Thomas in his shirtsleeves, in the study, standing near the fireplace, reading a document. He looked up as she entered, his sharp gaze immediately locking onto hers.

"What is it?" he asked, reading the urgency in her expression.

Bridget closed the door behind her and stepped closer. "I just spoke with Catriona. She told me something that changes everything."

Thomas straightened. "Go on."

Bridget took a breath. "Killian saw Alastair on the course that morning. He had tethered his horse. It was out of place. All along, Alastair was eager to participate in the chase. Killian stopped to ask if something was wrong. That's when Alastair gave him a package and told him to take it to the barn. He planned to retrieve it afterward."

Thomas's brow furrowed. "A package?"

Bridget nodded. "Killian doesn't know what was inside. But he said Alastair was serious about it. As if it was important."

Thomas set the document on the desk. "And Killian heard the scream shortly after?"

"No. He didn't know what had happened to Alastair until someone came looking for assistance."

Thomas ran a hand through his hair and exhaled slowly. "If Alastair sent something away before the chase, it wasn't just important; it was something he didn't want to be found on him." His voice sharpened. "Whatever he gave Killian might explain why he was killed. We must speak to him now."

Bridget didn't hesitate. "I thought the same."

Thomas grabbed his coat from the back of the chair, already moving. "Then let's not waste time."

Bridget followed him, her pulse quickening.

THE STEADY RHYTHM of the forge hammer echoed through the yard as Bridget approached the stables. The scent of horses and hay mingled with the sharp tang of heated iron. Inside, Killian worked methodically, his sleeves rolled up, revealing arms dusted with soot. He barely glanced up as she and Thomas entered, but Bridget didn't miss the way his grip tightened around the metal he was shaping.

She paused a few feet away, watching as he worked. "It's been a long morning," she said, her voice calm but deliberate. "I imagine you've had little time for anything but work."

Killian adjusted the iron in the glowing embers. "Work keeps a man's hands busy," he muttered.

Bridget nodded. "And his mind." She let the words settle before stepping closer. "Killian, I need to ask you about his lordship."

His hammer stilled, but he didn't look at her. Instead, he placed the iron back into the forge's embers. "A shame what happened," he said gruffly.

She exchanged a glance with Thomas before speaking again. "Catriona told me you saw him that morning. That he gave you something."

"She shouldn't have said that." Killian exhaled a short, forceful breath, the kind a restless horse gives when unsettled.

Thomas uncrossed his arms. His tone was even but firm. "But she did. And now we need to know what it was."

Killian finally turned to them, his blue eyes shadowed. "His lordship helped me and my wife escape Scotland when no one else would. I owed him everything." He hesitated. "If he asked me to keep something safe, I wasn't about to question him."

Bridget stepped closer, her gaze steady but kind. "You trusted him, and he trusted you. But whatever he left with you, it may be the reason he was killed." She let that settle before adding, "If we can find out what was so important, we might be able to find the person who did this."

Killian's throat bobbed in a hard swallow. He looked at the forge for a long moment before exhaling. "Up there. I put it where no one would find it."

They climbed into the loft, the air thick with the scent of dry hay. Killian pulled aside a stack of grain sacks, revealing a wrapped bundle tucked between the wooden beams.

Bridget's breath hitched. Her fingers hesitated for the briefest moment before she unwrapped it. Inside, several sheets of parchment, worn at the edges, lay folded together.

The inked letters were unmistakable. Alastair's handwriting was bold and precise.

Bridget exhaled slowly, smoothing the first page open, but her stomach dropped. The text was filled with numbers, symbols, and notations in Latin, Old Scots, and something else entirely.

"This isn't just notes written in different languages," he muttered beside her. "It's coded."

She scanned the pages, her fingers tracing the inked script. "Alastair must have been trying to decode something himself. Some of this looks familiar, but..." She exhaled, shaking her head.

"I don't understand all of it."

Thomas's brow furrowed. "Then we need someone who does."

Bridget refolded the pages carefully, her mind racing. "Tresham."

Thomas met her gaze. "He's the best chance we have of making sense of this."

She turned to Killian, her expression softening. "Alastair trusted you to keep this safe. And because of you, we have a chance to figure out what happened to him."

Killian nodded, his eyes somber. "I want justice for his lordship."

Thomas extended a hand, gripping Killian's forearm firmly. "So do we. Thank you."

Bridget nodded in agreement. "We won't forget this."

Killian gave a slight nod of understanding as Thomas turned toward the door.

"Then we go to Tresham. Now."

"Where?" Bridget stood facing him with her eyebrow raised.

"The library, of course." Thomas grabbed her hand and pulled her along.

Chapter Eighteen

Bridget and Thomas found Professor Tresham in Alastair's library, surrounded by dusty tomes and stacks of parchment. The room smelled of the faintest trace of pipe smoke. He looked up as they approached and adjusted his spectacles with an absent-minded flick of his fingers.

"Ah, Lady Bridget, Captain. Come join me," he said, his voice tinged with excitement. "I confess I had planned on a quiet weekend, but with Alastair's collection here... Well, it's impossible not to get drawn in."

Bridget didn't hesitate, setting the bundle of parchment onto the desk before him. "This belonged to his lordship. We believe it may explain why he was killed."

Tresham's hand hovered over the pages for a moment before he carefully unfolded them. The moment his gaze fell upon the first lines, his breath hitched.

"Good heavens," he murmured, his fingers tracing the text as though he could feel its significance through touch alone. His enthusiasm grew with each passing second. "This... this is exactly what Alastair told me about. He suspected he had found something remarkable, but he struggled to translate it fully."

Bridget and Thomas exchanged a glance.

"What do you mean?" Thomas asked.

Tresham leaned back slightly, eyes still locked on the parchment. "One of the old tales about the Order, one of the more persistent legends, suggests that they, like the Knights Templar, possessed something of great value." He exhaled, shaking his head. "But unlike the Templars, their purpose was not preservation. It was control."

He tapped a passage with a single finger, his excitement evident. "The Order's influence didn't fade with time but rather adapted. It hid in plain sight, weaving itself into institutions of power, ensuring its legacy was never truly lost."

Bridget's stomach tightened. "And you believe this treasure still exists?"

Tresham hesitated. "'Treasure' is the wrong word. It's not gold or riches. It's knowledge. Leverage." He glanced at the notes again, a furrow forming between his brows. "And if Alastair was right, this document hints at something that has remained hidden for centuries."

The air between them grew heavier, a charged silence settling over the room.

Bridget swallowed hard. "Can you read it?"

Tresham's brow furrowed as he leaned closer, studying the scrawled words beneath the notations. "Some of this is Latin... some, Old Scots... and this here..." He paused, adjusting his glasses. "This is something older. It's deliberately obscure, meant to be read only by those who already understood its meaning."

He muttered to himself, flipping through a reference book at his side. The candle beside him flickered as he turned the pages, his brow deeply furrowed. "Alastair mentioned this language to me before. He thought it was related to an older dialect, one used only in specific circles." He tapped the parchment. "This was not meant for casual eyes."

His finger halted over a particular phrase. His lips parted. "Ah. Here. This phrase, *Coille Dubh.*"

Bridget frowned, but before she could react, Thomas went still.

THOMAS FELT THE name like a physical blow. *Coille Dubh.* He had heard it whispered in the dead of night, traced in coded letters delivered under the cover of darkness. It was more than a name. It was a shadow that had loomed over Scotland for years. He forced himself to remain still, to keep his breathing even, though his pulse thundered in his ears.

But it wasn't just the past he feared. It was her.

Bridget stood beside him, unaware of how deeply this cut. If she knew, if she ever discovered his part in the Clearances, would she see him as a man or only as his father's son?

He had survived the war. Survived guilt. But the thought of losing her trust? That was a wound he didn't know how to fight.

"*Coille Dubh* has been referenced before in historical accounts," Tresham went on. "It's been whispered in connection with the Order's more violent dealings. But its true meaning has never been fully understood. Some believe it was the name of a place where a great treasure was buried, while others believe it's an enforcer, a shadowy figure who carried out the Order's will."

His past collided violently with the present.

He knew the name. He had heard it spoken in the dead of night, written in coded orders. He had known what Coille Dubh had done during the Clearances, what men like him had been ordered to do.

But no one, not even Barrington, knew Thomas had been involved.

Thomas stood rigid beside her. Though he had schooled his expression into neutrality, she could sense the effort it took. His silence, his stillness, it wasn't indifference. It was restraint.

Her gaze dropped to the parchment. She traced the inked letters lightly, the phrase pulling at something buried in her mind. A whisper of recognition teased at the edge of her thoughts.

And then, her breath caught. She looked up sharply. "I know what it means."

Tresham raised an eyebrow. "Oh?"

BRIDGET FROWNED, TRACING the letters again, speaking the phrase aloud under her breath. The words felt familiar, but not because she had seen them written before.

"*Coille Dubh…*" she repeated, narrowing her eyes. It wasn't the phrase itself but rather the way it was spoken. The rhythm of it, the way it lingered in the ear. It was something she had heard in passing, in conversation.

Her breath caught as realization crashed over her.

"*Coille Dubh* means Blackwood."

Silence fell like a hammer.

Bridget's mind spun, the name taking on a sharper, more ominous meaning. Across from her, Thomas remained silent, his posture stiff, but she barely registered it, too caught up in the revelation itself.

Tresham removed his glasses, his expression thoughtful. "If Blackwood's family was involved with the Order, we may be dealing with something far more dangerous than we realized."

The name sat uneasily in her mind, nagging at something just out of reach. A conversation, one she had barely noticed at the time. Then she remembered.

"*We all serve something greater than ourselves, Lady Bridget. Some of us simply understand that better than others.*"

The memory surfaced unbidden, taking on a more ominous meaning now.

She turned to Thomas, her voice low. "If Blackwood's family had been entwined with the Order for centuries, then he's not just another obstacle." She hesitated, the weight of the realization settling in. "He might be the key to all of this."

Thomas's jaw tensed. "Or the greatest threat we've faced yet."

Bridget nodded, the silence stretching between them. It wasn't ominous, but reflective. The kind of quiet that accompanied understanding.

Tresham, sensing the shift, quietly returned to his notes. No one rushed to speak again.

The fire crackled softly. The parchment lay open between them. At last, the truth had a name; it was Blackwood.

Chapter Nineteen

A ROUND THE BROAD oak table, Bridget, Thomas, Barrington, Townsend, and Tresham studied the brittle pages spread before them. Their edges curled with age. Professor Tresham adjusted his spectacles, fingers hovering over the faded script, his brows knitted in intrigue.

"This text isn't just a record. It's a cipher," the professor cleared his throat, "an instruction on how power is maintained. Not wealth or land, but influence. It speaks of leveraging alliances, toppling adversaries, manipulating rulers, and all from the shadows. To possess what's written here isn't about owning a kingdom. It's about ensuring that whoever does remains in your debt."

His fingertip traced along a particular line until he came to a stop, tapping the document where his finger landed. "Alastair must have believed this referenced something tangible, but it's more than that. It speaks of something lost, something that must not fall into the wrong hands. Something that could change the course of nations if wielded properly."

Barrington leaned forward, his gaze sharp. "Lost? Are we speaking of an artifact? A document? A person?"

Tresham hesitated. "That's the question. The Order's legend speaks of a source of power so influential that to possess it would mean absolute control. There are references to lost histories, rewritten accounts, and carefully placed figures of authority. But the wording is frustratingly cryptic. It speaks of 'the key to dominion hidden in plain sight, veiled by knowledge itself.'"

"Are you certain of your interpretation?" Barrington interjected, his expression skeptical. "Men have misread prophecies before. Could Alastair have seen danger where there was none?"

Tresham pursed his lips. "I would argue the opposite. If anything, the wording is deliberately confusing. Someone didn't want this knowledge to be easily accessible."

Bridget nodded. "That's common in oral traditions, layering meaning so only those with the right knowledge can decipher it. My father used to say the oldest truths were hidden in plain sight."

Thomas shot her a glance, something flickering in his eyes before he looked away.

Bridget frowned, leaning closer. "Some of these markings don't translate directly," she murmured, running her finger along the text. "It's an older dialect, likely a blend of Latin and Old Scots, but there are regional symbols I don't recognize."

Thomas removed a sheaf of parchment from his pocket and laid it on the table. He tapped the brittle page, his brow furrowing. "Professor, we found this hidden in Alastair's desk. Is there any chance you could decipher more of this? If Alastair believed this document was important enough to hide, then we need to know why." His voice was calm, but urgency simmered beneath it."

Tresham exhaled through his nose, adjusting his spectacles as he studied the page again. "Given time, possibly. But I'll need reference materials. Some of these symbols are unfamiliar, and the blend of Latin and Old Scots is inconsistent. If this was meant to obscure meaning, it was done skillfully. Leave it with me and I will see what I can do."

Bridget hesitated. "My father used to tell a story about the lost words of the Druids. Some of this reminds me of that."

Townsend exhaled sharply. "Are we chasing a ghost, or do you truly believe this is worth bloodshed?"

"The Order doesn't waste their efforts." Thomas's voice was

firm. "If they want this, there is a reason."

Townsend rubbed his jaw. "That sounds like something Scofield will want to see. If this document outlines how the Order has infiltrated key institutions and how they have controlled policies, wars, and even sovereigns, then this isn't just history. It's an active threat. If they still have access to these people, they're still pulling strings. That's not something the Crown can afford to ignore."

Bridget studied the text carefully. "It's not just about information. It's about control. The Order doesn't simply seek knowledge. They seek to own it, bend it, wield it like a weapon. If Alastair has pieced together that truth, it's no wonder they wanted him silenced."

A sharp rap at the door interrupted them. Mr. Simmons entered, his expression uneasy as he presented a sealed envelope. "This just arrived, Lord Barrington. There was no name on the delivery." Mr. Simmons hesitated before stepping back. "It was left at the servants' entrance, my lord. No one saw who delivered it."

Barrington took the letter and broke the seal. As his eyes scanned the contents, his jaw tightened. He handed it to Townsend without a word.

Townsend read aloud. *"The price of secrets is blood. Surrender what was taken or more will be spilled. There are no second chances."*

Bridget exhaled, the chill creeping through her bones. The words on the parchment felt like a promise, not a warning. Her breath caught. Without thinking, she took a half step closer to Thomas, drawn by his quiet intensity that steadied her even now. She could feel the heat of his presence, the quiet intensity that had become familiar. But he said nothing, only tilting his head slightly as Townsend spoke.

"Do you believe they'll act soon?" Townsend's voice was sharp, controlled. "Or is this meant to rattle us?"

"They wouldn't threaten if they weren't prepared to follow through," Barrington muttered. "We need to be ready."

Thomas's fingers curled into a fist before relaxing again. "Then we don't wait for them to act. We make the first move." His voice was calm, but the edge beneath it was unmistakable.

The room went still, each of them absorbing the veiled threat.

Barrington exhaled sharply. "The Order doesn't make idle threats. This means they are watching."

Bridget's breath quickened. "They know we have what they want even if we're not certain what Alastair's notes say."

Thomas set his hands flat against the table, his expression unreadable. "Then we make them think they're getting what they want."

Bridget turned to him. "You mean a trade?"

"Not exactly." His gaze met hers, understanding flickering between them. "A deception. We don't need to give them the real document. We just need them to believe we have it."

Bridget straightened, her mind racing. "A decoy."

Tresham frowned. "That's a dangerous gamble. If they realize the ruse—"

Barrington frowned. "And how exactly do you plan to age a document to match something centuries old?"

Bridget shook her head. "We don't have to. It's not the parchment they want. They want the translation. They already believe we've done the hard work for them. If we present them with what looks like a complete transcription, they'll think they've won."

Bridget's lips parted as the idea took shape. "We craft a replica, something close enough to convince them they've retrieved what they want. If we control the circumstances of the exchange, we can lure them into revealing themselves."

Tresham gave her a questioning gaze. "And how do you know they'll accept the decoy? Surely, they will verify it."

"They won't need to," Thomas said, his voice measured. "They're already convinced we've done the hard work. If we play this carefully, we dictate the terms of the exchange."

"And if they realize it's false?" Townsend pressed, his tone sharp. "Then we've just made ourselves the next targets."

"Then," Bridget said, lifting her chin, "we ensure they have no reason to doubt us. The key isn't the pages themselves. It's the illusion that they got what they wanted." Her confidence rang clear, though a glimmer of uncertainty coiled deep inside.

Thomas studied her, a flicker of something unreadable in his eyes. "A dangerous gamble, Bridget."

"A calculated risk," she corrected. "And one we need to take."

Their gazes held for a moment, charged and unspoken. There was more between them than strategy and survival. He saw her determination, and she saw his loyalty. And something warmer pulsed beneath it.

Thomas's expression was unreadable, but there was something else in his gaze, something deeper. His eyes lingered on her, something between admiration and exasperation flickering beneath the surface. "That is a bold plan."

Barrington crossed his arms. "And incredibly reckless."

Townsend nodded slowly. "But it might be our best chance to flush them out."

Bridget met Thomas's gaze again, heat creeping up her spine. "You don't approve?"

He hesitated, tilting his head slightly, watching her. "I wouldn't dare underestimate you." His voice was low and smooth, and something about it sent a thrill through her. "But that doesn't mean I won't be standing right beside you if this plan goes wrong."

Her lips twitched just slightly. "Is that a promise, Captain?"

His mouth curved, though his eyes still held that warning gleam. "A certainty."

Barrington cleared his throat. "Then we best start planning. We don't have much time."

Townsend leaned back, considering. "I'll get ready to take a copy of this to Whitehall. If there's even a fraction of truth in what we suspect, they need to know."

Barrington nodded. "Not until we make the exchange. They are watching, and I don't want to give anything away."

Townsend nodded.

Thomas turned to Bridget. "We don't have time to second-guess this. We start now."

Bridget looked away from Thomas, but his words lingered, curling through her thoughts. He would be standing beside her. And for the first time in days, that truth didn't just steady her. It made her feel strong.

Chapter Twenty

T HE SUN ROSE as it always did, casting a golden glow over the estate and illuminating the gardens with its gentle light. Birds sang their morning serenades, blissfully unaware of the grim events that had transpired within the grand manor. Servants bustled about, attending to their morning duties with practiced efficiency, as if nothing had changed. But for those who knew the truth, the day held a darkness that not even the brightest sunlight could dispel.

Barrington, Grenville, Tresham, and Bridget gathered once more in Alastair's library. The gravity of their task was clear. Townsend was ready to leave for Whitehall on a moment's notice, armed with a copy of the translation. Everyone else worked to plan the groundwork for their deception.

The decoy manuscript was Tresham's responsibility, but the success of their plan depended on how well they could convince the Order that they had what they wanted.

Barrington stood with hands clasped behind his back. "If we want them to take the bait, we need to make them believe the book is still within reach, somewhere hidden, waiting to be retrieved. We cannot simply hand them a target. We have to make them work for it."

Thomas leaned against the desk, arms crossed, his gaze thoughtful. "There are a few ways we could accomplish that." He drummed his fingers once against the wood, considering.

"We could leave an anonymous message, something cryptic,

just vague enough to stir their curiosity. But that could backfire if we misjudge their reaction."

He shook his head slightly and pushed off the desk. "Another option is to plant a false lead in the correspondence of someone they already watch. A letter intercepted at the right time might give them the impression that the book was hidden somewhere before Alastair's death."

Thomas paused, then added. "But the simplest, and perhaps the most effective, is to let the rumor grow organically. We don't feed them the direct information. We let them overhear whispers, half-truths, and fragments of conversations until the idea takes root. If they think the book has merely been misplaced rather than taken outright, they'll keep searching."

Bridget nodded, considering. "We need to be subtle, though. If it's too obvious, they'll know we're leading them. We should let the rumors arise naturally."

"And how do you propose we do that?" Barrington asked, arching an eyebrow.

A slow smile formed on Bridget's lips. "The house staff. They hear everything, and their gossip reaches further than any of us could. A misplaced word, a half-heard conversation between guests, if the idea takes root in the right way, the Order will act."

Tresham adjusted his spectacles. "A clever approach, but we must be mindful. If we fabricate the wrong rumor, they may search in the wrong places and figure out the ruse. It must be just believable enough to entice them."

Barrington nodded. "Then we start with a simple premise, that Mark Alastair kept a record of his findings, separate from the book itself, and that it may still be within the house."

"Not just a record," Thomas added. "A journal. Something personal, something only he would have hidden away. That will make them desperate to find it."

Bridget crossed her arms, intrigued. "And how do we convince them without being obvious?"

Thomas's lips curved in a knowing smile. "We let them overhear. Gossip and theories are already forming about Lord Alastair's death. All we need to do is add the idea of his journal to the mix."

Bridget tapped her fingers against the desk, considering. "We need someone who can speak naturally about the idea, someone the Order wouldn't suspect of working with us."

A thought struck her, and she looked to Thomas. "Catriona and Killian."

He gave her a puzzled expression.

"They're trusted," Bridget said. "They move about the estate without raising questions, and they owe Alastair their safety. If they speak of a missing journal, it won't look like a planted rumor. It'll look like a discovery."

Barrington nodded slowly. "A clever approach. But they must be cautious."

"I'll speak with them," Bridget said. "They'll understand what's at stake."

⟫⟫⟫⟫⟪⟪⟪⟪

LATER THAT MORNING, with the plan still settling in her thoughts, Bridget stepped into the corridor in search of Catriona. She found her just as she was setting a bundle of linens on a hall table.

"Good morning, my lady," she said softly. "Are you looking for something?"

"Actually, I am looking for you." Bridget paused and took a breath. "I need your help. You see—"

"Tell me what needs doing." Catriona's voice was steady and confident.

Bridget exhaled, pulling her into a quiet alcove. "It's about Lord Alastair's journal." At Catriona's sharp intake of breath, she pressed on. "We need people to believe it's still here, hidden, misplaced, waiting to be found."

Catriona's brows pulled together, her expression cautious.

"But it's not, is it, Lady Bridget?"

"That doesn't matter." Bridget waited. Catriona was a clever woman. She would get Bridget's meaning quick enough. "What matters is that the people responsible for his lordship's murder think it is. We need to draw them out."

Catriona hesitated, her loyalty to Bridget warring with her instinct for caution. "And you need someone to spread the whispers?"

Bridget allowed a small smile. "You and Killian. You're trusted. You move about the estate without raising questions. If you mention a missing journal in passing, it won't look like a contrived piece of hearsay, but like a discovery."

Catriona nodded slowly, understanding dawning in her eyes. "A bit of Scottish mischief, is it?"

Bridget's lips twitched. "Something like that."

"We need to speak to Killian," Catriona said. "He'll want to hear this." She took off her apron. They both left for the stable.

A short while later, Bridget, Catriona, and Killian stood behind the stable, hidden away from prying ears. Killian rolled his shoulders, casting a wary glance toward the house.

"If this will help find who murdered his lordship," he said at last, "I'll gladly help. How do we make sure they believe it?"

Bridget let out a relieved breath. "Keep it simple. A passing remark, something about how his lordship never went anywhere without his journal. And that if it was lost," Bridget added, "it would have to be somewhere within the house."

Killian nodded, his expression settling into one of grim determination. "Aye. I can manage that."

Catriona leaned in. "And what if they start asking questions?"

Bridget's expression hardened. "Then we'll know we're close."

Bridget thanked them both, but the unease lingered. Spreading rumors was one thing, watching them take root was another. As she and Catriona walked back toward the manor, the impact of what they'd set in motion settled on her shoulders. It was a dangerous game they were playing, one that required more than clever words.

That thought followed her up the stone steps and through the halls, all the way to Marjory's door.

When she arrived, she found her friend sitting by the window, gazing out at the fields. The light streaming in caught the shadows beneath her eyes. Bridget was startled to see the deep hollows. Mrs. Simmons stood nearby, a pot of tea in hand, her expression pinched with worry.

"You should eat something, my lady," the housekeeper urged gently. "You'll make yourself ill."

Marjory barely seemed to hear. Her hands rested awkwardly on the armrest of her chair. "It feels like he's still here," she murmured. "If I turn around fast enough, he'll be standing in the doorway, smiling at me."

Bridget's heart sank. "That feeling doesn't fade easily." Bridget moved closer and sat on the ottoman in front of Marjory. "But you don't have to face it alone."

Marjory turned to her then, her gaze sharp despite her grief. "Mark always said secrets had a way of surfacing at the worst times."

Bridget hesitated. "We're looking for the truth. Rumors and gossip are already swirling."

Bridget stilled. The quiet melancholy in Marjory's eyes shifted, sharpened. There was less grief now, more something else. Marjory gave her a long, unreadable look. "Be careful, Bridget. Whispered secrets have a way of turning into weapons."

Bridget frowned slightly. "What do you mean?"

Marjory sighed, her expression pained. "I've seen it happen before. Innocent whispers can turn into dangerous rumors, and those with ill-intentions can twist the truth to suit their purposes. Just… tread carefully."

Bridget felt a chill settle over her. This wasn't grief speaking, it was experience. Marjory wasn't hinting. This was a warning. The wrong word in the wrong ear could undo everything.

Bridget didn't have to wait long. By midday, the first murmurs drifted through the halls, servants exchanging hushed speculation about Lord Alastair's journal. A passing footman remarked that his lordship never went anywhere without it. A chambermaid whispered that perhaps it had been misplaced rather than lost forever.

Marjory's words lingered, quiet but insistent, even as Bridget went about the day.

By evening, the whispers had found their way to the guests. Over tea, a lady's maid confided to her mistress that some believed his lordship's journal still lingered somewhere within Alastair Court. At supper, a guest offhandedly questioned whether anyone had searched properly.

The next morning, the rumor had taken hold. Growing tendrils had reached the right ears.

Bridget overheard Blackwood scoffing at the notion, his tone dismissive. "If such a journal existed, Alastair would have safeguarded it, not left it lying about like a forgotten letter."

Lady Worthington, however, hummed thoughtfully. "But what if he did? Men grow careless when they believe they have time."

Bridget met Thomas's gaze from across the room. The trap was set. The snare had been laid. Now, they would learn just how far the Order would go to retrieve what they believed was theirs.

Chapter Twenty-One

THE NIGHT AIR was cool but gentle, carrying the faint scent of salt and heather as Bridget stepped onto the cliffs, the vast stretch of ocean unfurling before her in silver and shadow. The manor was far behind her now, its candlelit windows barely flickering in the distance.

She should have stayed inside, should have tried to rest, but the house had felt suffocating. The air within its walls had grown thick with too many voices, too many unspoken fears.

Her footsteps had carried her here without thought, drawn to the place where the wind was sharp and clean, where the endless horizon stretched beyond the reach of secrets and grief. She inhaled deeply, letting the salt air fill her lungs, willing it to wash away the burden of the past days.

And yet, even here, the restlessness remained.

She didn't hear him approach over the wind and waves, but somehow, she knew he was there before he spoke.

"I wasn't expecting company," he murmured.

She glanced up at him, her pulse already picking up. "Did you follow me?"

His lips quirked slightly. "I was already out here."

Bridget studied him in the moonlight, the pale glow highlighting the sharp angles of his face, the shadowed edge of his jaw. There was something about him in this moment, unburdened, raw, unguarded.

The wind played with the loose tendrils of her hair as she

looked back out to sea. "I used to come to places like this as a girl, staring out at the horizon and imagining what lay beyond it."

Thomas's voice was quiet. "And now?"

She let out a slow breath. "Now, I wonder what I will lose before I ever have the chance to find out."

The gravity of the past days was a burden to both of them, but Thomas did not speak of it. Instead, he simply watched her, as if memorizing every detail of this moment.

She turned to face him, and the world seemed to shift.

The moonlight turned his eyes to steel and smoke, their depths drawing her in until she forgot the cold, the wind, even her own name. She stepped closer, her heart racing, her breath shallow, pulled toward him not by reason but by need. She felt his warmth even before her fingers brushed against the front of his coat, hesitant yet sure.

"I do not wish to be alone tonight," she whispered.

Something flickered in his gaze, something dark, something restrained.

"You are not alone," he murmured. And then his hands were on her, pulling her against him with the certainty of a man who had tried to resist and failed.

Her breath hitched as his mouth found hers, a soft gasp escaping as desire lit like a spark along her spine. The kiss was slow at first, deliberate, as if he were memorizing the taste of her. But need burned beneath his restraint, threading through the tension in his body, in the way her fingers curled against the rough fabric of his coat, clutching it to anchor herself for the moment. The kiss deepened, fierce and sweet, and for the first time in days, she felt something other than loss. She felt alive.

She arched into him, fingers sliding up his chest, feeling the rapid beat of his heart beneath her palm. He groaned softly, a sound of surrender and warning all at once.

Her world narrowed to sensation, the heat of his body, the wind whipping at her skirts, the way his lips parted against hers with aching reverence.

It was intoxicating. It was inevitable.

She gasped as his mouth left hers, only to trace a path down the delicate column of her throat, his breath warm against her skin. His grip tightened at her waist as she pressed closer, as if testing how much space truly remained between them.

And then, suddenly, his hands stilled.

He exhaled sharply, his forehead coming to rest against hers, his breath uneven. His fingers flexed against her waist before he pulled back, just slightly, enough to cool the fever between them.

"Bridget." His voice was raw, the single syllable a plea, a warning.

She shivered, though not from the cold.

His hand lifted to cup her cheek, his thumb brushing the curve of her lips, swollen from his kiss. "I want you." The admission was hoarse, stripped bare of pretense. "But not like this. Not here. Not now."

There was more he could not say, truths that lived behind his eyes, truths he feared would undo everything. But not tonight. Not while her trust still shone in the moonlight. Not until he found the courage to face what came next.

Bridget hadn't been prepared for this. For him.

For the way her body answered his touch, for the way his lips moved against hers with a purpose that set fire to every nerve in her body. The sea air was sharp and cool against her skin, but his warmth wrapped around her, sinking beneath her defenses as if he had always belonged there.

Thomas wasn't holding back this time.

His hands skimmed the curve of her waist, his grip firm, possessive. She felt the raw power in him, the restraint slowly unraveling as she pressed closer, threading her fingers into the dark waves of his hair.

A low sound rumbled in his throat as he tilted her chin, deepening the kiss, as if trying to brand her with it, as if he had already accepted that there was no undoing this.

She gasped against his mouth as his hands skated over her

ribs, sending tremors of heat through her. Her eyes fluttered closed, and for an instant, there was no grief, no guilt. There was only the undeniable truth of his touch and what it awakened in her. It was as though a dam had broken inside her, releasing everything she'd tried to hold back. His thumbs teased the sensitive skin just below her corset's edge, drawing another breathless sound from her lips. Her pulse pounded, a slow, insistent thrum of awareness that had nothing to do with fear.

This wasn't a stolen moment in the dark. This was something more.

She pressed against him, the need spiraling inside her, her mind unable to think past the sensation of him. Every kiss, every touch, every shift of his body sent a new rush of heat through her.

The moment hung between them, taut and breathless, until he stilled, control overtaking desire in a heartbeat.

His breath was uneven, his grip still tight at her waist, but his muscles tensed beneath her touch. A battle waged behind his eyes, one she had no doubt was taking every ounce of his control.

His thumb brushed the hollow of her throat, lingering there for just a moment, feeling the rapid beat of her pulse.

He swallowed hard. "Bridget…"

Her name was a warning, a plea, a promise all at once.

She could feel the way his body strained against the pull of logic, the way he wanted her, the way he was fighting it.

Slowly, he pulled back, just enough to break the spell.

She exhaled sharply, her body still singing with the remnants of his touch. "You regret this," she whispered, barely able to find her voice.

His hand cupped her cheek, his touch gentle but unyielding. "Never."

Her breath caught, but before she could speak, he leaned in, pressing one last kiss to the corner of her lips, soft, reverent, a promise of what would come.

Then, with great effort, he stepped away.

"We can't," he murmured, raking a hand through his hair.

"Not here. Not now."

She studied him in the moonlight, not hurt, not wounded, but knowing.

He wouldn't always stop. And when that moment came... neither of them would hold back.

She swallowed, her body still thrumming with the remnants of pleasure, but she understood.

He was not rejecting her. He was protecting something between them, something fragile, something not yet spoken.

She nodded once, unable to speak, but he must have seen her acceptance, because the tension in his shoulders eased.

Still, he did not step away entirely. His fingers trailed down her arm, lingering at her wrist before his hand finally dropped to his side.

The sea whispered below, steady and unrelenting like the pull between them, impossible to ignore.

"Come," he said softly. "It's late."

But as they walked back toward the manor, the night air between them crackled with something unfinished, something not yet claimed.

Something that neither of them would be able to deny much longer.

Chapter Twenty-Two

B RIDGET SAID NOTHING as she and Thomas made their way back toward the manor, the silence between them rich with everything unspoken. The moment on the cliffs still lingered in her thoughts, impossible to set aside. Something between them had shifted, and there was no turning back.

By the time she reached her room, the house was quiet, the echoes of the day settling into stillness.

The following day, the house seemed determined to return to its usual rhythm. The weekend guests resumed their entertainments, some out of genuine distraction, others out of obligation. The gravity of the past day was pushed aside, at least on the surface, but a subtle tension still wove itself into the fabric of their gatherings.

Lady Carlisle presided over a lively game of cards in the drawing room, laughing as she playfully accused Lord Davenport of cheating. Miss Gray and Miss Hathaway, having abandoned their earlier debate over the weather, had taken to the pianoforte, filling the air with the soft strains of a duet. Lady Worthington, her embroidery hoop in hand, stitched with an intensity that suggested her mind was elsewhere.

Bridget and Thomas observed from the periphery, careful to blend in while remaining alert. Though the guests entertained themselves, none were truly at ease. The investigation had delayed their departures, and while no one openly voiced their frustrations, an undercurrent of unease settled over the house.

They were all waiting. Some for answers, some for the moment they could leave without suspicion clinging to their names.

By mid-afternoon, the men had moved to the billiards room, where Barrington and Blackwood engaged in a quiet but pointed match. Lord Davenport, having lost a game earlier, nursed a glass of brandy while listening to Townsend discuss the latest developments in London. Outside, a handful of guests ventured onto the damp grounds for a stroll, cloaks drawn tight against the gusts of wind as they wandered the paths leading toward the gardens.

Meanwhile, the ladies busied themselves with less strenuous pursuits. Lady Carlisle arranged for a small poetry reading in the afternoon parlor, where Miss Hathaway took great pleasure in reciting Lord Byron with a dramatic flourish. Tea was served, polite conversation resumed, and for a while, the house resembled any other gathering of its kind.

Yet beneath it all, a quiet watchfulness remained.

Bridget's attention drifted as she watched Thomas, who stood at ease near the mantel but missed nothing. His gaze frequently flicked toward Blackwood, assessing, calculating. She had learned to recognize when his mind was at work, turning over details and seeking patterns in the noise.

"Oh, bother! Where is it?"

Lady Worthington twisted in her seat, patting at the folds of her gown with increasing urgency. "It was right here," she muttered, her brows knitting together. She shifted her embroidery hoop aside, peering at the space between the cushions.

Lady Carlisle, in the midst of whispering a particularly scandalous theory to Miss Hathaway, frowned. "Evelina, whatever is the matter?"

"My bodkin," Lady Worthington huffed, her frustration clear as she searched the small table beside her chair. "It was just here not a moment ago!"

Thomas, who had been watching Blackwood's reaction to a circulating rumor about the missing journal, exhaled sharply, rubbing his temple. The timing could not have been worse.

Bridget, standing near the hearth, forced a polite smile. "Would you like some help looking?"

Lady Worthington barely seemed to hear her. "It has a sapphire set in the cap, a family heirloom," she added, her voice growing more clipped. She cast a glance toward a footman lingering near the doorway. "Did someone move it? Are you certain none of the maids disturbed my chair?"

The footman straightened, clearly uncomfortable. "No, my lady. I haven't seen anything."

Lady Worthington's lips pressed into a thin line. With a frustrated exhale, she upended her work basket onto the table, spilling a small pair of scissors, silk threads, and embroidery floss. But no bodkin.

Miss Gray, attempting to lighten the moment, let out a delicate laugh. "Lady Worthington, I do believe that your bodkin has seen more excitement tonight than any of us."

Lady Worthington didn't laugh. Instead, she exhaled sharply and stood, brushing off her skirts with clipped efficiency. "It must be somewhere," she murmured, as if convincing herself. "I'll look in the library."

Before anyone could respond, she swept toward the door.

Thomas leaned toward Bridget, his voice low and dry. "Could this evening be any more chaotic?"

Bridget barely resisted a smirk.

Barrington, who had been quietly observing, rubbed his chin in thought. "Perhaps a little distraction works in our favor," he murmured.

Across the room, Lord Blackwood had shifted, his fingers tapping against the armrest. He was either bored, or the rumor had reached him.

A murmur of conversation swelled and receded, the household settling into a deceptively normal rhythm. Footmen moved about the room, offering refreshments, while Lady Carlisle dealt a fresh hand of cards with a flourish.

Then came the steady clatter of hooves up the drive. The rhythmic sound cut through the noise, drawing only the briefest flickers of interest from those nearest the windows. A lone rider approached Alastair Court. His livery bore no crest, but his posture was upright, his manner purposeful. A proper messenger, then, not a tradesman.

Mr. Simmons answered the door, his usual composed expression never wavering as the man extended a letter. "A note of condolence from Lord Seaton," the messenger announced.

Simmons took the missive with a nod. "Her ladyship will receive it in due course."

The messenger hesitated for a moment, glancing around the entrance hall before shifting his stance. "Busy house," he observed conversationally.

Simmons remained impassive. "Naturally. Her ladyship has many guests."

The man adjusted his gloves and turned slightly as if about to leave, but then paused mid-step. He hesitated, then glanced back at Simmons.

"Forgive the inquiry," he said, lowering his voice slightly, "but I overheard something on the road here. A gentleman at the coaching inn mentioned a missing journal belonging to the late Lord Alastair. He seemed rather insistent that it was important. Would there be any truth to that?"

Simmons's posture remained impeccable, but his tone cooled. "Idle speculation is hardly fitting at a time of mourning."

The courier held up his hands in mock surrender. "Didn't mean to offend, sir. Just found it curious, is all."

He tipped his hat and strode back toward his horse.

Simmons stood in the doorway, watching him mount and ride off. His grip on the letter tightened slightly before he turned back into the house.

Bridget and Thomas watched from the drawing room. As they walked down the corridor, Thomas exhaled sharply, hands settling on his hips. "We wanted whispers, but we need to be certain they don't spiral beyond our control."

Bridget nodded. "If we guide the gossip properly, we can keep attention focused where we want it."

Thomas glanced toward the butler's study. "Mr. Simmons already knows every bit of talk in this house before it reaches the guests. If anyone can steer the rumor, it's him."

Bridget hesitated for a moment before nodding. "He won't like meddling in gossip."

Thomas's mouth quirked slightly. "No, but he'll do what's best for the household. If we explain what's at stake, he'll manage it."

Bridget squared her shoulders. "Then we should speak with him now."

Thomas rapped his knuckles against the door. There was a pause, and then the butler's steady voice called. "Enter."

Bridget stepped inside first, followed by Thomas. Mr. Simmons was already rising from behind his desk, smoothing the front of his coat. "Captain. Lady Bridget."

Bridget inclined her head. "Mr. Simmons, we appreciate you seeing us."

The butler dipped his head slightly. "How may I assist you?"

Bridget hesitated only a moment. "You must have heard the rumors circulating. About Lord Alastair's missing journal."

Simmons clasped his hands behind his back. "I make it a point not to entertain gossip, Lady Bridget."

Thomas stepped forward, his voice even. "We need you to do more than ignore it. We need you to guide it."

Simmons's brows lifted just slightly. "Guide it?"

Bridget nodded. "Not to stop the rumors. But to direct them."

The room was silent. Simmons dropped his arms to his side. "You wish for me to let them believe it was merely misplaced. That there is nothing of consequence left to find."

Thomas crossed his arms. "Would that be possible?"

Simmons considered them both for a long moment before

inclining his head. "Quite."

Bridget exhaled, relief easing the tightness in her chest. "That would be most helpful, Mr. Simmons. We appreciate your discretion."

Thomas gave a nod of approval, his voice measured. "You'll be doing Lady Marjory and his lordship a great service, guiding the conversation. It won't go unnoticed."

Simmons's lips twitched with something akin to satisfaction. "A well-placed word at the right moment can often achieve more than outright declaration. If the goal is to keep curiosity alive, subtly, of course, then I shall see to it."

Bridget met his gaze, understanding the delicate balance of suggestion and silence. "Then perhaps an offhand remark about how misplaced things have a way of turning up in unexpected places?"

Simmons's expression brightened, as if pleased by the challenge. "Ah, yes. A lingering question left unanswered is far more tantalizing than a blatant search. A discovery just out of reach."

Thomas smirked, arms still crossed. "As long as it keeps the right people searching and the wrong ones second-guessing."

Simmons tipped his head. "Consider it done."

Bridget offered a grateful smile. "Then we are in your debt."

Simmons gave a small bow. "Think nothing of it, my lady. Some stories beg to be buried. Others, well… sometimes it is far more interesting to leave them just beneath the surface."

With that, they took their leave, knowing they had left things in Mr. Simmons's capable hands.

BY MIDDAY, THE first hints of unease rippled through the house. Not everyone seemed concerned about rumors of a missing journal, but those who were had grown increasingly restless. Bridget and Thomas watched as subtle shifts took place, whispers exchanged in the halls, lingering glances toward the study, and the unmistakable tension among those who thought no one was looking.

Yet, it was not only the journal that stirred commotion. Lady Worthington's bodkin was still missing.

Bridget and Thomas had just left Mr. Simmons's study when they passed a pair of footmen searching beneath the sideboard in the hall. A maid stood nearby, carefully lifting the cushions from a settee while another straightened the drapes as if expecting the bodkin to appear tangled in the folds of fabric.

Bridget arched a brow. "The entire house is searching now?"

One of the footmen, a young man with an earnest face, straightened. "Lady Worthington insists it was misplaced here in the drawing room, but we've yet to find it there."

"Or anywhere else," the maid added with a slight huff. "It's as if it vanished into thin air."

Before Bridget could reply, Lady Worthington herself swept into the hall, her usual poise slipping beneath the clear agitation in her expression. "You've checked the writing desk?"

"Yes, my lady," the footman replied promptly. "And beneath the rugs."

Lady Worthington turned, her fingers pressed to her temple. "It cannot simply be lost." Her tone sharpened, frustration clear. "It is a family heirloom, irreplaceable. The sapphire on the cap alone—" She broke off, shaking her head. "It must be here somewhere."

Bridget softened her voice. "Perhaps you set it aside somewhere unexpected. Have you checked your reticule?"

"I did. Twice." She exhaled sharply. "I've looked everywhere I can think of."

A housemaid hesitated before speaking. "Might you have left it in the library, my lady? You were there yesterday morning with Miss Gray."

Lady Worthington's lips parted as if to dismiss the idea, but then she stilled. "Perhaps." Her expression remained troubled.

Bridget caught Thomas's slight smirk, and she nudged him lightly.

"Shall I continue searching here, my lady?" the maid asked.

"Yes. Yes, of course," She said, waving a hand. "And send someone to check the library thoroughly. If it is not found soon, I will have to assume one of the maids put it away."

She turned on her heel, her gown rustling as she strode off.

Thomas leaned in slightly. "That woman is determined."

Bridget let out a small laugh under her breath. "You would be too if it were something important to you."

Thomas hummed. "If she keeps this up, she may have the entire household in an uproar by supper."

Bridget glanced toward the house staff, still searching beneath tables and along shelves, and felt a small pang of amusement. The woman's bodkin truly had become the most sought-after object in the manor.

But at least, for now, it was only a distraction.

That evening, over brandy and conversation, Lord Blackwood scoffed at the speculation.

"A lost journal, is it?" He leaned back in his chair, swirling the amber liquid in his glass. "It's fascinating how easily people are led by whispers. If such a thing existed, it would have been found already. The dead do not hide secrets."

Across from him, Lord Davenport chuckled, shaking his head. "At this rate, I'm not sure which has caused more disruption, the journal or Lady Worthington's missing bodkin. If you ask me, the latter seems to be winning."

Blackwood's expression didn't change, but he tilted his glass slightly, watching the amber liquid swirl. "That depends," he said, his voice calm, measured. "Value is determined by the one who wants it most."

Bridget held her glass steady, keeping her expression neutral as the conversation shifted around them. The air inside the drawing room had grown thick with speculation and glances traded like silent wagers. She had spent the better part of the evening listening, watching, and waiting. Yet now, she found herself restless.

Thomas leaned slightly toward her, his voice pitched low enough for only her to hear. "Would you care for some air?"

She set her glass aside. "I think that would be wise."

They slipped from the drawing room unnoticed and she took his offered arm as they stepped into the quiet hush of the night. The summer air was cooler than expected, the lingering warmth of the day tempered by the whisper of an evening breeze. The scent of damp earth and fading blooms clung to the air, a stark contrast to the tension simmering inside the house.

Thomas's expression was unreadable. "Do you think Blackwood knows more than he lets on?"

Bridget exhaled, considering. "He's too controlled to reveal anything outright. But he didn't dismiss it entirely. That tells me he's listening."

Thomas hummed in agreement, his gaze flicking toward the shadowed estate grounds. "And if he's listening, others are as well."

As they rounded the corner of the house, faint movement near the tree line caught Bridget's eye. The flicker of a lantern, a quiet shift of shadow, subtle but intentional. Her breath hitched, her fingers squeezing his arm.

He didn't miss the touch or the slight panic in her eyes.

"It's all right," he murmured, his voice low and steady. "Barrington positioned his men along the perimeter. If the Order plans to make a move, they won't get far."

Bridget exhaled, some of the unease coiled in her chest loosening. "Then we're not the only ones waiting to see what happens next."

Thomas's lips quirked, though his gaze remained sharp. "No. We're not."

The tension in the air hadn't faded. It had merely increased. Whatever came next, the night was far from over.

He turned to her then, his face partially illuminated by the distant glow of candlelight from the manor. "Are you ready for this?"

Bridget met his gaze, something unspoken passing between them. "You should know by now that I do not shrink from what must be done."

A slow smile tugged at his lips before he turned back toward the house. "Then let's see who comes looking next."

Bridget swallowed, pulse thrumming. "Either way, we make sure they don't escape."

Thomas didn't respond immediately. His gaze lingered on her, searching, as if seeing something in her he hadn't allowed himself to before. The distant glow of candlelight from the house flickered across his features, casting deep shadows and making his expression unreadable.

"Bridget—" He stopped himself. The sound of her name on his lips sent an unfamiliar thrill through her.

She tilted her head, curiosity stirring beneath the tension that stretched between them. "Yes?"

His jaw tightened slightly as if evaluating the risk of his next words. Then, softer, almost as if the words weren't meant to leave his lips, he murmured, "Sometimes, with you, it's too easy to forget there are things I haven't said… things I can't say. Not yet."

The admission sent a shiver down her spine, though the evening air was still. "Careful?" she echoed, her voice barely above a whisper. "Of what?"

He let out a breath, but it wasn't exasperation. It was something else, something quieter, more dangerous. "Of this."

His fingers moved deliberately, brushing against hers, then lingering. A single touch, but it might as well have been a spark in dry kindling. It would have been so easy to pull away, to let the moment slip into nothing. But she didn't. And neither did he.

Her heart pounded. "You think too much, Thomas."

The corner of his mouth twitched, though his eyes still held that unreadable depth. "And you don't think enough."

"Then stop thinking," she whispered.

It was all the invitation he needed.

His hand came up, brushing along the side of her face, his fingers trailing the curve of her jaw before tangling in the loose strands of her hair. His touch was careful, as if he wasn't sure he had the right to be there, but when she didn't pull away when her breath hitched, and she leaned just slightly toward him, his hesitation vanished.

His lips met hers.

Warmth surged through her, unexpected yet entirely right. There was no fleeting hesitation in his kiss, no uncertainty. He kissed her like a man who had spent too long resisting what he wanted and had finally decided to stop fighting it.

Bridget's hands slid up, gripping the lapels of his coat as she deepened the kiss as if grounding herself in the reality of it. He made a small sound in the back of his throat, something between restraint and surrender, but he didn't pull away.

The night, the danger, the mission, all of it blurred. For a breath, for a moment, nothing else mattered.

Then reality surged back.

The truth of what they risked crept in, cooling passion with the chill of consequence. Thomas broke the kiss, his forehead resting lightly against hers as his breath came uneven. His hands remained on her waist as if reluctant to let go.

"That—" His voice was hoarse, filled with something she couldn't quite name. "That should not have happened."

Bridget's lips parted, her pulse still pounding in her ears. "I disagree."

His laugh was quiet, but the warmth in his eyes had shifted. "Of course you do."

She reached up, brushing her fingers lightly along his jaw. "We can discuss it later."

A flicker of something passed through his gaze, something raw, something unspoken. Instead, he exhaled, stepping back just slightly, though his fingers lingered at her waist before finally falling away.

"Tomorrow," he said, voice steadier now, though not quite neutral. "We set the trap."

Bridget swallowed the words that threatened to rise, her thoughts still tangled in the feel of his mouth against hers. She only nodded.

"Tomorrow."

Chapter Twenty-Three

T HE HOUSE STIRRED early the following morning, the soft clatter of trays and murmured voices signaling the start of another day. Sunlight streamed through the tall windows of the breakfast room, dappling the crisp linens with warm golden hues. Guests filtered in at their leisure, some bleary-eyed from the late evening's conversations, others keenly alert.

Bridget had barely taken a seat before a sharp huff of frustration cut through the room.

"This is intolerable," Lady Worthington snapped, pressing her napkin against the table with far more force than necessary.

Bridget glanced up in mild surprise as the woman sat stiff-backed, her gaze darting over the breakfast spread as if she expected to find something hiding among the tea services.

Lady Carlisle, delicately spooning jam onto her toast, arched a brow. "Evelina, must you look as though you intend to wage war against the morning rolls?"

Lady Worthington barely heard her. "I still haven't found my bodkin," she declared, looking pointedly toward the nearest footman. "Hasn't it turned up anywhere?"

The footman stiffened under her scrutiny. "I'm afraid not, my lady. The maids searched the drawing room again this morning."

She pursed her lips, clearly unimpressed. "Well, they must not have looked thoroughly enough. A sapphire set in silver does not simply vanish."

Davenport, who had been buttering his toast with meticulous

care, let out a chuckle. "A needle lost in a grand estate. What a tragedy. We should all abandon our breakfast at once and form a search party."

A flicker of irritation crossed Lady Worthington's face. "Very amusing, my lord."

Davenport merely smirked. "I do try."

Lady Carlisle took a sip of her tea, eyes twinkling with amusement. "Perhaps it will turn up in an unexpected place. Things often do."

Lady Worthington exhaled sharply. "I need it found."

Lady Worthington, always the epitome of grace and poise, now paced like a woman unraveling. The elegant composure she had worn like a second skin was gone, replaced by clipped words and harried glances. She scoured the breakfast room with restless energy, her hands fluttering over cushions and candelabra alike, as if decorum itself had betrayed her. It was not just a missing bodkin. It was the breach of something deeper, something she could not name but could not tolerate.

The morning had been a flurry of quiet disruptions, muttered rumors, exchanged glances, and the ever-present tension simmering beneath the civility of the house. But no disturbance had been more persistent than Lady Worthington's frantic search for her missing bodkin.

"Turn the cushions again," she directed a footman, her usual composed manner fraying at the edges. "It must be here somewhere!"

Across the room, Davenport exchanged an amused glance with Miss Gray, who had long since abandoned any pretense of interest in her needlework.

"If I disappear before luncheon," he murmured, "tell them I was last seen beneath a pile of misplaced embroidery."

Miss Gray stifled a laugh while Lady Carlisle attempted to soothe Lady Worthington. "Perhaps you left it in your chambers? Or the morning room?"

Lady Worthington's sharp exhale made it clear that such a

possibility was both absurd and unacceptable. "It was right here," she insisted, scanning the room once more before turning on her heel. "I shall check the drawing room again."

As she stormed away, the tension she had stirred remained. The footman hesitated, unsure whether to continue upending cushions, and several guests shared knowing glances, some sympathetic, while others were entertained.

Barrington, who had been standing by the window observing the exchange in silence, finally sighed and moved toward one of the vacant chairs. "Well," he muttered, "if I'm to witness an unraveling, I may as well be comfortable."

He started to sit, then abruptly stopped.

Something hard pressed against his palm as he adjusted the cushion.

Frowning, he reached down and pulled a small, ornate silver bodkin from the crevice between the fabric. The cap gleamed in the soft morning light, the embedded sapphire winking at him.

Barrington turned it over between his fingers. An impressive piece of finely worked silver filigree along the slender case, the cap fitted snugly to protect the delicate needle tip. A fine thing to lose, he mused, though he suspected Lady Worthington's distress was less about the embroidery tool itself and more about the sentimental value attached to it.

"Well, that settles that," he said to no one in particular, standing again. He glanced toward the doorway through which the woman had disappeared. Should he return it to her now or later?

His fingers absently turned the cap. It was stuck firm.

Probably from being wedged in the chair, he reasoned. With a slight shrug, he slipped the bodkin into his pocket, intending to return it when she was in a more reasonable mood.

For now, there were more pressing concerns. He finished his breakfast, casting one last glance at the room before rising. The library would provide the solitude he needed to think.

He stepped inside, the quiet space a welcome reprieve from the morning's activity. Crossing to the nearest shelf, he let his fingers drift absently over the spines of the books, his mind already turning over the puzzle before him.

A sharp knock at the door drew his attention. Barrington looked up as Townsend stepped inside, his expression unreadable.

"We need to talk," Townsend said without preamble, closing the door behind him.

Barrington gestured toward the chair across from him. "I assume this isn't a social call."

Townsend's mouth twitched in amusement, but the humor didn't reach his eyes. "Not unless you consider the Order's latest move a lively topic of conversation."

As the library doors closed behind them, Bridget approached from the corridor, a stack of correspondence balanced in her hands. The soft murmur of voices drifted through the slightly ajar door, drawing her pause.

The deep timbre of Barrington's voice carried clearly in the quiet corridor, followed by Townsend's measured response.

"If the information is accurate," Barrington was saying, his tone thoughtful, "it confirms the Order's involvement. They've been working to destabilize the Highlands for years. Huntington's actions were just the beginning."

Bridget froze, her heart hammering in her chest. The name struck her like a thunderclap, dredging up memories she had tried to bury. From the eviction notices to the burned cottages, all the way to the pleading voices of her clansmen as their lives were torn apart. She leaned closer, her breath shallow, and listened.

"It's a dangerous web," Townsend replied. "And not one easily unraveled. Huntington's presence in the Highlands was no coincidence. It's clear now he wasn't acting alone. The question is, how much does Grenville know?"

Barrington's voice hardened. "Grenville would never involve himself in his father's dealings. He's spent years distancing himself from that legacy."

Townsend hesitated before speaking again. "That may be true, but the Order isn't interested in his innocence. They've sent a message requesting a meeting at the clearing by the river, and not with Grenville, but with me."

Barrington's sharp intake of breath was audible even through the door. "Do you think it's wise to go? They're not asking for you by chance."

Townsend's tone grew resolute. "It doesn't matter. If this is the only way to get closer to what they're planning, I'll take the risk. As soon as I have my things together, I'll leave."

Barrington's reply was clipped. "Then we'll be ready for what comes next. But Townsend… be careful."

Bridget was shaken by the truth she'd just learned. The name alone had knocked the air from her lungs. But it was the truth beneath it, the unbearable collision of past and present, that left her unmoored.

Bridget's grip tightened on the letters, her knuckles whitening. Her vision blurred for a moment, the corridor tilting at the edges. It was as if she had been thrust back into the past, standing among the ruins of her home, smoke thick in the air, her father's grim silence cutting deeper than any words.

Grenville's father. The man whose orders had turned her world to ash. The architect of the Clearances. Of her clan's ruin. And now his legacy stood in the room beside her.

Her knees threatened to buckle, but she forced herself upright, retreating a step before the men inside could notice her presence. Her mind raced, conflicting emotions warring within her: betrayal, anger, and a confusing pang of sorrow.

She stumbled back a step, her fingers numbing around the forgotten letters. She had to leave before her presence was noticed and before her legs gave out beneath her. But moving felt impossible, as if the years-old grief had suddenly turned to iron around her chest.

The moment Barrington's and Townsend's voices faded behind her, she turned on her heel and walked swiftly through the house, the words she had just overheard burning through her like fire. Each step fueled the storm rising inside her. She didn't need time to think, to process, she needed answers.

She found him in the sitting room, standing near the hearth, flipping absently through a book as if this were just another day. As if nothing had changed.

"Bridget," he said softly, rising from his chair.

"Why didn't you tell me?" Her eyes were blazing.

"Tell you what?" The words left him more cautiously than he intended. His shoulders squared, but his stance remained rooted, as if bracing for a blow he knew was coming.

"How long were you going to let me stand beside you and not know?" Thomas froze, his chest tightening. The accusation in her voice was a blade's edge poised to cut deep. He took a careful step forward.

"Huntington," she said, at last. The name left her lips like a curse. "Viscount Everard Huntington."

Realization flickered in his eyes, and with it, something close to anguish. "Bridget—"

"Do you have any idea what that name means to me? To my people?" She cut in, her voice as sharp as glass, honed by years of unspoken grief. "You bear his name. The same name that sent Catriona's family fleeing for their lives. That left my people scattered and broken. And you—" She inhaled quickly steadying herself against the wave of emotion rising in her chest. "You said nothing," her voice breaking.

His jaw tightened, but he remained silent, his gaze steady, unyielding.

Bridget stepped forward, fury burning beneath her skin. Her hands curled into fists at her sides, but it was nothing compared to the tightness in her chest. "You've stood beside me, knowing what your father did. Knowing exactly what his name would mean to me. And still, you held your tongue."

Her breath came in shallow bursts, anger and something dangerously close to betrayal twisting inside her like a vice. "What was your plan, Thomas? To let me care for you, to let me trust you, while you kept this hidden?"

He exhaled slowly, his voice steady but something raw slipped through. "It's not what you think."

"Don't," she snapped, holding up a hand. "There is nothing you can say. Nothing that will erase what your father has done. Nothing that will make me forget the lives destroyed under his orders."

Bridget searched his face, willing him to fight back, to defend himself, to give her something, anything, that could make this betrayal sting less. But he simply stood there, the pain in his eyes a mirror of her own.

"Say something," she demanded, her voice breaking against all she was trying to hold back. "I dare you to defend yourself."

His mouth parted as if he had words, explanations, defenses, but none came. Instead, his fingers curled at his sides, knuckles white.

The quiet was worse than any denial, worse than any excuse. His silence confirmed everything he had known, and he had chosen to keep it from her.

Bridget turned away, her hands shaking as she pressed them against the window frame. A memory surged. Smoke rose over the glen, a child's cry cut short, her father's shoulders still with defeat. The past suddenly felt too near, too real, and the grief she'd fought so long to master roared back with sharp, aching teeth. "There is nothing you can say," she whispered, her voice hollow now, empty of all the fire it had burned with moments before.

A long beat passed before she heard him shift behind her.

He wanted to speak. The words pressed behind his teeth like a rising tide, but none felt worthy. Not when the truth had already torn through her so violently.

Still, he said nothing.

Bridget's breath caught at his silence. The quiet felt like a blow, knocking the wind from her chest. She had expected resistance, anger, anything but this. She turned slightly, just enough to glimpse the conflict etched into his features. For the first time, uncertainty crept in, whispering that she had miscalculated, that the man standing before her was not as simple as the sins of his father.

But before she could speak, Thomas turned sharply, moving toward the door. He paused, just for a breath, as if considering some last words. He paused, his breath catching, his hand lingering on the doorframe as if words teetered on the edge, but none came. He chose silence instead. Without a sound, he left, the door shutting behind him with quiet finality.

As the door clicked closed, her shoulders sagged, and her composure cracked. A single breath shuddered out of her, unsteady and raw. She pressed a trembling hand to her chest, as if to hold the pieces together, but they scattered like ash in the wind.

Bridget pressed her forehead to the cool glass, hoping for relief, for clarity, anything but the hollow ache creeping through her chest. But the room was empty now, and Thomas had left her with nothing but silence.

Chapter Twenty-Four

B RIDGET STORMED INTO her chambers, her pulse a relentless drumbeat in her ears. The heavy air of summer offered no reprieve, thick and suffocating, but it was nothing compared to the chill settling deep in her chest. She hadn't felt this kind of betrayal in years, not since the Clearances stole everything from her family.

And now she knew why.

Thomas Grenville. Son of Viscount Huntington.

A man who had walked beside her, stood beside her, and kissed her while carrying the name of the man who had ruined her people. She had vowed never to trust an Englishman again. And yet… She clenched her fists, her breath uneven. How could she have been so blind?

A soft knock at the door barely registered before Catriona stepped inside, a folded linen draped over one arm. She studied Bridget for a long moment before setting the cloth down. "I heard you pacing from the hall. Are you trying to wear out the floorboards?"

Bridget exhaled sharply. She turned away, staring at the flames as if their heat could burn away the fury in her chest. "I don't have patience for jests, Catriona."

The humor faded from Catriona's eyes. She took a step closer. "Aye, I can see that. What's happened?"

Bridget shook her head, pacing to the window. The reflection in the glass showed her own rigid posture, with her shoulders tight and her jaw clenched. "Thomas—" She stopped, swallowing hard. "Grenville. I should have known there was something he wasn't telling me. That his name—" She forced the words past the lump in her throat. "That name has haunted my family for years. I just never thought it would be his."

Catriona's brow furrowed. "His name?"

Bridget turned sharply. "His father. Huntington. The Huntington." The name felt bitter on her tongue. She whirled back toward Catriona, her voice raw with emotion. "The man who carried out the Clearances. He—" Her breath caught. "He took everything from us."

Catriona went very still. Something flickered in her expression, an emotion Bridget couldn't place.

Bridget's pulse pounded. "I let him stand beside me, Catriona," she whispered. "I let him get close. And all the while, he knew. He knew. And he never said a word."

Her chest tightened, rage battling against something far more dangerous, a pain not like anything she had ever experienced. How could she have let herself forget who she was, what she'd lost? It would be easier if she hated him outright, if she could erase every shared moment from her mind. But the warmth of his touch, the way he had looked at her beneath the stars, the way he had kissed her as if she was his salvation…

Bridget shook her head sharply. She couldn't afford such thoughts. Not now. Not ever.

Catriona exhaled, her gaze unreadable. "And what did he say when you confronted him?"

Bridget's jaw clenched. A fresh wave of anger rose in her chest. "Nothing. He didn't even try to deny it."

He hadn't denied it. But he hadn't looked triumphant or indifferent. He had looked… broken.

Catriona tilted her head slightly. "And did you give him the chance to explain?"

Bridget faltered. "What?"

Catriona's voice softened, but her words cut straight through.

"Did you let him explain? Or did you decide you already knew what he would say?"

Bridget stiffened, a sharp retort ready on her lips, but it never came because Catriona was right.

Bridget had confronted Thomas and had pushed him to speak, but she had never really given him the chance. She had wanted an apology, a defense, something to make the betrayal make sense. But his silence had been more damning than any excuse. And yet…

No. She shook her head sharply. This wasn't about excuses. This was about the truth. And Thomas had kept that truth from her.

"It doesn't matter," Bridget said, the words tasting like ash. "Nothing he could say would change the past."

Catriona watched her, but she said nothing else.

For once, Bridget was grateful. She turned away, pressing her hands against the cool wood of the dressing table, forcing herself to breathe. The sunlight casting long shadows across the room. But none of it could chase away the darkness curling in her chest.

"Did you ever wonder how Killian and I made it here?"

Bridget blinked, caught off guard. "What?"

"How we escaped? How we found safe passage?"

Catriona's voice held a credence Bridget hadn't heard before. Bridget frowned. "Alastair arranged it."

Catriona's lips twitched, but there was no amusement in it. "Aye. And who do you think arranged it for him?"

Bridget's breath stalled. "What are you saying?"

Catriona folded her arms. "I'm saying it wasn't just Alastair who got us out, Lady Bridget. It was Thomas."

The words landed like a blow. Bridget stared at her. "That's not possible."

"Oh, but it is." Catriona's voice softened, but it didn't waver. "You think Alastair could have arranged that without help? That he, on his own, knew how to get Scots out under the very nose of the men driving them from their homes? That he could have smuggled us through without a single notice?" She shook her head. "It was Thomas. He gave Alastair the means. The contacts. The routes. The coin."

Bridget's breath stalled in her chest. "No."

"Yes," Catriona said firmly. "And he didn't just help us. There were others. Whole families who made it out because he made sure they had a way."

Bridget's knees felt weak. She reached for the edge of the dressing table, gripping it tightly. "Why didn't anyone say anything?"

"Because Thomas didn't want to be known." She met Bridget's gaze. "Sometimes the truest acts are the quietest."

Bridget swallowed hard. She wanted to deny it. Wanted to hold on to her anger, her sense of betrayal. But the words wouldn't come because Catriona was telling her the truth.

He had risked everything. Not just his coin, but his name, his position, his safety. All to undo what his father had done.

The truth settled uncomfortably in her chest. A small, unwelcome part of her whispered that maybe, just maybe, she had known all along.

Her fingers curled into the folds of her skirt, frustration rising. She had been so certain, so absolute in her anger. And now? She exhaled sharply, pushing to her feet. Sitting here would accomplish nothing. She needed to find him.

Bridget strode toward the door, pausing only briefly to steady herself before stepping into the corridor. The hush of the house pressed in around her, and her own realization slowed her steps. Where would he have gone?

She checked the study first, then the library. He wasn't there.

As she passed the stairwell, she spotted Barrington lingering near the hall, his gaze sharp as he took her in.

"Looking for Grenville?" he asked casually.

Bridget hesitated, then lifted her chin. "Yes."

Barrington studied her for a long moment before nodding toward the open doors leading outside. "He left an hour ago. If I had to guess, he's down by the cliffs."

The cliffs. Where they had last stood, where she had wanted him, where she had let herself feel something beyond duty and loss.

Bridget's pulse quickened, but she squared her shoulders. She had been wrong about him, and now she had to face that truth.

She nodded her thanks and turned toward the cliffs.

The wind tugged at her skirts as she made her way toward the rocky outcrop. The path was familiar, the same one she had walked with him before. Her heartbeat pounded in her throat, equal parts nerves and anticipation.

But when she arrived, he wasn't there.

Bridget stood motionless, scanning the jagged cliffs, the restless sea below. She had been so certain she would find him here. Her stomach twisted, disappointment cutting sharper than she expected.

For a long moment, she stood there, listening to the crash of the waves, letting the wind whip at her hair. The wind bit through her gown, but it was the absence of him that chilled her most. He wasn't there. And now, she had to face what came next, alone.

Chapter Twenty-Five

T HE DRAWING ROOM held an uneasy calm. Conversations had turned polite but subdued, the usual vibrancy of the house party dulled considerably. The guests might have resumed their usual distractions, but tension simmered beneath the surface.

Barrington, standing near the fireplace, let his gaze sweep the room, ensuring he had everyone's attention before he spoke.

"I will not keep you long, but there is something you all should be aware of."

The low murmur of conversation ceased, heads turning toward him in expectation.

"Mr. Townsend has received a request for a meeting and will be leaving the estate briefly."

A flicker of unease passed through the guests. Lord Davenport leaned forward slightly, his brows drawing together. "A request from whom?"

Barrington's expression remained carefully neutral. "A party that may have information regarding Lord Alastair's death."

Miss Hathaway set down her teacup, fingers tightening around the saucer. "And he's going alone?"

"He is more than capable," Barrington assured them. "This is not a reckless decision."

Blackwood, seated near the window, let out a quiet chuckle, shaking his head. "And we're simply to accept this without question?"

Barrington met his gaze with practiced patience. "I do not

answer to speculation, Lord Blackwood. I am telling you this as a courtesy. You will notice Townsend's absence, and I would rather not encourage unfounded gossip."

Lady Worthington's lips pursed. "If this is connected to Lord Alastair's death, shouldn't the magistrate be involved?"

Barrington's response was measured. "Judge Scofield has already taken steps to ensure this investigation is properly handled. Mr. Townsend's meeting is part of that effort."

An unsettled murmur rolled through the guests, but no one dared to challenge him outright.

Blackwood, however, leaned back in his chair, his smirk returning. "Curious, indeed. First, you assume authority over this house, and now, you send men off on mysterious errands. Tell me, Lord Barrington, just how much more do you know than the rest of us?"

Barrington's jaw tightened slightly, but his voice remained calm. "I am ensuring that order is maintained, Lord Blackwood. Nothing more."

Blackwood exhaled, his smirk unwavering, but he said nothing further.

Barrington turned back to the room. "I see no need for alarm. Townsend is a cautious man, and this meeting is a necessary step toward understanding what has transpired."

The guests exchanged uncertain glances, their unease lingering, but there were no more objections. Barrington had given them just enough to satisfy curiosity without feeding panic.

With that, he inclined his head slightly. "I suggest you continue as you see fit."

The conversation resumed, though with a distinct edge of tension.

By evening, the household was thrown into quiet disarray as Townsend prepared to leave. The staff moved briskly to assist him, gathering what he needed and saddling his horse while the guests whispered among themselves. Everyone sensed the gravity of the moment.

Bridget stood near the entrance, her arms crossed tightly, her face carefully composed. She hadn't spoken much since the afternoon, since overhearing the truth about Thomas's father. But even with her thoughts storming inside her, she couldn't ignore the tension that gripped the house.

Barrington caught Townsend near the stables, his expression tight. "Are you certain about this?"

Townsend nodded, adjusting the strap on his satchel. "If I don't go, we lose our best chance at uncovering what they're planning. This might be the only way to stay ahead of the Order."

Barrington's jaw clenched. "And if it's a trap?"

Townsend exhaled, steady as ever. "Then we'll know just how far they're willing to go."

Silence stretched between them before Barrington gave a reluctant nod. "Be careful. If anything feels off, don't play the hero. Get out."

Townsend let out a quiet chuckle. "I'll try to restrain myself." He clasped Barrington's shoulder, his expression losing its usual humor. "We'll see this through. Together."

Barrington gave a small nod, saying nothing, but his grip tightened briefly on Townsend's arm before letting go.

ACROSS THE COURTYARD, Bridget noticed Thomas stood motionless, his eyes fixed on Townsend. There was something in his stillness, calm on the surface, but a coiled readiness beneath it all. It made something tighten in her chest.

But before she could make sense of it, Townsend swung into the saddle. The gathered household fell silent, as if the unspoken fears held them all. Bridget's stomach twisted. She told herself it was nothing, but the unease lingered.

The horse's hooves struck against the damp earth, the sound fading into the night as Townsend disappeared down the road.

Across from her, Thomas didn't move.

BRIDGET CROSSED THE threshold to find the room already full, though no one truly seemed present. Conversations flickered and faltered, everyone pretending not to feel the tension thickening like mist before a storm.

Bridget sat near the window, her gaze fixed on the garden, though her thoughts were anywhere but the quiet scene beyond the glass. Barrington stood near the mantel, arms crossed, his expression unreadable.

The hushed clinking of teacups and the occasional shuffle of playing cards filled the space, a poor attempt at maintaining the appearance of normalcy. Lady Worthington sat primly in her chair, her embroidery hoop resting in her lap, still without her bodkin.

Lady Carlisle, never one to tolerate prolonged silence, set her cards down with a flourish.

"This won't do at all," she declared, glancing around the room with an expectant look. "We cannot simply sit here, wringing our hands like nervous schoolchildren. We need a distraction."

Miss Hathaway hesitated, then offered a tentative smile. "Perhaps a riddle game? Something to keep our minds occupied."

Lady Carlisle considered this, then shook her head. "Too somber. What we need is something to lift the spirits." Her gaze flickered to Miss Gray. "A song, perhaps? Music always restores the mood."

Miss Gray blinked in surprise, glancing around as if hoping someone else would protest first.

Lord Davenport, leaning back in his chair, chuckled softly. "Music or no, I suspect you'll have trouble rallying enthusiasm for a proper evening of entertainment, my lady."

Lady Carlisle sighed dramatically. "So we are to sit in silence all evening? How utterly miserable."

Miss Hathaway smothered a smile. "I think we have little choice."

Lord Blackwood, seated near the corner with a glass of brandy in hand, watched the exchange with mild amusement. "If you're set on amusement, Lady Carlisle, might I suggest a wager? Something to make the evening less… tedious."

Lady Carlisle's brows lifted with intrigue. "Oh? And what do you propose?"

Before he could answer, the door opened.

The hush was immediate.

Townsend strode into the room, his expression unreadable. Whatever had been said before no longer mattered. The room stilled around him.

Lady Worthington's fingers stilled on her embroidery, her surprise obvious in the tight grip she had on her needle.

Bridget felt herself tense. He wasn't supposed to be here. Her gaze swept instinctively across the room, searching for some reason behind his return—some sign of what had changed.

Barrington stood. "What are you doing here? I thought you'd be halfway to the meeting by now."

Townsend shook his head, stepping further into the room. "I was stopped."

The hush deepened.

"Stopped?" Barrington's voice was low. "By whom?"

Townsend's gaze swept the room and, for just a moment, paused on Bridget. Long enough to set her nerves thrumming.

"Grenville," he said. "He intercepted me on the road."

The air left Bridget's lungs.

Barrington's voice was sharp. "What do you mean he intercepted you?"

Townsend exhaled, setting his satchel down. "Grenville insisted that he take my place. He said it wasn't the other party's decision who they dealt with. It was ours. He believed his name and presence would draw out more information than I ever could."

Barrington's face darkened. "And you let him go?" His voice was sharp, but it couldn't mask the flare of alarm in his eyes. For the first time since this began, Barrington looked truly unsettled.

"I didn't have much of a choice," Townsend replied, his voice calm but edged with something that sounded like regret. "Grenville made it clear this was his responsibility. Barrington had called him to this, asked him to do what others could not. He wasn't going to back down."

Barrington exhaled sharply. "Then at least tell me he had the book."

Townsend hesitated. "He wouldn't take it."

Bridget's stomach clenched. If Thomas had nothing to bargain with, then what was he walking into?

Townsend turned to her, his expression softening. "He's capable, Lady Bridget. And he's determined. I tried to argue, but he wouldn't hear it."

Bridget shook her head. "He's walking into a trap," she whispered, barely able to force the words past her throat.

Townsend hesitated before nodding. "He knows the risks. But he also knows what's at stake."

Barrington's fingers curled into a fist. "We need to be ready. If this goes wrong, they will have the upper hand."

But Bridget barely heard him.

Her fingers brushed her arm, finding the place where he had once rested his hand, a touch that had once felt like a promise. The ache in her chest deepened, twisting into something she couldn't name. She had pushed him away. And still, he had chosen to fight. Now, it was a reminder of everything she might lose.

Bridget's breath came fast and uneven. She had been so consumed by her own hurt that she hadn't seen the truth sooner. Thomas was walking into a trap.

The realization slammed into her chest. She could not wait

for permission, nor hope someone else would act. She had to be the one.

And she would not stand by and let it happen. Not again. Not to him.

Steeling herself, she turned and slipped out of the room. No one would stop her. By the time they realized she was gone, it would be too late.

Chapter Twenty-Six

THE NIGHT WAS cool and still, Bridget smoothed her gown, then tested the grip of her sgian-dubh.

The weight was familiar and comforting. She had carried it since she was a girl, a reminder of where she came from and of what she was willing to fight for.

Bridget moved swiftly, stuffed the small dagger into her boot, and picked up a book of poems by William Blake that was next to her bed. The chamber was dark, but she didn't dare light a candle. Every sound seemed amplified in the silence. The rustling of fabric, even the soft creak of the floorboards beneath her hurried steps, signaled she was leaving.

Her heart pounded against her ribs, each beat a reminder that she was running out of time. Thomas was out there, alone. Facing men who had no reason to bargain with him, not when they had the power to destroy him instead.

Bridget reached for the door latch, but the soft sound of foot-steps in the corridor froze her in place. She barely had time to step away before the door swung open, and Catriona stood there, brows drawn, lips pressed into a thin line.

Bridget swallowed back a curse.

Catriona's sharp gaze swept over her, the traveling cloak, the sturdy boots, the barely concealed tension in her stance. Her expression darkened. "Where are you going?"

Bridget didn't answer. She reached for her gloves instead, but Catriona stepped further inside, closing the door behind her.

"No," she said softly. "No, you're not fooling me. You're leaving, aren't you?"

Bridget's fingers curled around the leather of her gloves, her jaw tightening. "I have to."

Catriona exhaled sharply. "You're going after him."

Bridget didn't deny it.

Catriona took another step closer, lowering her voice. "You don't know what you're walking into. This isn't a reckless chase through the Highlands. These men are killers. They killed his lordship. You're not talking any sense."

Bridget lifted her chin. "I can't just stand here and do nothing. Thomas—" She stopped herself, but Catriona's knowing gaze didn't waver.

"If you go," Catriona continued, her voice tight, "then I'm going with you."

Bridget's heart twisted, but she forced herself to stay firm. "No, you're not."

Catriona let out a frustrated breath, shaking her head. "You cannot do this alone."

Bridget's fingers clenched into fists. "I have to."

The silence stretched between them, thick with unspoken words.

Then, as if sensing the shift, Catriona took a slow step back, eyes narrowing in realization. "You planned this," she murmured. "You weren't going to tell anyone."

Bridget's throat tightened.

Catriona reacted quickly, but Bridget was faster. Before she could reach the door, Bridget lunged, shoved her inside, slammed the door, and turned the key in the lock. The soft click was like a hammer in her chest.

"Bridget!" Catriona's hands slammed against the wood.

Bridget's fingers trembled as she pressed her forehead to the door. "I'm sorry," she whispered. "But I can't let you stop me."

"Bridget, don't do this." Catriona's voice turned urgent. The muffled sound of her pushing against the door broke through the quiet. "You'll get yourself killed!"

Bridget closed her eyes for a brief moment, willing herself to shut out the doubt creeping into her chest. "I won't," she said, forcing the conviction into her voice. "I won't let that happen."

Catriona's voice was muffled but fierce. "Bridget! Open this door. I swear if you—"

"I'm sorry," Bridget whispered, pressing her palm against the wood for just a second before she forced herself to step back. She hesitated, then left the key in the keyhole, right where Catriona would find it.

"Lady or no lady. I will throttle you when I get out of here!" Catriona shouted.

A smile flickered across Bridget's lips as she stepped away. "Then I'd best make it worth the trouble."

She hurried down the corridor, her pulse racing.

The night air hit her like a slap as she stepped outside. The estate was quiet. Most of the guests had retired, and the few who still lingered were gathered in the drawing room, speaking in hushed tones about Thomas's absence.

Bridget moved carefully through the shadows, her destination already set in her mind. Townsend's horse.

She found him still saddled near the stables with his reins looped loosely over the hitching post. She untied the reins, soothing the beast with a gentle murmur as she checked the girth. It was a fine animal, bred for speed and endurance, precisely what she needed.

Swinging up into the saddle, she adjusted her cloak, casting one last glance toward the manor. There was no turning back now.

With a sharp nudge of her heels, she sent the horse into motion, guiding him onto the path leading away from the manor. The cool night air bit at her cheeks, the world around her narrowing to the rhythmic pound of hooves against damp earth.

Shadows stretched long beneath the moonlight, the towering trees forming a dark tunnel ahead. She leaned forward, urging the horse onward, her breath steady despite the storm raging inside her. Somewhere beyond the bend, beyond the river's winding path, was the clearing. And Thomas.

She didn't know how long she'd been riding before she noticed a faint glow flickering in the distance, just beyond the tree line. Smoke curled upward, thin but visible against the inky sky, a beacon leading her to the heart of what had been set in motion.

She eased the horse to a stop as the trees thinned around her. Sliding down the saddle, her boots sank into the softened ground. The clearing ahead was shrouded in an eerie stillness, the silence broken only by the soft hiss of lanterns swaying from low branches.

Bridget pressed a steadying hand against the book beneath her cloak. Her pulse pounded, fear and determination battled for dominance. But her back remained straight, her stance unwavering. She was Lady Bridget McConnell, daughter of Laird Duncan McConnell of Glencross, Chief of Clan McConnell. She was Highland born, Highland bred. She lifted her chin and walked into the clearing.

Across from her, a tall man with sharp, calculating eyes stepped forward, his long, dark cloak shifting as he moved. His smirk was one of cruel amusement.

"Well, well," he drawled, eyeing her with a mixture of curiosity and suspicion. "You're not who we expected. Where is Townsend?"

Bridget forced a measured breath, meeting his gaze. "Plans changed."

The leader's eyes narrowed slightly, his smirk twitching. "Did they? And who might you be?"

She ignored the question. Instead, she shifted her grip on the book beneath her cloak. "I have what you want," she said evenly.

That caught his attention. His gaze dropped and tracked what she was holding. Around him, the others tensed, their hands inching toward their weapons, alert and suddenly still.

"You've brought the journal," he murmured, his tone suddenly more interested. "I must admit, I didn't think Townsend would be fool enough to send someone else in his place. And certainly not—" He eyed her with amusement. "You."

Bridget slowly withdrew the decoy from beneath her cloak, lifting it just enough for the lantern light to catch the leather cover. A ripple of tension passed through the group.

"You seem surprised," she said, voice edged with irony. "You didn't expect someone to be so obliging, did you?"

The leader's lips curled into a thin smile, though his eyes flickered with suspicion. "Perhaps not. But if you're here, you know its value."

She took a step forward, closer to the fire. "I know enough to realize you'll stop at nothing to get it."

A murmur ran through the men behind him, but the leader merely tilted his head. "A clever girl. But I wonder, why risk coming here alone? Surely someone like you has more... expendable options."

Bridget lifted her chin. "Sometimes, if you want something done right, you do it yourself." Then, after a deliberate pause, she added coolly, "Or did you think I would grant you what you want without making you earn it first?"

A flicker of irritation passed over the leader's face, his smirk fading. The men around him shifted, growing restless.

"Enough games," he snapped. "Give me the journal."

Bridget hesitated just long enough for tension to increase. She had only seconds now, seconds before everything turned to chaos.

She extended the journal just beyond his reach, her fingers tightening around the leather cover. "If you want it, you'll have to give me something in return."

His expression darkened. "You're in no position to negotiate, my dear."

Bridget's grip didn't waver. Her voice dropped, deliberate and steady. "Maybe not. But the question is, are you willing to take that risk?"

A shadow moved at the edge of the clearing.

"Enough!" A voice cut through the tension like a blade, sharp and commanding.

Bridget's breath caught.

Thomas stepped into the clearing, his expression carved from stone.

The leader turned, amusement flickering across his face. "And here I thought tonight couldn't get any more interesting." His eyes gleamed. "Lord Grenville, I presume?"

Thomas ignored the taunt, his gaze snapped to Bridget, ensuring she was unhurt before shifting back to the leader. "Step away," he said, his voice dangerously calm.

Bridget hesitated, every instinct telling her to stand her ground.

The leader sighed, shaking his head. "You two are more trouble than you're worth."

Movement stirred in the shadows.

Grenville didn't hesitate. His boot scraped against the gravel as he lunged.

The attack came fast. A fist struck hard, snapping Grenville's head back. He staggered but barely lost a step before driving forward with practiced precision.

Bridget's heart lurched as the Order's enforcer, a hulking brute with a scar down his cheek, threw another brutal swing.

The fight was fast and vicious. Fists met flesh, gravel scuffed beneath their feet, and the sounds of struggle echoed in the clearing. Thomas was fast, but the brute was strong, his blows heavy and punishing.

A glint of steel, low in the shadows caught Bridget's attention.

A figure burst from the shadows, steel flashing in his grip. The knife gleamed under the swaying lanterns as he closed in fast, silent, swift, and deadly. He moved swiftly, closing the distance between himself and Thomas, his blade poised for a lethal strike.

She tossed the book into the fire and ripped the sgian-dubh from her boot. Gripping the handle with practiced ease, she threw it.

The blade whistled through the air, striking true.

The man let out a strangled yell as the knife sank into his shoulder, planted deep. His body jerked backward, his weapon slipping from his grasp falling uselessly to the ground.

A collective gasp rippled through the Order's ranks. The man staggered, his injured arm limp at his side, blood spreading rapidly through his coat. He let out a guttural curse, glaring at Bridget through pained, narrowed eyes.

Bridget stood her ground, meeting his glare with cold defiance. From the corner of her eye, she caught the glint of steel, the knife he had dropped in the scuffle.

Slowly, deliberately, she stooped down, fingers closing around the weapon's worn handle. The blade was still warm from his grip. She straightened, the knife firm in her grasp.

"Stay down," she warned, her voice like steel. She lifted the blade just enough for the firelight to catch along its edge. "Or the next one goes through your throat."

The leader stared at the fire as he realized what was in it.

"The journal." His voice was low, deadly. "What have you done?"

Bridget took a slow, deliberate step forward, her voice unwavering. "I've ensured you'll never get what you came for. This is over."

The leader's jaw clenched, his fury barely restrained. The flickering firelight cast long shadows across his face, deepening the scowl carved into his features. His hands curled into fists, the barely contained rage of a man whose carefully laid plans had just crumbled before his eyes.

Before he could speak, another voice cut through the night like a blade.

"I believe she said this was over."

Bridget knew that voice. Barrington.

A series of sharp, deliberate clicks shattered the silence. The unmistakable sound of dozens of flintlock pistols being cocked in unison sent a ripple of unease through the clearing. The Order's men froze. They were surrounded.

Barrington stepped forward, his silhouette framed by the firelight, his gaze locked onto the leader. "Drop your weapons."

The leader's lips pressed into a thin line, his hand hovering near his belt, but he wasn't foolish enough to draw. His men hesitated, their gazes darting between the pistols trained on them and their leader as if waiting for a signal.

Barrington lifted his chin. "Make no mistake. You are not walking out of here on your own terms."

The leader's fury twisted into something colder. Calculating.

One by one, the Order's men dropped their weapons.

"Bind them," Barrington ordered.

Ropes bound their hands, their weapons kicked aside. The leader didn't resist, but his gaze was sharp and calculating. Even in defeat, he was already calculating his next move.

Barrington turned to Townsend. "Get them to Sommer Castle. The militia can deal with them from there."

Townsend nodded, already moving toward his horse.

Bridget turned, her pulse still unsteady from the fight, only to find Thomas watching her. His gaze traced her face, lingering on the faint smear of soot near her cheekbone.

"You could have died," he said quietly. Not with anger, but with something raw.

She managed a breathless laugh. "So could you."

He stepped closer, his fingers brushing the soot from her cheek, slow and deliberate. "I don't think I could have endured that."

The words stole whatever response she might have had. Instead, she reached for his lapel, anchoring herself against the rush of emotion. "Then it's a good thing neither of us plans on dying anytime soon."

He held her gaze, something flickering beneath the surface. Was it relief, restraint, something deeper?

"You were supposed to stay behind," he murmured, his voice rough but without reprimand. Just something softer.

Bridget swallowed hard. "And let you face them alone? You should know me better by now." Her voice wavered, but she pushed forward. "You think I don't understand risk? That I don't know what it means to lose?" She exhaled shakily. "I grew up watching everything I loved taken from me, piece by piece. And now—" She hesitated, her breath catching. "And now, you almost became another loss. And that, I truly could not bear."

Thomas took a slow step forward, his hands curling at his sides as if holding something back, something powerful that he had been fighting for too long.

Bridget hesitated, then reached out, brushing her fingers along the torn edge of his coat. He tensed slightly beneath her touch, but he didn't pull away.

"I thought I lost you," she whispered.

His breath hitched, and then, slowly, he straightened, his face inches from hers now, the firelight catching in his eyes, turning them molten.

Bridget's heart pounded. She knew she should step back, should say something clever, something to break the moment before it swallowed them whole. But she didn't.

Instead, Thomas reached up, his fingers brushing over the loose strand of hair at her temple, tucking it behind her ear. His touch lingered, warm against her skin.

Her pulse thrummed.

He searched her gaze as though waiting for a sign, waiting for her to push him away.

She didn't.

So he closed the space between them.

The kiss was slow, deliberate, not stolen in battle or born of desperation, but rich with everything unspoken. A kiss that said I see you. I choose you. I won't let you go.

Bridget's breath caught as his hands slid to her waist, pulling her closer. She could feel the strength beneath the exhaustion, the quiet promise in the way his lips moved against hers. She melted into him, her fingers gripping his coat, holding him there as though grounding herself.

He deepened the kiss slightly but not demanding. Never demanding.

Just… them. Just relief and unspoken truths and something dangerously close to devotion.

When he finally pulled back, neither of them spoke.

Thomas exhaled a quiet laugh. "This time, you can't say I think too much."

Bridget smiled softly, her hands still fisted in his coat. "No. This time, you finally did something right."

He let out a breath, his thumb tracing over her cheekbone, a quiet tenderness in his touch.

Footsteps crunching in the distance reached their ears.

They both tensed, instinct snapping them back to reality. The world came rushing in again, Barrington, the Order, the danger still lingering in the shadows.

Bridget took a slow step back, immediately feeling the absence of his warmth.

Thomas's expression hardened slightly, but not with regret. Never regret.

The fire had burned low, its embers casting a flickering glow across the clearing. The acrid scent of charred parchment lingered in the air, mixing with the damp earth and the distant rustle of retreating footsteps. It was over. The Order had been driven back, and for now, they were safe.

But Bridget couldn't move.

"You were never supposed to be part of this," he said roughly.

"And yet here we are," she whispered.

He shook his head, his jaw tightening. "I swore I would never let you get caught in my world. That I would protect you from it."

Bridget let out a sharp, humorless laugh. "You think you can protect me from myself? Her voice held a hint of bitter amusement. "You've no idea what that even means."

His lips quirked, but there was no amusement in it. Just heat.

Then suddenly, he was right there, too close, too much, not enough.

"Bridget," he murmured. Her name on his lips sent a shiver down her spine.

Her breath hitched. She wanted to fight him, to tell him she wasn't ready for this, that loving him would be her undoing, but she couldn't.

Because she was already undone, she was already his.

His hands came up, framing her face, rough fingertips brushing her skin as if he couldn't believe she was real. "I tried," he murmured. "I tried to keep my distance. I tried to stay away, to be what you needed—"

"You're what I need." The words slipped out before she could stop them.

Thomas sucked in a breath, his grip tightening ever so slightly. His gaze was fierce, searching, disbelieving. "Say it again."

Bridget lifted her chin, letting him see everything she had tried to hide. "I need you." Her voice was quieter now, the fight draining out of her. "I love you, Thomas."

The words left her lips before she could reclaim them, and in the silence that followed, she felt something shift inside her. No fear. Only truth.

A ragged sound escaped him, something between relief and surrender.

And then he kissed her. It was not a soft kiss, not tentative or questioning. It was fierce, desperate, edged with everything they had held back for too long.

Bridget rose onto her toes, fisting her hands in his coat, pulling him closer. His arms wound around her, solid and unyielding, as if letting her go was no longer an option.

The world blurred. The fire crackled. Somewhere in the distance, the night stretched on. But here, at this moment, there was only them.

When they finally pulled apart, Thomas tucked her into his

side.

"This changes everything," he murmured.

Bridget smiled, finally unafraid of what that meant.

"No," she whispered. "This changes nothing. Because I was always yours."

"We should go back," he said.

She nodded, but before she turned, she caught his wrist, squeezing it lightly. She released his wrist, letting her fingers trail away before turning toward the path.

With one last lingering look, they stepped into the night, leaving the clearing and the danger behind them.

Chapter Twenty-Seven

BARRINGTON SAT AT the wide mahogany desk in the study, the single candle casting flickering shadows across the neat stacks of parchment. The house was still, hushed with the weight of everything that had transpired. The confrontation with the Order had been a victory, but it had cost them. Thomas and Bridget had not yet returned, and while Barrington suspected their delay had nothing to do with danger, he knew the next few hours would be crucial.

With a steady hand, he dipped his pen into the inkwell and began drafting a report. Townsend would leave for London soon, and the Home Office would need a full account of the Order's movements, their failed attempt to recover the journal, and the implications of what remained hidden.

His fingers brushed against his coat pocket absently, and something cool and metallic met his touch.

Frowning, Barrington withdrew the small object, the dim candlelight glinting off the delicate silver filigree. Lady Worthington's bodkin.

A soft, knowing smile escaped him. He'd meant to return it to her. In all the chaos, it had completely slipped his mind. He turned it over in his palm, studying the fine craftsmanship, the intricate design curling around the slender casing. The sapphire glimmered atop the cap, its deep blue catching the light.

He started to set it aside when a faint, almost undetectable scent reached him. Something sharp. Faintly floral, yet bitter.

He frowned, lifting the bodkin closer. The scent wasn't embroidery thread, nor was it the mild fragrance of scented gloves or handkerchiefs common among ladies of her station. It was something else. Something… familiar. Belladonna.

The realization sent a slow chill through him. Carefully, he twisted the cap, revealing the gleaming tip of the sharp bodkin. He held it up to the candlelight and saw it, a dark, dried stain nestled in the fine engraving near the base. Blood.

A knock at the door broke his thoughts.

Townsend entered, brushing off his coat as he crossed the room. "The horses are being readied for dawn. I trust you've noted everything that needs to be included in the report?"

Barrington didn't answer. He held up the bodkin instead.

Townsend paused at the sight of Barrington holding the bodkin up to the light.

"Have you taken up needlework, Barrington? Should we be concerned?"

Barrington gave him a flat look. "I'm considering a new hobby. Poisoned embroidery tools seem quite the statement."

Townsend let out a low whistle. "Fashionable and deadly. Lady Worthington always did have refined tastes."

Barrington's expression turned grim. He crossed to the bell-pull and gave it a sharp tug. Moments later, Simmons appeared.

"Have the rest of the houseguests gathered in the library," Barrington said. "Now, please."

Simmons bowed. "At once, my lord."

The library was dimly lit, the late evening glow barely filtering through the heavy drapes. A single lamp burned on Barrington's desk, casting long shadows against the bookshelves. Tension filled the room.

Barrington stood behind the desk, the bodkin still in hand. Townsend leaned against a nearby chair, his arms crossed.

A soft knock came, followed by Mr. Simmons's steady voice. "As requested, my lord."

The door opened. Thomas entered first, his expression wary.

Bridget followed, her eyes scanning the room. Behind them came the others, Miss Gray, Lady Carlisle, Lord Davenport, and Miss Hathaway, each wearing a mixture of confusion and unease.

Blackwood strode in behind them, his gaze sharp.

Lady Worthington entered last, composed, though irritation flashed across her face. "This is highly irregular," she said, smoothing a hand down the front of her gown. "If this is about my bodkin, I would prefer to speak privately. I assume you found it?"

Barrington lifted the delicate silver instrument between his fingers. "Wedged into the seat of one of the chairs in the drawing room." He turned it slightly, then removed the cap with a deliberate motion.

Bridget inhaled sharply. She recognized that smell. Belladonna.

Lady Worthington's posture remained steady, but her lips thinned. "Well. I suppose that explains why I couldn't find it. I trust you have not damaged it?"

Townsend let out a humorless chuckle. "Damaged it? No. But we did examine it rather carefully."

Barrington set the bodkin on the desk. Its tip bore a near-invisible stain.

Bridget stepped closer. "There's blood on it."

Lady Worthington's fingers twitched before she clasped them in front of her. "Blood? Don't be ridiculous. It's an embroidery tool."

Barrington's gaze sharpened. "Then perhaps you can explain why it smells of poison."

The room stilled.

Lady Worthington let out a soft laugh. "Poison? Surely you jest."

Townsend shook his head. "Belladonna. A slow but effective toxin when used in small doses. Lethal in larger ones. Mark Alastair was stabbed with a thin, pointed blade, one much like this."

Lady Worthington's chin lifted. "You can't be serious."

Blackwood stepped forward. "Evelina, if you know something, now is the time to speak."

She turned to him. "I don't know anything, Cedric."

Barrington picked up a square of linen and pressed it against the bodkin's tip. A faint trace of blood stained the cloth. "You've been in distress over this bodkin since it disappeared. You claimed it was a cherished heirloom, yet it's connected to murder."

Lady Worthington's breathing quickened. "It was stolen from me!"

Bridget folded her arms. "By who?"

"How should I know? Someone in this house."

Townsend stepped closer. "When did you notice it was missing?"

She hesitated. "I—"

Bridget narrowed her eyes. "The morning the rumors started about the journal?"

Lady Worthington swallowed. "Coincidence."

Thomas finally spoke. "You weren't worried about the sentimental value. You were worried that someone might look too closely."

Lady Worthington glanced toward the door. "You cannot truly believe—"

Barrington cut her off. "Mark Alastair was murdered by someone desperate to keep the journal hidden. What did you think he was going to uncover?"

The room fell silent.

Her fists clenched. "This is preposterous."

Blackwood took a step toward her. "Evelina."

She looked at him. "I did what was necessary."

Bridget's breath caught.

Lady Worthington's composure cracked. "Alastair was careless. He was going to ruin everything."

Townsend straightened. "The Order."

Lady Worthington let out a sharp breath. "This is absurd—"

"You stabbed him," Barrington interrupted holding up the bodkin.

"I had no choice!"

The room froze.

Blackwood exhaled and stepped back. His face was unreadable.

Bridget stared. The elegant woman was now trembling with fury and desperation.

Barrington's tone remained level. "You murdered him, and tried to recover the weapon."

Lady Worthington's gaze darted between them. "This isn't over."

Townsend stepped in. "Oh, I think it is."

Lady Worthington trembled, realizing she had no escape.

Blackwood turned away from her, silent.

Bridget let out a long breath. It was done. The accusation, the confession, the arrest, yet none of it felt like resolution. Only exhaustion.

The door creaked open.

Professor Tresham entered, his scholarly air strikingly out of place amid the remnants of tension still thick in the room. He carried a folio in his hands and approached the library table with quiet purpose.

Barrington gestured toward the folio. "You have something for us, Tresham?"

"Yes. And I'd like to show it to you." Professor Tresham carefully smoothed out the worn parchment on the large library table. The edges were curled slightly with age. He adjusted his spectacles.

"This document has been altered multiple times," he began, running a careful fingertip over the layered script. "It was common practice to scrape ink from parchment and reuse it. I suspected as much the moment I examined the texture."

Bridget leaned in to see the document. "And what was beneath it?"

Tresham lifted his gaze. "Something far more concerning."

He reached for a small scraping tool and brushed away the faintest layer of ink. Beneath the writing, a symbol began to emerge. It was faded, but unmistakable, a raven, its wings spread wide over a diamond.

Bridget gasped.

Grenville cursed.

Barrington's jaw tightened. "The Order of Shadows."

Tresham nodded. "The mark was hidden beneath more recent entries."

"What is this parchment?" Bridget asked.

Tresham angled the candlelight, revealing the faint remnants of a title at the top.

"Registry. A Record of Members," Barrington read aloud."

Tresham traced his finger down the faded list. "These are the names Alastair was trying to uncover."

"There are dates next to these names." Thomas looked up at Tresham.

"Entry dates into the Order."

"Kerrington," Blackwood said, tapping one of the names. "It's dated 1785." He glanced at Lady Worthington. "That's your father."

Lady Worthington's breath hitched. "My father was a historian… he advised powerful men, but he never spoke of such things."

Tresham read aloud. "The notation next to his name reads 'Senior Advisor.'"

Thomas's voice was cold. "Your family has served the Order for generations."

She met his gaze, something proud in her eyes. "It was never a choice. It was my duty."

Barrington's voice dropped. "Your duty? Was it your duty to murder Mark Alastair?"

Lady Worthington smiled. "He lost his conviction. That made him a liability. I did what had to be done."

Bridget inhaled sharply. There was no remorse. No doubt. Only certainty.

Lady Worthington glanced at the bodkin. "It's rather poetic, isn't it? An instrument of creation… and death."

Thomas said quietly, "You poisoned him."

Lady Worthington didn't answer. But she didn't deny it, either.

Barrington turned to Townsend. "Lock her in the east guest room. Post a guard. Search her belongings. Remove anything that looks suspicious."

Townsend inclined his head. "Consider it done."

Lady Worthington lifted her chin. "I did what was necessary."

"So will we," Bridget said softly.

Townsend led Lady Worthington away, and the door clicked shut behind them.

Tresham returned his attention to the document. "I saved one name for last." He took the torn corner that Bridget had found in Alastair's hand and carefully aligned it with the torn edge of the parchment.

Bridget froze.

"Baron Lucius Ellington."

"Ellington?" Blackwood took a slow step forward. "That's Marjory's maiden name."

Bridget's pulse roared in her ears.

Barrington muttered a curse. "Alastair must have suspected his wife's family had ties to the Order."

Blackwood laughed bitterly. "That sounds familiar."

Grenville asked the professor. "Did Alastair ask you to research the Ellington line?"

Tresham exhaled. "Yes. But I never delivered my full findings. This Lucius Ellington is not part of Marjory's family line."

Bridget's fingers gripped the edge of the desk. "Then who is he?"

Tresham met her gaze. "That is the question we must answer."

⟫⟪

THE LIBRARY HAD fallen into a hush. Grenville stood near the edge of the table, watching Blackwood.

Blackwood's gaze lingered on the parchment. Once. Twice. A third time.

Grenville watched him closely, waiting for a true reaction, not the man's usual charm. What he saw was a flicker of disbelief.

"Something wrong, Blackwood?" Barrington's voice was smooth, but Grenville recognized the deliberate probe.

"I was given a name, a false one, it seems." He let out a bitter laugh. "All this time, I thought I was chasing truth."

His mouth curled into a smile, but Grenville saw the pain. "Turns out I was just like Alastair. Another fool, discarded."

"They used you." Bridget's voice was quiet, but firm.

Blackwood's head snapped up. The fury in his eyes was raw. "That they did."

"And what will you do with that knowledge?" Grenville asked quietly.

Blackwood glanced at the parchment one more time. Then his voice turned cold. "I suppose that depends."

"On?" Barrington asked.

Blackwood's fists unclenched. "On whether or not they come calling again. And if they do… I'll be ready."

Grenville studied him. There was no bluster, no dramatics, just certainty.

Townsend asked. "And if they don't?"

Blackwood shrugged. "Then I'll consider myself fortunate and be on my way."

He turned for the door. "Just don't mistake absence for inaction," he said over his shoulder. "The shadows have long memories. But should you ever need another blade against the Order… If you're willing to look in the shadows."

Grenville let out a breath. If the Order ever sought Blackwood again… they'd regret it.

As Blackwood exited, a tense silence lingered. The others remained frozen, caught between the shock of what had unfolded and what had yet to come.

Lady Carlisle shifted uneasily, dabbing at her brow with a lace-trimmed handkerchief. Lord Davenport muttered something about brandy and made for the drinks cabinet, while Miss Gray stood very still, eyes fixed on the parchment. Miss Hathaway whispered a prayer, fingers clenched tight.

Grenville remained still, the names echoing in his mind. The Order was wounded, but far from finished, and so were they.

Chapter Twenty-Eight

THE MORNING AIR was warm, the drawing room bristled with quiet tension, a stillness that felt out of place. Conversations were hushed, the usual chatter replaced with quiet speculation. Though sunlight streamed through the tall windows, it did little to dispel the tension that had settled over the house. What had begun as a weekend of sport and leisure had turned into something far more unsettling.

Lady Carlisle smoothed her skirts, glancing nervously at Miss Hathaway. "I suppose we should have expected some sort of explanation," she murmured.

Miss Hathaway sighed, her fingers twisting the edge of her handkerchief. "But do we truly want to hear it?"

Davenport, who stood near the window, let out a quiet breath. "It's better to know the truth than continue pretending nothing happened."

Barrington stood near the mantel, his expression solemn but composed. At his side, Townsend and Grenville flanked him, their presence reinforcing the gravity of the moment. Bridget stood nearby, her hands clasped before her, her gaze looking over the faces of everyone assembled. Marjory sat stiffly, her fingers tangled together in her lap, eyes downcast but listening.

Scofield was notably absent. His discreet presence had become a fixture over the past few days.

The hush deepened as Barrington cleared his throat, drawing everyone's attention to him.

"As you are all aware, we have been investigating the tragic death of Mark Alastair," he began. "I regret that this weekend, meant to be one of sport and leisure, has been marred by something far more sinister. But now, we have answers that we can share with you."

A heavy silence followed, expectant and uneasy.

Barrington continued, his voice steady. "Mark Alastair did not suffer a fatal accident." Barrington paused, letting the words settle. "He was murdered, and the culprit was among us. Lady Evelina Worthington," he paused, allowing the name to settle over the room, "was responsible for his death."

Gasps rippled through the gathering. Miss Hathaway pressed a hand to her mouth, while Lady Carlisle's fingers tightened around her handkerchief.

"God's teeth," Davenport muttered under his breath.

Blackwood remained expressionless, his arms crossed as he absorbed the statement.

"Evelina?" Marjory's voice cracked. "But she was my friend… why would she do this?" Her voice wavered, caught between shock and disbelief.

Townsend stepped forward, his gaze sharp. "Lady Worthington was a member of the Order of Shadows, a clandestine organization that seeks to manipulate those in power for their own ends. Mark Alastair, through his research into his family's library, stumbled upon a book containing their secrets. When he refused to give them what he had found, he became a liability."

Barrington's expression hardened. "She used her bodkin, a seemingly innocuous embroidery tool, coated with poison to end his life. And she did so without hesitation."

Miss Gray shuddered, her eyes darting to her friend. "Good heavens, we dined with her."

Davenport let out a slow breath. "And where is she now?"

"She has been taken into custody and will be transported to London for trial," Barrington confirmed. "Along with the other members of the Order that Grenville and Lady Bridget captured yesterday." Barrington glanced at Grenville, his expression softening for a moment, an unspoken acknowledgment of their shared risk. He turned back to the others. "The Order will not escape scrutiny."

A hush settled over the room, expectant and uneasy.

Bridget took a steadying breath before she stepped forward, her voice gentle but firm. "There is one more matter." Bridget looked around the room. "I kept wondering why Alastair refused to sell the book. Why was it worth his life. It held more than secrets. It contained a list of people. Families. Members of the Order whose ties go back to the late 1600's. It was where we found Lord Kerrington, Lady Worthington's ancestor." She turned to Marjory. "He also found Baron Ellington."

As gasps swelled and murmurs began, Marjory's head snapped up, fear flickering in her eyes. "What?"

Professor Tresham, who had been silent until now, retrieved a document from his coat. "Alastair found your maiden name, Ellington. But," he hesitated, "we discovered a different Ellington line. Your family was not affiliated with the Order. Alastair wanted to prove it before coming to you. I brought him the final documentation when I arrived on Friday."

Marjory inhaled sharply, her hands shaking. "So… he was trying to protect me."

Bridget reached out, squeezing her hand. "Yes. And he succeeded. It is why he wouldn't give them the book or the list."

Marjory let out a shuddering breath, relief and sorrow warring in her expression. "He died protecting me."

Barrington inclined his head. "Indeed. His actions ensured that the truth was uncovered."

The guests absorbed the information in stunned silence. Lady Carlisle dabbed her eyes with a lace handkerchief. Miss Hathaway, usually so composed, whispered something to Miss Gray, who nodded solemnly.

Davenport exhaled. "Then it is over."

Barrington's gaze swept the room. "Yes, my friends. You are

all free to leave this afternoon. The investigation is complete. Those responsible will face justice in London."

A murmur of conversation rose among the guests. Lady Carlisle sat back in her chair, exhaling deeply, while Miss Hathaway exchanged a relieved glance with Miss Gray. Davenport rubbed the back of his neck, as though still absorbing the gravity of what had been revealed.

Blackwood, who had remained silent, finally pushed off from where he leaned against the fireplace. "The Order will not let this lie," he said grimly. "You know that."

Barrington met his gaze. "We've set events in motion. But for now, this house is safe. And those who need to answer for their crimes are on their way to London."

Bridget turned to Thomas, their eyes meeting. No words were needed. The cost had been steep, but today, they had won.

Chapter Twenty-Nine

THE REMNANTS OF the past days still lingered in the drawing room, not in the form of spoken words but in the careful way the guests moved and the glances they exchanged. Though the immediate danger had passed, a quiet tension remained, a collective understanding that the events of the weekend had changed more than just their plans. The air, once thick with tension, now held a sense of quiet relief. Though the shadow of the Order still lingered, they had won a battle, and for now, that was enough.

Bridget stood near the fireplace, her fingers tracing the rim of a delicate porcelain teacup. Across the room, Thomas spoke in low tones with Barrington and Townsend, their expressions measured but not grim. Their work was not yet done, but for the first time in days, there was no immediate danger and that was a relief.

Marjory sat with Miss Hathaway and Miss Gray, her posture relaxed in a way it had not been since Alastair's passing.

"I'm still deciding what to do," she admitted, offering them a small smile. "Alastair Court is mine now, but I cannot decide whether to stay or return to London."

Lady Carlisle stirred her tea thoughtfully. "Perhaps a bit of both? You deserve time to heal, but that doesn't mean you must hide away in the countryside forever."

Marjory's gaze flicked to Bridget, something unspoken passing between them. "Perhaps."

Before another word could be said, the butler appeared in the doorway. "My lady," he announced, "Viscount Huntington and Laird McConnell have arrived."

The room was filled with a heavy silence.

Bridget stiffened. Her teacup nearly slipped from her grasp, and across the room, Thomas straightened sharply in his chair. He quickly glanced at her. Their fathers had arrived together.

The doors swung open, revealing the two men laughing as if they were old friends. McConnell clapped Huntington on the back, clearly pleased with himself.

Bridget nearly choked.

Thomas, braced for a confrontation, looked as though someone had just knocked the wind from him.

"Ah, Grenville!" McConnell greeted warmly. "Or should I say, Thomas? We've much to discuss, lad."

Thomas blinked. "I—pardon?"

Huntington's gaze settled on Bridget with surprising familiarity. "And you, Bridget," he said, his tone almost indulgent. "I hope my son hasn't given you too much trouble."

Bridget opened her mouth. Then closed it.

Thomas stared at the two men, his brows drawing together as if he'd misheard. His father and Laird McConnell, laughing, speaking as though they were old friends? The very idea unsettled him, knocking the breath from his lungs.

His father, the man who had built a reputation on measured control and political maneuvering, stood shoulder to shoulder with McConnell, the very embodiment of the Highland resilience Thomas had spent years trying to understand. It didn't make sense.

A strange tightness settled in his chest. He'd spent years carrying the weight of their silence, of their absence. And now, to find they'd been allies all along. It felt like betrayal laced with relief. How could they have kept this from him? And why did part of him want to forgive them anyway?

His jaw tightened. "You've been working together?" His

voice was quieter than he intended, rough with disbelief.

Neither man hesitated.

McConnell clapped Huntington on the back once more, unfazed. "Aye, lad. And for longer than you'd think."

Thomas shook his head slowly. "No. That's not possible." His father had been absent, indifferent. And McConnell? His contempt for the English had been clear. For years, Thomas had thought, had *known,* exactly where these men stood.

And yet, here they were.

Bridget's voice cut through his thoughts, sharp and incredulous. "But you... you *hated* him," she accused, gesturing toward Huntington. "You blamed him for everything—"

McConnell sighed, his expression softening. "I never hated him, Bridget. I hated what happened. I hated the suffering. But your mother—" His throat worked for a moment before he continued. "She made me promise not to let hatred blind me to the good in men. Huntington had power. I had knowledge. Separately, we could do nothing. Together, we could help."

Thomas exhaled slowly, his thoughts still catching up to the truth unfolding before him. "And you never thought to tell us?" The words came out sharper than intended, but his father met his gaze without flinching.

"Because it was too dangerous."

McConnell nodded. "The Order had already taken too much from our people. We couldn't risk them turning their attention to you and Bridget. Keeping you in the dark kept you safe."

Bridget stiffened. "So you just decided for us?"

McConnell's eyes softened, but his voice remained firm. "Aye, lass. And I'd do it again if it meant keeping you alive."

Huntington sighed. "It wasn't an easy decision. But we knew the burden of what we were doing. We chose to carry it alone."

Thomas exhaled again, but this time it came with a bitter smile. "All those years I thought you were distant out of disapproval. Turns out, you were just hiding secrets."

Huntington stepped forward, his gaze steady. "I may not

have shown it, Thomas, but I was always proud of the man you became. That strength came from within you."

Later, when the others had left the room, Thomas remained behind.

Bridget lingered near the door, watching him. "You're taking this better than I would."

He shook his head slowly. "I'm not. I just... I've spent so long resenting him. I don't know what to do with this version of the truth."

Bridget stepped closer, not touching him, just close enough to share the silence. "Maybe you don't have to do anything with it. Not yet."

"Maybe." He glanced at her. "But I know one thing."

"What's that?"

He gave a ghost of a smile. "If my father and McConnell conspired to bring us together... I can't find it in me to be angry about that."

Thomas glanced at Bridget, his expression softening.

"You had help. Just not from the ones you expected."

Thomas exhaled slowly, the tension in his shoulders easing slightly. "Did Alastair know the truth?"

"No, lad," McConnell said. "He told us about his mission to find the books that his library once had. He told us about the Order, and we advised him—"

"To burn the blasted thing," Huntington said. "It was only a few months ago that he told us he found the Ellington family on the list. If I had known what he planned to do, I would have burned the book myself."

A heavy silence settled over them.

Finally, Barrington cleared his throat. "The Order may be weakened, but they are far from finished." He looked to Townsend, who nodded.

"I'll take what we have to Whitehall," Townsend confirmed. "The arrests will hold, but the network runs deeper than we can see."

Marjory exhaled, rubbing her temples. "I just want the books out of my house. I don't care if the room goes back to being empty." She turned to the professor. "I'm certain you can find some that you would want. Professor, feel free to take what you like."

Professor Tresham offered her a thoughtful look. "Lady Alastair, I'd be honored to take a few volumes."

Marjory offered a small, genuine smile. "Then let's see to that before you leave."

The room lightened just a fraction. Miss Gray turned to Marjory. "You won't be alone."

Marjory's smile was grateful. "Thank you. I received a message from our solicitor, Mr. Hughes, regarding the settlement of the estate. It will be lovely to have you both here."

Simmons appeared at the doorway. "Breakfast is served, my lady."

A sigh of relief rippled through the guests. The ordeal was over. As they rose to leave, Marjory linked arms with Tresham and led the way, calling over her shoulder, "The minister's cat is an admirable cat."

Tresham chuckled. "The minister's cat is a benevolent cat."

"The minister's cat is a clever cat," Miss Hathaway added.

Bridget caught Thomas's eye as the game continued into the dining room. She lingered near the window for a moment before he stepped beside her, his voice low. "You still look as if you're thinking too hard."

She huffed a quiet laugh, shaking her head. "Not thinking, realizing that some truths sneak up on you. And when they finally hit, they change everything."

He lifted a brow, watching her closely. "And what revelation has you looking so serious?"

Bridget turned to him fully, her fingers tightening around his. "That I've spent so much time fighting what was inevitable."

Thomas stilled, his gaze locked on hers. "And what do you see now?"

She exhaled, searching his face, seeing not just the man who had challenged her, stood beside her, and stolen her breath more times than she could count, but the man she could no longer picture a life without.

"That I don't want to imagine a future without you."

His fingers laced through hers, a slow smile touching his lips. "Then don't."

Bridget swallowed hard, her heart pounding against her ribs. There was no hesitation left, no doubt, only the truth of what she wanted. What she had always wanted.

"Thomas…" She drew a breath, steady and sure. "Will you marry me?"

His breath hitched, his grip tightening before a quiet chuckle rumbled from his chest. "I was going to ask you."

She arched a brow, smirking. "Too slow, Captain."

He laughed, shaking his head as he pulled her into his arms. "Then I suppose I'll just have to say yes."

She smiled against his shoulder, holding on to him, knowing that for all the twists and turns their journey had taken, this was exactly where they were meant to be.

"You'll know it's love when the rest of the world fades, and there's only the two of you."

Catriona's words echoed in her mind, clear and certain. And in Thomas's arms, Bridget knew she had known it from the start.

He drew back just enough to search her face. "They really did meddle, didn't they?"

Bridget let out a soft laugh. "From the very beginning. Your father with his letters, mine with his estate visits…"

"Do you think they're smug about it?"

"Oh, definitely." She glanced toward the door, lowering her voice. "Which is why we'll never admit they succeeded."

Thomas grinned. "Agreed. Let them wonder if we figured it out despite them."

She leaned in, her smile wry. "Let them wonder who truly outmaneuvered whom."

Their laughter mingled, quiet, full of relief and something deeper. Whatever lay ahead, they would face it together.

And if their fathers overheard from the hallway, neither of them said a word.

The End

About the Author

There was never a time when *USA Today* Bestseller, RUTH A. CASIE hasn't had a story in her head. When she was little, she and her older sister would dress up and act out the ones Ruth creative. Today, Ruth writes exciting and beautifully told legendary historical romances that are both rich and engaging. Her stories feature strong women and the men who deserve them, endearing flaws and all. Her stories are full of, 'edge of your seat' suspense, mind-boggling drama, and a forever-after romance.

She lives in New Jersey with her hero, three empty bedrooms and a growing number of incomplete counted cross-stitch projects. Before she found her voice, she was a speech therapist (pun intended), client liaison for a corrugated manufacturer, and vice president at an international bank where she was a product/ marketing manager, but her favorite job is the one she's doing now—writing romance. Ruth hopes her stories become your favorite adventure.

Fun facts about Ruth:

1. She filled her passport up in one year.
2. She has three series. The Druid Knight is a time travel romance. The Stelton Legacy is a historical fantasy about the seven sons of a seventh son. Havenport Romances are contemporary romantic suspense stories. She also writes for the Pirates of Britannia connected world.
3. She did a rap with her son to "How Many Trucks Can a Tow Truck Tow If a Tow Truck Could Tow Trucks."

4. When she cooks she dances around the kitchen.

5. Her sudoku books is in the bathroom and that's all she'll say about that!

Social Media Links:

Website:
ruthacasie.com

Instagram:
instagram.com/ruthacasie

Facebook private reader's page, Casie Café:
facebook.com/groups/963711677128537

Facebook Author Page:
facebook.com/RuthACasie

Twitter:
twitter.com/RuthACasie

BookBub:
bookbub.com/authors/ruth-a-casie

Amazon:
amazon.com/author/ruthacasie

Goodreads:
goodreads.com/author/show/4792909.Ruth_A_Casie

YouTube:
bit.ly/3hI5eQr